**Praise for USA T‍[...]
Ju[...]**

"The 411 is that KCPD rocks and so does Miller."
—*RT Book Reviews* on *Nanny 911*

"Miller's characters are so well drawn they feel like family, and the book is the beginning of a new ongoing mystery, peppered with pitch-perfect dialogue, intriguing suspense and perfectly paired partners."
—*RT Book Reviews* on *The Marine Next Door*

Praise for Dana Marton

"Marton wraps up the ongoing Wind River County mystery with deft fingers, snappy dialogue and an adventure so tense it will knock readers off their feet."
—*RT Book Reviews* on *The Black Sheep Sheik*

"Sassy, smart and sexy, with pitch-perfect action and two feisty, funny and dedicated agents, *Spy* is going to get three cheers from readers."
—*RT Book Reviews* on *Last Spy Standing*

Praise for Paula Graves

"As always, visiting the battling Cooper family is a real treat, and Graves folds in yet another tricky FBI chase and simmering romance, taking fans on a satisfying adventure."
—*RT Book Reviews* on *Secret Hideout*

"Readers won't be disappointed."
—*RT Book Reviews* on *Secret Identity*

ABOUT THE AUTHORS

JULIE MILLER attributes her passion for writing romance to all those fairy tales she read growing up, and to shyness. Encouragement from her family to write down all those feelings she couldn't express became a love for the written word. She gets continued support from her fellow members of the Prairieland Romance Writers, where she serves as the resident "grammar goddess." This *USA TODAY* bestselling and award-winning author and teacher has published several paranormal romances. Inspired by the likes of Agatha Christie and Encyclopedia Brown, Ms. Miller believes the only thing better than a good mystery is a good romance. Born and raised in Missouri, she now lives in Nebraska with her husband, son and smiling guard dog, Maxie. Write to Julie at P.O. Box 5162, Grand Island, NE 68802-5162.

DANA MARTON is an author of more than a dozen fast-paced action-adventure romantic-suspense novels and a winner of a Daphne du Maurier Award of Excellence. She loves writing books of international intrigue, filled with dangerous plots that try her tough-as-nails heroes and the special women they fall in love with. Her books have been published in seven languages in eleven countries around the world. When not writing or reading, she loves to browse antiques shops and enjoys working in her sizable flower garden, where she searches for "bad" bugs with the skills of a superspy and vanquishes them with the agility of a commando soldier. Every day in her garden is a thriller. To find more information on her books, please visit www.danamarton.com. She loves to hear from her readers and can be reached via email at DanaMarton@DanaMarton.com.

PAULA GRAVES Alabama native Paula Graves wrote her first book, a mystery starring herself and her neighborhood friends, at the age of six. A voracious reader, Paula loves books that pair tantalizing mystery with compelling romance. When she's not reading or writing, she works as a creative director for a Birmingham advertising agency and spends time with her family and friends. She is a member of Southern Magic Romance Writers, Heart of Dixie Romance Writers and Romance Writers of America. Paula invites readers to visit her website, www.paulagraves.com.

USA TODAY Bestselling Author

JULIE MILLER

DANA MARTON

PAULA GRAVES

THREE COWBOYS

HARLEQUIN®

entertain, enrich, inspire™

ISBN-13: 978-0-373-69658-1

THREE COWBOYS
Copyright © 2012 by Harlequin Books S.A.

The publisher acknowledges the copyright
holders of the individual works, as follows:

VIRGIL
Copyright © 2012 by Julie Miller

MORGAN
Copyright © 2012 by Dana Marton

WYATT
Copyright © 2012 by Paula Graves

Recycling programs
for this product may
not exist in your area.

CONTENTS

JULIE MILLER
VIRGIL

CAST OF CHARACTERS

Virgil "Bull" McCabe—The second son of Justice McCabe. He's as tough as his nickname. But this big-city detective left the family ranch he loved when his mother died and his father pushed him away. It would take a serious kind of trouble—and a special woman from his past—to convince this cowboy to come home.

Tracy Cobb—The girl next door was Bull's best friend growing up. But the tomboy he remembered is now the prettiest high-school teacher he's ever seen. She's on a mission to rescue a troubled student she's taken under her wing—Bull's little sister. Tracy's stubborn determination could get her killed—but Bull is just as determined to keep her safe…and make her his.

Brittany Means—The half sister the McCabe brothers hadn't known they had.

Justice McCabe—Bull's estranged father. Wealthy rancher and self-made man. He runs his family the way he runs the J-Bar-J: he's the boss.

Julio Rivas—Another student missing from Miss Cobb's class.

Sol Garcia—Thug number one in the *Los Jaguares* drug cartel has the brains and a mean streak.

Manny Ortiz—Thug number two in the *Los Jaguares* gang has the muscle. You'd think you would see him coming.

Javier Calderón—Leader of the *Los Jaguares* cartel. He doesn't care who gets hurt when he wants something.

Morgan McCabe—Virgil's older brother has spent years away on commando missions. Will the McCabes be able to track him down and bring him home to help out in this family emergency?

Wyatt McCabe—Bull's younger brother, the Serpentine, Texas, sheriff, will do anything it takes to help bring their sister home.

For all my readers. Thank you!

Prologue

"Amiga." Brittany Means rubbed her cheek against the itchy burlap of her pillow and tried to reclaim the blank oblivion of sleep. But a swat on her bottom jolted her from her drowsy state. "Wake up!"

She sat bolt upright on the crackling straw mattress. "Hey! What's…?" Her stomach churned at the sudden movement and she leaned over the edge of the bed and retched onto the dirt floor. She nearly tumbled over the edge herself when her hands refused to move where she wanted them to. Brittany steadied the ball bearings ping-ponging through her skull before opening her eyes again. Straw mattress? Dirt floor? Her hands weren't working because they were bound together at the wrists with several loops of gray duct tape. Alarm replaced the turbulence in her stomach as she awkwardly pushed herself back into a sitting position to face the black-haired man sitting at the foot of the bed. "What's going on? Where am I?"

"At the end of your little joy ride with my nephew." The man's Latin accent was thick, but his words were sharply articulate, his English perfect. He was a lot older than she, in his forties or fifties, probably. She supposed he was good-looking, the way somebody's dad might be. But his black eyes were hard. And cold. This small room in the middle of nowhere had to be ninety-plus degrees and smelled of man sweat. But Brittany shivered at the chilling lack of compassion in the man's dark eyes.

What had happened to her? The last thing she remembered was speeding across the Mexican border just outside Serpentine, Texas, where she'd grown up. She and her impromptu date for the day, Julio Rivas, were delivering hay to his uncle's alpaca ranch.

Her life had been in absolute upheaval the past few months since her mother's death. She'd had a blowup with the man who claimed to be her father that morning about staying home for Christmas break instead of going on a skiing trip with her friends at school. Brittany had jumped at the opportunity to cut classes and get to know the mysteriously aloof senior a little better. Feeling the wind in her long, dark blond hair, and snuggling up beside Julio's bad-boy body had been the perfect antidote for the raging hurt bottled up inside her. They'd stopped for lunch. Julio had kissed her. And then…?

She cursed at the big blank spot in her memory. Panic pumped her heart faster as she tugged against the duct tape and took in the adobe walls, wood beams and stone fireplace of the room. It was like one of the old kitchens she'd seen on a field trip to the Alamo in San Antonio. Only that room had been well-preserved in the name of history as students and tour guides filed past. This room was used and dirty and filled with several men—two big bruisers at the door, a man wearing enough silver and turquoise and cologne to tell her he thought he was a player and a couple more who wore guns on their belts and rifles strapped over their shoulders. There was one scruffy old guy who looked like he might be the only one who actually knew about alpacas and ranch life. And even he was armed. But there was no one her age here, and certainly no sign of Julio. If she was a bound prisoner, what had happened to him?

The player in the black felt hat flashed a bright white smile and laughed. "The sedative has worn off and the *muchacha* is back with us now, *patrón.* I see it in her eyes—she is afraid."

That fear pricked goose bumps across her skin. Brittany pulled her gaze from his leering grin and turned to the man with the cold eyes who was clearly in charge of this gathering. "You're Julio's uncle?"

"Many people call me that. Julio has a cousin who works for me. I am Javier Calderón."

Javier Calderón? Mexican-drug-lord Calderón? The-reason-she'd-been-warned-to-stay-out-of-certain-neighborhoods-in-Serpentine-after-dark Calderón? How did she…?

She might have a wild streak and abandonment issues, but she was just a kid in high school. And she didn't do drugs. This had to be a joke. Only, the duct tape and guns and raging headache left over from whatever they'd given her were no joke. "Where's Julio?"

"The boy does not matter. I sent him away yesterday."

"Yesterday?" How long had she been here? Why couldn't she shake this groggy lack of focus? "What do you want with me?"

"A simple phone call." Her bound wrists wouldn't cooperate when Javier Calderón scooted across the bed and she tried to retreat. Rough hands saved her from falling, but pushed her forward while Calderón thrust a cell phone into her fingers. The number was already ringing. "Talk to your daddy. It's time he started cooperating with us."

She was in trouble. Grounded for life kind of trouble. She'd-be-lucky-if-grounding-was-the-worst-thing-that-happened-to-her kind of trouble.

"I want Julio," she begged, as each ring of the phone counted down like a death knell in her hands.

"We don't care what you want." Player boy, with all the shine on his clothes and hat, sank onto the bed behind her, his hand settling far too familiarly on her thigh, his body brushing against her back and blocking any chance of escape.

But she was more afraid of the unblinking threat in Calderón's cold, dark eyes. "Talk to your papa, *amiga*. Tell him you are my prisoner. Say exactly what I tell you to."

Brittany didn't know whether to be mad at Julio for handing her over to these horrible men, or worried that the betrayal hadn't been his fault—that he'd been drugged the way she must have been, or beaten up…or something worse. Calderón hadn't said exactly where he'd sent Julio, or what condition he'd been in when he left.

Out of desperation, her spine solidified with the stubbornness that had gotten her into a lot of trouble during her seventeen years. She didn't know where that toughness came from, but she'd talked her way out of worse than this. Well, not really. But she wasn't going to submit to their pawing and bullying without a fight. She tossed the phone to smack Pretty Boy's offending hand away. "Don't touch me!"

The man laughed. "Ah, she is definitely Justice McCabe's daughter."

Oh, how she loathed that name. Up until three months ago, Justice McCabe had simply been a wealthy rancher who raised cattle and horses on the outskirts of Serpentine. An old cuss whom people gossiped about and revered. He'd been a nebulous entity with a town library and a barn at the county fairgrounds named after him.

And then the cancer took her mother and she'd learned the truth.

She was Justice McCabe's bastard daughter from some stupid affair. A child who'd never meant more to him than a monthly paycheck to support her mother.

"Get with the program, *amigo*," she mocked, her turbulent emotions getting the better of her common sense. "My father barely even knows me. I only live with him now because my mom died. She always told me my father was dead—until she realized I'd have no place else to go. I wish he *was* dead."

Calderón's answer was frightening with his calm tone and precise movements. He picked up the phone and dialed the number again. "That was your mother's choice, not his."

"Whatever. He doesn't care about what happens to me. What if he doesn't answer?"

"Enough with your poor-little-me whining." With the darting accuracy of a rattlesnake, he pinched her chin in a hard grasp and shoved the phone against her ear. "The only thing Justice McCabe values more than his land is his family. He will answer."

Chapter One

Things never changed.

At least here on the southern edge of Texas at the J-Bar-J ranch where Virgil "Bull" McCabe had grown up, they didn't.

Before pulling through the arching stone gate that marked the ranch's entrance, he slowed his black pickup on the dusty gravel road to take a good look at the sprawling landscape, dotted with cacti and scrub pines, where he'd grown up. Somehow he'd thought ten years and 1300 miles would make a difference. But they hadn't.

His barrel-size chest expanded with a painful breath as he tapped on the brake and the memories came flooding back. All the hard work that he'd been a part of from boyhood to make an operation of this size a success—breaking and moving and birthing livestock, battling the elements, building and repairing fence lines. The connections he shared with his older brother, Morgan, and younger brother, Wyatt, the harsh criticisms and hurtful secrets that had forced them to stand as one. His mother's tragic death.

His father.

That painful breath eased out on a wry laugh.

His father had been keeping a doozy of a secret this time. This wasn't just another affair he'd had while married to their mother. Justice had fathered a daughter. A girl who was now a teenager. Another casualty from Justice McCabe's selfish, womanizing ways. And, as usual, Bull and his brothers had been called on to put a bandage on the wounds Justice's choices inflicted on those around him.

The gray limestone hills grew more rugged and rocky as they

dropped off toward the Rio Grande River valley and its tributaries to the west. The land to the east, sectioned off by a network of irrigation canals, flattened out to succulent green pasture where hundreds of fat brown cattle and horses grazed. The gently sloping hills to the north led to a dammed-up reservoir and the neighboring Cobb ranch where he'd taken his horse on many rides to escape the arguments in the main house and stables. And behind him, about a mile to the south, was Mexico.

Pulling off his sunglasses, Bull scrubbed his hand across the dark brown stubble that peppered his square jaw and peered through the windshield. The barren landscape where he stood taller than almost any tree was a stark contrast to the crowded streets and steel high-rises of the Chicago neighborhood where he worked as a detective. He tucked his fingers beneath the unbuttoned collar of his damp, white shirt and wished for the snow and cold and biting lake wind he'd left up north. Even in mid-December with the A/C on in his truck, he could feel the sun beating down on him and heating his emotions.

This was a mistake. Why the hell had he let Wyatt talk him into this? He didn't belong here anymore. Their father had made that painfully clear. The two of them had gotten into a shoving match out in the barn that day during spring break.

"You're gonna learn to do things my way, Bull McCabe. And if you don't like my rules, you don't have to stay."

He hadn't.

But now he was back. He'd traveled down here from the northern edge of the country in just over twenty-four hours. His muscles were stiff and his neck ached. He was beat. But he needed to shift his truck into Drive and finish the last half mile of his journey. Someone needed him.

As Bull crossed through the gate, he recognized the familiar, two-story white house with its wraparound porch and pine-shingled roof. Framed by whitewashed barns and metal outbuildings, the house stood like a lonely beacon of civilization on the endless horizon of J-Bar-J land. This was Justice McCabe's own little country, west of the Texas town of Serpentine.

And Bull had stopped being a citizen there ten years earlier.

He'd never envisioned himself coming back home to this place, to his father—he'd never wanted to.

But the phone call from his brother Wyatt had him handing off cases and leaving early for his holiday vacation. *"Bring your gun and your badge, Bull,"* Wyatt had said. *"We need to save her."*

Bull didn't intend to be here any longer than he had to be. Morgan, Virgil and Wyatt McCabe might have lost their beloved mother, Jeanne, to a traffic accident a decade ago, but she'd been dying inside long before that because of their father's cheating. He'd be damned if he'd let another family member be hurt because of his father—even a sister he never knew they had.

"What the hell?" Bull pulled up behind a pair of departmental SUVs parked in the circular drive near the bottom of the front-porch steps. He recognized the dark-haired man in the blue jeans and cowboy hat, wearing a gun at his waist and a sheriff's badge on his shirt pocket. That was his brother Wyatt. He could even guess the dark-haired woman arguing with him was some kind of law enforcement, judging by the brown-and-tan uniform she wore.

What he didn't recognize was the evergreen garland, strewn with lights and red bows that draped around the porch railing and twisted up each post to another row of lights anchored to the gutter. And beyond the couple at the top of the steps, just to the right of the door, a tall pine tree, hung with ornaments and lights and an angel on top was framed in the front windows. What kind of game was this? There hadn't been a Christmas celebrated at the J-Bar-J since their mother had died.

Maybe some things did change. But the unexpected decorations only made him suspicious. What was Justice up to? Did he think a few imported greeneries and sparkly lights could convince Bull to make this emergency visit a permanent move home?

He pulled his gun from the glove compartment and slipped it into the shoulder holster he wore beneath his left arm before opening the truck door. The heated debate that was mostly one-sided felt more like the home he'd left behind than the brightly colored holiday decor did. Bull shook his head and reached back across the cab for his gray, Western-tailored blazer and shrugged into it, making sure his badge was visible on his belt before approaching his brother and the dark-haired woman with the sharp tongue.

"We don't have time for family reunions and strategy meetings." Her Latin heritage was evident in the lilting fire of her voice. "The *Los Jaguares* and Javier Calderón are dangerous men. We need to get on this case right now."

"There's no point to chasing after rumors and shadows. More people could get hurt." Wyatt dipped his face toward hers and lowered his voice to a whisper. "Let me handle this." Then he turned to Bull and hoofed it down the steps to greet him. "Hey, big man."

"Pipsqueak." Bull caught his brother's outstretched hand and pulled him in for a hug that included slapping backs and nods acknowledging the years they'd been apart and the bond they'd forged long before that. Despite the four inches and fifty pounds he had on his younger brother, the storm-gray eyes that looked back at him were the same as when they separated. Trouble was brewing on the J-Bar-J. Or maybe just on the J-Bar-J's front porch. Bull arched a curious eyebrow toward the woman pacing at the top of the steps. "You two need a room?" he teased. "To duke it out or, um, resolve your personal issues in some other way?"

"We do not have personal…" The woman silenced her protest just as quickly as she'd turned to make it. "We were having a professional difference of opinion, that's all."

Uh-huh.

"Give it a rest, Bull," Wyatt warned. "Things have been pretty tense around here the past few days."

"Is Morgan here?"

"Not yet."

"Where the hell is he? Why doesn't he have to deal with this latest McCabe family Christmas crisis?"

"He's on a mission out of the country somewhere. I've called in every favor I can to try and track him down. But he's off the grid for now. Once I get a hold of him, though, he'll be here. I'm sure of it. You're the one I was worried wouldn't show up."

"Yeah, well, just know I'm doing this as a favor to *you*. I'm not staying any longer than I have to."

"I'll take what I can get." Wyatt motioned for Bull to follow him up the steps. "This is Elena Vargas, a local ICE agent. We serve together on the Border Security Task Force. My big brother, Bull McCabe. He's the Chicago PD detective I told you about. He's worked a lot of drug cases over the years. And nobody knows this land the way he does. If there's any track to follow, any place to hide, he'll find it."

"A big-city cop?" The woman looked skeptical.

Bull looked down—way down—to meet the agent's dark eyes. He hadn't earned his nickname just from the rodeos he'd competed in back in high school and college. He was the biggest and brawniest of the three McCabe brothers, and he was impressed that Elena Vargas didn't seem intimidated by that fact.

"Agent Vargas." They shook hands. "Immigration and Customs Enforcement. Does that have something to do with the girl's disappearance? Is she an illegal?"

"She's blond-haired and has eyes the same color as you and your brother." She propped her hands on her hips and challenged him. "Think you can find a girl like that around here with your tracking skills, detective?"

Bull ignored the sarcasm. "Things don't change much around this part of the country, Agent Vargas. I remember it well."

Wyatt backed him up. "There's probably not an inch of this ranch Bull hasn't covered on horseback, ATV or on foot. And he knows how these kind of people operate. We need his expertise."

"*You* need it," Elena insisted. "There's no time for random searches through the countryside. Calderón and his *Los Jaguares* are dangerous men. I believe this kidnapping is related to a drug-smuggling operation I've been investigating. I'm willing to work with the sheriff's department on this, Wyatt—to let you handle it personally to protect this foolish sister of yours. But I'm not willing to wait forever."

"I haven't even had a chance to talk to my brother Morgan. At least let me give Bull a briefing so he's up to speed on what's happening here. He could probably use some food and a few hours sleep, too."

With an impatient huff, Elena marched past both men down to her ICE vehicle. She didn't stop until she opened the door to her SUV and turned to give them an ultimatum. "I'll give you one hour, Wyatt. I hope the reinforcements you've called in *can* help us. But Calderón and his *criminales* won't wait. The task force needs to move on this. So one hour. Call me."

Wyatt was still staring as the dark-haired beauty drove away in a plume of dust.

Bull glanced over at the steely clench of his brother's jaw. He could see that Agent Vargas had wormed her way beneath Wyatt's cool, calm and collected facade. And that, apparently, wasn't a good thing. "Are you running this show, Sheriff, or is she?"

Wyatt flashed him a snarky glance before hiding his face beneath the brim of his hat. "Come on inside. I'll explain everything I know about the kidnapping and…Brittany."

Bull followed him to the door. "What's to explain? The old man never could keep it in his pants. Broke Mom's heart more than once. You're probably too young to remember much of that."

"I remember enough. But you can't hold a grudge forever, Bull," Wyatt explained. "Brittany's in the kind of trouble that supersedes family secrets and the bad history you share with Dad." Wyatt opened the door and halted before stepping inside. "She needs us. She needs the kind of help that you, Morgan and I can give her."

"Not the kind of help that Agent Vargas can?"

"Protecting Brittany and getting her safely home isn't Elena's priority."

"But it has to be ours, right?"

Wyatt's shoulders lifted and he looked Bull square in the eye. "Brittany's a good kid. But she's got nobody but us. This family is fractured enough as it is. I intend to protect whatever we have left. Are you in?"

Bull nodded, impressed with how the pipsqueak had grown up, even if his ideology was a little too rose-colored-glasses for Bull's taste. "I'm in."

Catching the door, Bull followed his brother into the front entryway. But his purposeful stride slowed as another wave of memories washed over him. The pungent scent of fresh pine tickled his nose. The tree he'd seen through the front window must be freshly cut. It matched another garland of greenery and lights that looped through a peg board running along the foyer wall that held hats and keys and jackets.

Bull's breath lodged in his chest. Other than the new decorations, this place was like a museum frozen in time. A black Stetson, wide-brimmed and shaped to fit his own head, hung from a wooden peg. Wyatt disappeared around the corner into the main room, calling for their father while Bull reached out to brush his fingertips over the soft crease in the Stetson's crown. He'd left the hat hanging there that last day he'd stormed out and driven off to his dorm in College Station without any intention of ever returning.

He knocked a layer of dust off the crown and then wiped his fingers on the leg of his jeans as his attention turned to the other keepsakes on display in the entryway. There was Morgan's state fair ribbon on the wall beside some academic thing Wyatt had won. And on the front table, nestled among family portraits and more greenery, stood a glassed-in shadow box on a small easel. His silver high-school rodeo champion belt buckle was mounted inside. A slow smile spread across Bull's mouth as he remembered the pride he'd felt the day he'd outlasted that giant Brahma and earned that championship. For a few days after that, he'd been on top of the world, invincible. For a few days, his dad had been proud of him.

Bull glanced around to take it all in. These were the good memories he had of growing up here. Their mother had proudly framed and shown off each of her sons' accomplishments. Automatically, Bull's gaze went to the image of the petite dynamo who had raised them. He touched his fingertip to the glass over her smiling face. "Miss you, Mom."

The one anomaly in the collection of family artifacts drew his attention to a lump of yellow clay, crudely molded with several stubby extensions protruding in various directions. Bull picked up the tiny sculpture and frowned. Unlike the other keepsakes on the front table, it was free of dust, clearly a new addition. Where had it come from? And who besides their mother had ever cared to put a piece of a child's art on display?

He heard the footsteps on the stairs and tensed.

"Welcome home, son."

Squeezing both sentimentality and curiosity from his veins, Bull turned to greet the man coming down the stairs. Other than the silvering hair and knees bent from too many years and too many injuries that shortened his height, Bull was every inch his father's son.

"Justice."

The older man bristled for a moment at the use of his given name by his middle son. But he curbed whatever he'd been tempted to say and smiled instead. "That's a horse. Don't worry, I had to ask what it was, too."

Was his father really joking around as though broken promises and ultimatums hadn't kept them apart for ten years?

"I'm glad Wyatt got ahold of you." Justice McCabe stretched his arm out, and for a split second Bull thought he was making an attempt to shake his hand. Instead, the older man plucked the lumpy representation of a horse from his fingers and set it down beside the photograph Bull had just touched. "Brittany helped Cody make that."

Bull tensed. Was a new grandchild part of the family now, too? "Who's Cody?"

The screen door in the kitchen at the back of the house slammed. Justice glanced toward the sounds of laughter and running feet and a woman's voice calling out. "Cody? Come back here. Wipe your feet."

"I think you're about to find out."

"Juh-tis!" A little boy, wearing dusty cowboy boots about a size too big for his feet, bolted from the kitchen and ran up to the two men. "I counted tree horses!"

To Bull's surprise, his father scooped up the thigh-high youngster and bounced him on his hip. "Three?"

"Yep." A stubby little finger shot up with each number. "One. Two. Tree."

"That's right." Bull felt like he'd stepped into an alternate universe. His father was playing with the boy, practically beaming. "And how old are you?"

The same fingers went up again. "Tree!"

Bull looked from the sandy-haired child up to the man he barely recognized. Surely this wasn't another offspring from one of Justice's more recent dalliances. "And Cody would be...?"

The child answered first by tapping his chest. "I'm Cody. I can count to tree. One. Two. Tree."

"Good job, buddy." It was impossible not to be charmed by the little boy's enthusiasm—or to stop the smile relaxing his own face. Bull held up three big fingers and the boy tapped each one, repeating his numbers again. "I'm Bull."

Cody's sweet round face squinched up in a frown. "I can't go where the bull is. He's very mean."

"It's the four-legged kind that's mean." He tweaked the boy's nose and winked. "I'm the two-legged Bull. I won't hurt ya."

The boy's confusion vanished in an instant and he counted off his fingers again. "One leg. Two—"

"I'm sorry, Justice." A tall, willowy blonde with a chic ponytail and an exasperated expression walked in from the kitchen. "He got away from me. I need to run these tax forms into town before the post office closes. I thought the cook might still be here to watch him."

She reached out to take the child from Justice's arms. But with a smiling insistence Bull scarcely remembered from his own childhood, his father shifted the boy onto the other hip. "I sent Maria home early today. You run along. I can take care of him for a little while."

The blonde straightened the sealed manila envelope she'd tucked beneath her arm and purse. "I know you have other priorities right now. I don't want to be an imposition."

"Nonsense. I said I'd do it and I'll do it. Dakota, do you remember my son Bull?" The momentary sharpness of his tone eased to make the polite introduction. "This is Dakota Dayton and her son, Cody. She does all the accounting for me and the ranch now. Lives in old LeRoy's cabin out back. It's not the same homesteader's cabin you remember. We've completely redone the inside and updated everything—even put a studio apartment on the top floor."

"Of course, Bull, I remember you."

The memory of a woman much younger and less frazzled finally registered. The last name was different, but several years back, she'd gone out on a few dates with his brother Morgan. "Dakota. It's been a while. You're looking well."

"You're a good liar, but thanks." Her handshake was as smoothly professional as her smile. But the cool tone wavered a bit when she turned her gaze up to Justice. "Are you sure about watching Cody? I can take him with me if I have to."

"I don't mind. Hey, did you ever pick up that S-A-N-T-A gift I ordered for the boy?" The *no* had barely formed on her lips before Justice shooed her back to the kitchen. "Get out of here, then. You can pick that up after you run by the post office."

"Okay. Thanks." She planted a kiss on Cody's cheek before tossing Bull a wave and hurrying out the back door. "Good to see you again."

"Let's move this to my office." Justice carried Cody through the main room and past the decorated tree before setting the boy down inside the room where Justice ran both the ranching and business ventures that had made him a wealthy man. "Down you go, son."

Bull noted the box of toys that had been added to the bookshelves and leather furniture that lined the room. After watching the three-year-old dump out a pile of building blocks to begin construction on a tiny ranch of his own, Bull followed his father to the hand-carved walnut desk where Wyatt was pulling a sheet out of the computer printer.

"I got a copy of the transcription you asked for, Dad."

The little boy pulled a plastic horse from the toy box and knocked over the blocks with a toddler-size roar. Then, laughing with delight, he set the horse down and began reconstructing his buildings all over again. He looked so at home playing in the corner of Justice's office, like he had no doubt he belonged here.

"Is Cody yours, too?" Bull asked bluntly.

Wyatt groaned. "And here we go."

Justice swung around and thumped a finger in the middle of Bull's chest. "I'm going to pretend you didn't just say that."

Ignoring the taunt, Bull dropped down to pick up a block that had tumbled beneath one of the leather couches and handed it back to the boy. "But I'm supposed to pretend enjoying this kid's company is normal behavior for you? And decorating the house? Who are you trying to impress?"

"Understand this, Virgil McCabe. Mrs. Dayton works for me. It's good business to hire someone with her qualifications. Accommodations in the cabin for her and her son are part of her salary, nothing more."

Bull straightened to his full height. "Virgil? You're going to start calling me Virgil now? That honor was reserved for Mom."

"I don't have to impress anyone. The decorations are for the boy. Every child should have the chance to celebrate Christmas."

"Would you two stop going at it like rival stallions and focus on the more pertinent problem?" Wyatt got between them and thrust the printout into Bull's hands. "Brittany Means is seventeen years old and being held hostage by a Mexican drug lord who promises to kill her on Christmas Day if we don't give him what he wants or we can't find her first. That's a transcript of the ransom message he left on Dad's phone." He stuck a second printout into his hands. "That's her picture. Take a good look at her, Bull. *She's* the reason you're here."

Tearing his combative gaze from his father, Bull glanced down at the image in his hand. Brittany Means must have gotten her blond, wavy hair from her mother. But the dark gray eyes and strong jawline were uncomfortably similar to the angles he looked at in the mirror each day. The family resemblance was unmistakable.

Wyatt was smarter than Bull had given him credit for. He'd put a face to the problem at hand. This wasn't about Justice betraying their mother. This wasn't about some mistake he'd hidden from his sons for seventeen years.

Bull had a sister.

He had a baby sister.

And she needed him.

Bull ran his hand over the top of his short brown hair. Damn the pipsqueak, anyway, for making him care. It was easier to be angry. But when had Bull McCabe ever done anything the easy way? "I'm sorry if I insinuated anything about Dakota or Cody. Old habits are hard to forget."

"Old hurts, too," Justice conceded.

With a temporary truce in place, Bull smoothed out the paper he'd crumpled in his fist, dutifully adjusting his focus. He swore as he read the concisely worded threat. "Why didn't you ever tell us about this sister sooner?"

"Margaret—her mother—never wanted me to be a part of Brittany's life, and I respected that. She thought it'd be harder for Brittany if gossip got around that she'd slept with a married man and gotten pregnant. And she knew I wouldn't leave your mama." His father looked suddenly like a much older man as he sank down into the chair behind the desk. "Margaret was smart enough to know I wasn't good father material. I tried to do right by her, though. As long as I kept it anonymous, she let me help out financially. I even paid her medical expenses when she got so sick at the end." Pain deepened the lines of his face. "It was her decision to finally tell Brittany the truth. And then, when she was gone and there was nowhere else for the girl to go... I promised I'd take care of her. Look how well I've done so far."

Wyatt reached over to squeeze their father's shoulder. "You're not the same man who raised us, Dad. We'll get her back. And you'll have the chance to make things right with her."

Justice patted Wyatt's hand, then looked across the desk to include Bull. "What about you boys? Will I ever have the chance to make things right with you?"

Bull wanted to believe there was a chance at reconciliation. He might have believed it if he didn't have thirty years of life experience to remind him that Justice McCabe lied. Wyatt had apparently bought into their father's reformed ways. But Bull had come here braced to do battle. Maybe he had gone on the defensive far too quickly. The aging man sitting across the desk from him, the man who played with a little boy, wasn't the father he remembered.

A knock on the door curtailed the internal debate. "Mr. Mc-Cabe?"

Rusty Fisher, a longtime ranch hand at the J-Bar-J, stepped into the room. The deferential hat in his hand went by the wayside when he spotted Bull. A big, gap-toothed smile lifted the corners of his handlebar mustache. "Well, look who's come back home. Bull, how are ya?" He slapped his hand into Bull's for a hearty shake before stepping back. "Hear you're a big-city boy now. Other than being a little pale, you look as fit and ready to work as ever."

"Rusty, good to see you." The snakeskin belt was new, but the prized mustache and friendly welcome were the same as they'd always been. "There's not much call for herding cattle up in Chicago these days."

"Still roundin' up those bad guys?"

Bull pulled back the front of his jacket to let him see his badge. "I made detective a couple years ago."

"Well, don't that beat all."

"Rusty." Justice stood up, propping his fists on the desktop. "I'm having a meeting with my sons. Is there a reason for this interruption?"

Quickly remembering who was boss around here, Rusty glanced over at Cody. "I ran into Mrs. Dayton out back. She said her boy was in here, but that you needed to conduct some business. I can take him out to the stable with me for a bit. I know he likes looking at Missy's colt."

"Horsie!" Cody piped up.

Justice's stern face softened with a smile. "Good idea, Rusty. Thanks."

"Come on, little man." Cody eagerly latched on to Rusty's hand and headed out the door with him.

"Don't you take your eyes off him," Justice warned.

"I won't." Rusty tipped his hat to say goodbye, then hurried his pace to keep up with the excited child.

Instead of going back to the unsettling idea that his father's desire to make amends was sincere, Bull concentrated on the reason he was here—and summoned the investigative skills Wyatt had asked for. "Is this all we know so far?" He read aloud the ransom message in his hand. *"You have a deadline. By midnight Christmas Eve, you sign over usage rights to the river valley on the western expanse of your ranch to Javier Calderón, or your daughter will die."*

Wyatt added his report. "We know that she left school three days ago. One of her friends saw her get into a rusty old farm truck with a flatbed, and she hasn't been seen anywhere in town since."

"Any description of the driver?"

"Hispanic male was all I got. He wore a hat that shadowed his face. They didn't recognize the truck and nobody wrote down a license number."

That description was next to useless in this part of the country. "Does she have a boyfriend? Any other place in town or on one of the nearby ranches where she'd go to get away from things?"

"She's not old enough to date," Justice insisted. "Besides, she's been kidnapped. She hasn't run off with some boy."

Bull had to guess it was more wishful thinking than naïveté that made his father think a teenage girl wouldn't be interested in a boy. He turned to Wyatt for a more levelheaded answer. "Who does she trust enough to get into a vehicle with?"

"I've talked to some of her friends." His brother shook his head. "None of them say she's been seeing anyone."

"The friend or boyfriend might not be from here." Bull remembered the argument on the front porch when he'd first arrived. "Is that why you asked Agent Vargas to get involved? Does she have contacts over the border?"

"Something like that."

Justice wouldn't be left out of the conversation. "I own every inch of this land—from the Mexican border to the Cobb's spread up north and west to the river." He crossed to the map painting on the wall behind his desk, outlining the ranch and surrounding lands. "Calderón says he wants to use it as a shipping short-cut for his alpaca farm in Mexico. Alpacas, my ass. He wants to bring drugs into the country over J-Bar-J land. I make a lot of deals when it comes to running a successful business, but I won't help a criminal. I won't let that happen."

Bull narrowed his gaze. "Something tells me he's approached you before."

"He offered me money to transport his livestock and I told him no. His men slashed my tires in town and threatened that other accidents would happen if I didn't cooperate. That's when I knew this was about the drugs."

"And now he has your daughter," Bull said evenly. "Are you going to rethink saying no to him?"

"There has to be a way to rescue her and keep the *Los Jaguares* off my land."

"Not to mention keeping his drugs out of the country. Were there any other threats between the slashed tires and the abduction?" Ah, hell. That stony silence meant there had been. "Your stubbornness let the trouble escalate to this?"

"I thought I could handle it. I made it clear to Calderón that I wouldn't condone or be a part of what he does."

"So he found a way to bend the mighty Justice McCabe to his will."

"Here we go again," Wyatt muttered.

Justice pushed back his chair and stood. "What is that crack supposed to mean? You think this is my fault?"

"You almost had me there, with Wyatt throwing his sweet talk in on the argument. No wonder Morgan hasn't shown up yet. He's smart enough to keep his distance." Bull folded the printouts and stuffed them inside his jacket pocket. "You hurt everything you touch. All to save your land or your pride and reputation." He tapped his heart, where Brittany's image lay inside his jacket. "And now this girl is paying the price for being a part of your life."

Justice came around the table. "Still so angry? Holding on to hate like that wears a man down, son. I made mistakes—said and did things I deeply regret. I asked you boys to be men before you were ready to handle that responsibility, and then I cut you down when you couldn't live up to my impossible demands. But I'm trying to live a better life now. For Brittany. To honor your mother's memory. I've learned to ask forgiveness and move on."

Bull squared off against him. "Are you going to ask for my forgiveness, Justice?"

"When you're ready."

"Don't hold your breath, old man. You promised this place would be mine one day and then you threw me out."

"I was angry at the world. I was devastated by your mother's death."

"So was I. We all were. In the end I didn't care about the damn ranch. What I needed was my family. And all I had was you, smacking me around."

The weathered skin went pale. "I thought you could take it."

"I couldn't." Before any other emotion—guilt, regret, anger, love, pain—could blindside him, Bull stormed out of the office. "I need some air."

"Bull!"

The Christmas tree was a colorful blur as he headed back to the hallway. The faint hope that things might have changed on the J-Bar-J was blurring, too.

"Hold up, big man." Wyatt closed the office door and chased Bull into the hallway, falling into stride beside him. "You two are just alike. You know that, don't you?"

"Like that helps." On impulse, Bull grabbed the black hat, brushing the dust off on his pant leg as he headed out the door. If he was still a teen, right about now is when he'd be marching off to the stables to escape the latest conflict on a long ride into the countryside. Today, he'd settle for a fast drive in his pickup.

His brother's booted feet followed him down the steps and across the gravel to his truck. "You're tired. Your nerves are on edge. The old man hasn't slept much in the last couple of days, either—"

"Enough, Wyatt. You're not working any miracles here." Bull tossed his hat into the open window of his truck and spun around.

Alike or not, that man and I are never going to make peace. If I can't get past the resentment he stirs up in me, I'm not going to be any good to you. Or Brittany."

His glance back at the house took his gaze farther north across the rugged landscape. He remembered losing himself in the rocks and dust. He remembered finding solace there.

"If you're looking for Tracy Cobb, she doesn't live at her parents' ranch anymore."

"What?" Bull squinted into the rosy sunset and dragged his gaze back to Wyatt.

"I know how you and Dad would get into it, and then you'd go off to find her. The two of you would talk until the sun went down." The pipsqueak grinned. "Or came up. You know, she wasn't married."

His brother was matchmaking now? "Tracy Cobb and I were never more than neighbors. Friends. Classmates."

"You're tellin' me that all those times you rode over to the Cobb ranch you never once made a play for Tomboy Tracy?" What Bull and Tracy had done on their long rides together was nobody's business but theirs. And if anyone thought something had happened…it hadn't. They'd talked. They'd listened. They'd been each other's adolescent salvation. But it rankled to hear that his brother—or anyone else—believed Tracy had been anything more, or less, than his best friend. "Well, if you're looking for an old classmate to reconnect with, she lives in town now. Her apartment's a few blocks from where I live."

Bull opened the truck door and climbed in behind the wheel. "I'm not staying, Wyatt. I'm not reconnecting. All I need is a drink and some space to clear my head. Where do I go to find a cold beer around here?"

"I don't want to hear that one of my deputies pulled you over for a DUI."

"You won't." He closed the door and started the engine. "Let me know if you hear from Morgan. In the meantime, I'll call my contacts to see what I can uncover about Calderón's operation. I'll find you later tonight to compare notes." He held up his wrist and tapped his watch. He could do the innuendo thing, too. "Isn't it about time you checked in with Agent Vargas?"

"I recommend Margarita's over on Acuna Street," Wyatt advised, cleverly avoiding the question and backing away as Bull shifted the truck into gear.

Between Justice and the kidnapping, the memories he wanted to forget and the ones he wished he could hold on to, he definitely needed that drink.

THE SUN HAD SET BY THE TIME Bull found a parking space on Acuna Street. And while things hadn't changed all that much out at the J-Bar-J, the scenery here in Serpentine had. Apparently, lots of folks were getting a jump start on their holiday celebration this weekend. For a town of only 35,000, the downtown area was jumping.

The growing population of locals, immigrants and military personnel from the nearby air force base was reflected in the explosion of bars and restaurants here. Bull adjusted the black Stetson he'd reclaimed on top of his head before strolling down the sidewalk. The cop in him liked the idea of blending in with the other pedestrians and partiers, giving him the opportunity to take note of his surroundings without calling attention to himself any more than the Illinois license plate on his truck already did.

The temperature hadn't cooled all that much, but he left his blazer on to mask the gun he wore, and quickly sized up the hot spots. A saloon-styled bar dubiously named Shifty's had a line waiting outside to get in. Frankie's Cantina seemed to have a corner on the military clientele while a rare sighting of men and women in suits and business attire were smoking their cigarettes outside a sit-down restaurant called Miguel's.

Bull politely averted his head from the make-out session inside one of the cars parked on the street, and wondered if the trio of young Hispanic men claiming the right-of-way by walking side by side on the opposite side of the street were up to anything they shouldn't be, or if their boisterous conversation and flirty catcalls to every woman they passed just meant they'd started their drinking sooner than the rest of the crowd. It was good to get a feeling for the town again, see what he recognized, identify what was less familiar, so he wouldn't be at a disadvantage asking questions and looking for leads into Brittany's kidnapping.

The tension he'd felt at the ranch eased a little more with every step. He tipped the brim of his hat to a pair of raven-haired hotties who smiled up at him. And the mix of country music and Latin rhythms pouring out of Margarita's bar at the end of the street was calling to him like the thirst for something tangy and cold to drink.

The crowd thinned and the music grew louder as he neared the end of the block. His eye was drawn to a woman pacing near the alleyway next to Margarita's. Shooting darting glances at every man who passed, and underdressed for the town's nightlife in plain jeans and a blouse, she stood out like a wallflower at a junior high dance.

Still, there was something about her that kept distracting him from the street life he wanted to survey. Her hair wasn't just a brown ponytail hanging down her back. The shining neon from the bar's entrance reflected red highlights, giving the curling waves a sorrel sheen. And plain clothes didn't matter. There was plenty to admire in the rear view of her jeans when she turned and moved away.

Bull's blood warmed with the possibility of unwinding with something more than a cold beer. He meant what he'd told Wyatt—he wasn't back in Serpentine to make any lasting connections with anyone. But maybe he could persuade that sweet backside to go for a two-step spin around the dance floor with him.

"Or not."

Wasn't that just the way this trip back home had been going for him? The woman's entire posture changed from restless waiting to an eager greeting when a tall, black-haired Hispanic man walked out of Margarita's. Although dressed a little warmly for the night in a black leather jacket, he flashed a smile when she waved and he hurried over to join her. Miss Sweet Jeans was taken.

Bull's own pace slowed as he watched the couple's greeting unfold. Sweet Jeans straightened her shoulders and tipped her chin as the man approached. She was bracing for the encounter, not welcoming him. She reached into the front pocket of her jeans and pulled out a roll of money.

Seriously? A drug buy? He'd been lusting after a user?

A suspicious beat of alarm in his pulse pushed aside his disappointment as the man in black leather slapped his hand over her fist and pulled the money down out of sight between them. Bull lengthened his steps into a jog. Where was the dope? Where was the smooth handoff? Dealers didn't linger with their customers like this guy.

"Walk away, lady," Bull urged on a tight breath.

He recognized the signs of a drug buy going south. The dealer clamped his free hand around the woman's arm and pulled her into the alley with him. Sweet Jeans was in trouble.

Bull's interest morphed into concern. With a quick check for traffic, he bolted across the street and ducked into the shadows at the edge of the alley. All it took was a peek around the corner to see the woman yank her arm from the man's grasp and to see the gun holstered beneath the leather jacket.

"Well?" she demanded, rubbing her arm. "I brought the money."

With one hand, the bum stuffed the cash wad into his jacket pocket. With the other, he reached out and stroked the woman's cheek. She jerked away from his touch and he laughed. "What else do you have for me, *chica?*"

"You said—"

"Ma'am? Are you all right?" Spotting a second bulge at the man's ankle where another gun or knife was hidden, Bull stepped out of the shadows and made his presence known.

Startled, she whirled around, her eyes catching the light from the street. For a split second, Bull was struck by the blueness of her irises and just how pretty they were. Then the rest of her face registered.

Oh, no. There was a wholesome maturity to the dusting of freckles across her cheeks that hadn't been there a decade ago. Breasts and a butt softened the coltish figure he remembered.

One thing had definitely changed in Serpentine, Texas.

"Tracy?" Tomboy Tracy? The girl next door all grown up into this pretty woman? Buying drugs? "Tracy Cobb?"

"Bull?" She threw up her hands, gasped something distinctly unladylike, then pointed toward him. "Duck!"

Chapter Two

Bull heard the scrape of boots on the concrete behind him the second Tracy's odd reply registered. Bull spun around to see a trash can hurtling toward him.

"Vamos! Policía!"

Knowing Tracy was standing right behind him, Bull stood his ground and absorbed the brunt of the heavy plastic projectile with his shoulder. Paper and bottles and who knew what else flew through the air as he knocked the can out of his way and squared off against a second Hispanic man. This one, just as big as he was, charged through the debris.

With no time to do more than react, Bull absorbed the attack like an offensive lineman guarding the quarterback. He hit the ground hard, losing his hat as he dodged a punch and rolled the muscleman beneath him. "Tracy!"

"Mintió a mi." The dealer, smaller in stature than his *compadre,* but no less violent, shoved her to the pavement and ran.

"I didn't lie. I need your help. Stop!" Tracy scrambled to her feet and latched on to the dealer's jacket.

But the bastard swung around and backhanded her across the face, freeing himself.

"Tracy!" Bull shouted. He pushed himself up. "Trace—!" His attacker seized the advantage and looped a stout arm around Bull's neck.

"Don't leave! He's not with me. I just want to talk. Please!"

Ah, hell. She was chasing after the guy with the gun.

Enough.

Bull needed to end this mess before this guy strangled him unconscious or he was too beat up to protect her. Making his own advantage, Bull threw himself against the bricks, slamming the guy on his back up against the wall and loosening his hold enough to ram an elbow up into his gut. A second elbow to the face popped his attacker's nose, and the man finally let go, muttering all kinds of curses in Spanish.

"Sol!" Cradling his battered face, the man dropped to his knees and shouted for help.

"Manny?" The dealer in black leather reappeared, this time swinging a long stiletto. Stepping between Tracy and the knife, Bull raised his forearm to deflect the blow and was rewarded with a stinging brand of fire cutting through his sleeve and into his skin. "Who are you?" the man muttered in a thick accent, raising his knife again. "Why are you in my business?"

"Sol! *Vamos!*" Broken-nose guy dragged his friend out of the alley, pushing aside a young couple as they ran into the street.

The two thugs jumped into a double-parked car and sped away, scattering shrieking pedestrians as they careened through the crosswalk and disappeared into the night.

"Wait!"

Tracy darted around Bull's shoulder and chased them all the way to the corner before he could catch her by the arm and pull her back to the curb out of the path of a car screeching its brakes. "Tracy!"

While she waved an apology to the driver cursing her, Bull cinched his arm around her waist and lifted her onto the sidewalk, pulling her several steps out of the path of danger, and away from the curious glances and outright stares of the people around them.

"Well, that went real well." Tracy turned in Bull's grasp and nudged him back a step. His hands settled at the nip of her waist, lightly holding on when she would have pushed him completely out of the way so she could get a glimpse of where the dealer's car had gone. "Maybe they thought I was up to something when you showed up." Finally understanding that Bull wasn't going to let her loose to go after them again, she pulled open the front of his jacket and breathed out a heavy sigh of disappointment. "You're wearing your badge, aren't you?" She made a face at the gun and holster beneath his arm and quickly smoothed the jacket back into place. "They probably thought I was a cop, too. Or an informant or bait or whatever—"

"Tracy Cobb?" Bull repeated, the raw wound on his arm burning, his chest heaving to even out his breathing, his brain trying to wrap itself around the idea of seeing the classmate who'd lived on the ranch next to his all grown up. And hot. And meeting in an alley with two armed thugs. "Trace—"

She tilted her chin up to chide him. "If all you say is my name one more time, I'm going to smack you."

Bull grinned. At last, something he recognized—a friend half his size who wasn't afraid to tease him.

"Been beat up enough for one night already, thanks." Risking that she wouldn't bolt after their two attackers again, Bull let go to run his hands up and down her arms, feeling soft cotton and firm muscle underneath, checking for any sign of injury. He touched her chin and angled it up to the corner streetlight to get a better look at the puffy mark on her cheek where the man called Sol had struck her. "Are you all right?"

She brushed aside a chestnut tendril that had blown across her face and tucked it back into her ponytail. "I'm not hurt."

But something *was* wrong. A tiny frown marred the smooth skin of her forehead.

"Why are you buying drugs?" he asked.

She propped her hands on her hips, and tipped those true blue eyes up to his. "How else am I supposed to meet a drug dealer?"

Matching her stance, Bull blinked twice, three times, still trying to make sense of this unexpected reunion. Tracy's eyes couldn't be that intensely clear if she was using, so, "What's going on? What the hell are you doing messing with guys like that? They both carried guns, and they knew how to fight."

"Of course they would. They're members of the *Del Rey de los Jaguares.*"

"King of the Jaguars," he translated. Wait a minute. Drug cartel? Dealer? Enforcer? "How do you know thugs like that?" He cupped his hands over her shoulders and shook his head. "Sorry. Could we start this conversation over again?"

"Oh, Bull. You're hurt." With his arm in her line of sight, it was impossible to miss the sticky crimson staining the light gray sleeve of his jacket. She gently cradled his forearm between them with one hand, and started patting at the pockets of his jacket and jeans, probably searching for the bandanna she'd always known him to carry.

"Back pocket," he told her, reading her intention the way he'd once been able to. He liked the familiarity of her palming his backside to retrieve the dark blue cloth about as much as it surprised him to *notice* that he liked having her confident hands on him. The way a woman touched a man. Not the way two buddies who'd grown up together and shared each other's secrets made contact with each other. The bustle and noise of the music, people and traffic around them drifted outside the bubble of awareness that seemed to be drawing Bull closer and closer to the pretty tomboy and her tender ministrations.

What the heck was that about? This trip home to Texas was all out of whack. Justice playing with little kids and throwing out apologies? Tracy Cobb looking all pretty and feminine and like somebody he wanted to kiss?

She helped him shrug off his jacket and roll up his shirtsleeve so she could get a better look at the cut on his forearm. "I think you were bleeding the last time I saw you." She wadded up the bandanna and gently pressed the cotton against the three-inch long gash. "You're current on your tetanus shots, aren't you? What brings you back to Serpentine? After ten years, I figured I was never going to see you again. Are you home for the holidays?"

Ah, hell. She was being all friendly and tender just to distract him from the questions he'd asked.

"Uh-uh." Bull pulled away and brushed that wayward tendril of hair away from the freckles on her cheek. "We aren't pretending like something scary didn't just happen."

She knew he was onto her ploy now. Her touch and tone were more efficient nurse than tender lover when she grabbed his wrist and held it up to slow the bleeding. "It's a long story."

"Ow." He winced at the pressure on his cut. "I imagine so. But I want to hear it."

"Sorry." A sigh of confusion that must match his own lifted her shoulders. "Sounds like old times…you and me talking."

There was nothing old or familiar about the purely male interest and protective concern she'd stirred up inside him. But he did know how to be a cop and elicit answers when he needed them. If he shared some information, the witness or suspect he was interrogating was more likely to share something, too.

She was tying the bandanna around the wound when they both blurted out in unison.

"I've got a sister."

"It's about your sister."

Bull dipped his head, demanding an explanation. "You know about Brittany?"

"I'm a high school English teacher now. Brittany's a student of mine. She's been missing for three days. It's not unusual for some of the more troublesome kids to skip school the last day or two before a break. But she's not a problem student—at least not for me." Tracy finished tying off the square knot before meeting his searching gaze. "She's run away in the past—Brittany really rebelled when her mom died and she found out Justice was her father. Turned up at my place once. She needed a place to chill out and talk before I drove her back to the J-Bar-J."

"So you're a teacher now? You face down those teenage terrors we once were?"

"We weren't so bad. And neither is Brittany. I think she's just a confused, heartbroken girl. But she's never run away for this long before, and I'm worried. There are a few other kids the truant officer hasn't been able to track down yet, but I didn't think she ran with those…" An alarm went off in those clear blue eyes. "That's why you're here, isn't it, something *has* happened to her." Tight fingers curled into the sleeve of his shirt and the muscles underneath. "Bull? Is Brittany okay?"

This was no place to have this conversation. Once again aware of all the curious glances and potential eavesdroppers around them outside of Margarita's, Bull flipped his slashed jacket over his shoulder and took Tracy by the arm. He nodded toward the bar's flashing entryway. "Can I buy you a drink?"

She twisted around in front of him, stopping him with a palm at the center of his chest. "Whatever it is, you can tell me. Brittany and I were close. I worked with her at school. She had a real talent for writing and needed an adult she could trust. What's happened to her?"

He covered her hand with his own and gave it a reassuring squeeze. "Better make that drink coffee. Someplace private."

"KIDNAPPED?" TRACY UNLOCKED the door to her apartment and ushered Bull into the kitchen. "I knew it wasn't good for her to miss three days of school. Wyatt gave me the standard departmental line of 'I'll look into it,' when I reported her missing, and Justice wouldn't return my phone calls. So I was trying to buy information about your sister. Or any of the other missing students. I figured if anyone knows about the bad things that go on here in Serpentine, the *Los Jaguares* would."

"Your logic was good. As a cop, I probably would have done the same thing." She pulled out a stool at the eating peninsula and pushed him onto the padded seat. She took his bloodied coat and the black hat they'd retrieved from the alley and hooked them over the back of a kitchen chair. When she moved past him to get some clean towels and a first-aid kit, he caught her hand and pulled her back to face him. "Still, that was a pretty dangerous thing to do. Men like that, they don't like people poking around in their business. And back in that alley, away from any witnesses…? I hate to think of what could have happened."

Bracing her hand against his knee to keep herself from walking all the way into that broad, strong chest, Tracy summoned a smile she wasn't feeling. "You were always there for me when I needed you, Bull."

"Likewise." He angled his square face and gently brushed his fingertips over her bruised cheek. "Better get some ice for that while you're doctoring me up, too."

Adrenaline was quickly ebbing from her system, and the full realization of the danger she'd been in—and the danger her young friend Brittany was facing—gave her knees an embarrassing wobble, and the temptation to let Bull wrap all that strength around her was almost more than she could stand. But she and Bull were just friends—he'd made that clear when he'd left Texas. And no amount of wishing and wanting their relationship to be something more had ever once made him call or write or come back home.

Understanding that she needed to rely on her own strength, Tracy pulled away while she still could. "So how is Justice handling this? He and Brittany were still in the process of getting to know each other."

She heard Bull's deep sigh when she went to the sink to wash her hands and gather what she needed. "How do you think? He's Justice McCabe. He's not going to bow down to any drug cartel. It's all about his reputation and his precious code of right and wrong. To hell with whoever gets hurt. His own daughter. You."

"Shame on you, Bull." She leaned her hip against the counter as she dried her hands and looked across the room to those eyes that were as dark and unflinching as the gray limestone rock that studded the rugged ranch land where they'd grown up. His relationship with his father had always been a sensitive subject. But he'd been gone ten years. "You don't think he's worried sick about Brittany? You don't think he's regretted every day that you and Morgan have been gone? I'll give you that his pride makes for a pretty thick skin. It hides a lot. Your father isn't the same man he was when you left. He's not as hard. He's not as…indomitable as he used to be."

"Indomitable?" The wry sound he made wasn't quite a laugh. "You really are an English teacher, aren't you."

She wasn't going to let him change the subject any more than he'd let her avoid explaining the desperate stunt she'd pulled outside Margarita's tonight. "Justice has lost a lot of the people he cared about—your mother, Morgan. You. And he's not as young as he used to be. He's feeling his mortality, regretting the mistakes he made. I think he was…is…working to create a relationship with Brittany."

"Do better with his second family than he did with his first?"

Tracy knew that sarcasm was a thin veil for the pain he was feeling. Tossing the towel aside, she went back to Bull and cupped the sides of his face, wanting him to see the sincerity in her own. "Don't let the bitterness you feel toward Justice dictate all the choices you make. You need to find a way to forgive him, Virgil. Or it'll eat you up inside until there's nothing left." She smiled to take the sting out of her words. "And who'll come to my rescue if that happens?"

"Virgil, hmm?" His voice had dropped to a husky tone that vibrated from deep in his throat. He turned his face between her hands and pressed a kiss into her palm. Dots of tobacco-brown beard stubble tickled her fingertips, but his warm, firm lips gently soothed. Tracy's breath lodged in her chest at the sensations dancing across her sensitive skin. It was just a friendly kiss—spur-of-the-moment gratitude or teasing, perhaps.

But it didn't feel like a friendly kiss. It felt like…more.

Something about standing here in the shadows of her apartment, seeing those gray eyes locked onto hers, absorbing his abundant heat, feeling his lips on her skin, felt sensual, intimate. His deep-pitched whisper feathered against her eardrums like a husky caress, intensifying the hypnotic effect. "You know, there's only one other person who ever got to call me that."

She knew how dearly he'd loved his mother. "I'm sorry. I didn't mean—"

"No. You call me Virgil." He pulled her in between his knees and hugged her tight. His arms wound around her back and waist. Her toes left the floor. Tracy nestled her cheek against the sandpapery warmth of his neck and held on. Her body softened against the harder planes of his. She soaked up the heat emanating from his arms and chest. Her nose filled with the musky scent of the long, warm day that clung to his skin. Old memories resurfaced as every nerve ending awakened.

Virgil McCabe was bigger, more mature, more masculine—more everything than the boy she remembered. And that only made the schoolgirl crush she'd once had on him blossom into something more. She tightened her arms around his neck and whispered against his skin. "I've missed you, Virgil."

"I missed you, too. Coming home was about what I expected—conversations would be awkward, feelings would get hurt—I knew there'd be no reason to stay once the job of find-ing Brittany was done. But this is the first thing that's felt right since I've been here." He pulled back a few inches, letting her feet settle to the floor. He brushed aside one of those independent locks of hair that refused to do her bidding, stroking her cheek and the shell of her ear as he tucked it into place. His probing gaze studied the line of blushing heat created by his touch. And then his gaze dropped to her lips, making them feverish with antici-pation for his touch, too. But just as Tracy began to lean toward temptation ever so slightly, Bull retreated. He twisted her in his grasp and pushed her back a step, frowning as he untucked the side of her blouse and pulled it up between them to show her the seeping spot of blood staining the flowered cotton. "Oh, man. Sorry. I got some on your blouse. You'd better bandage me up before I bleed all over your apartment."

"Right. Um…" *Say something clever. Laugh this off.* She was the only one feeling the magic here. "Right."

As embarrassed by her sudden lapse of eloquence as she was by nearly throwing herself at an old friend, Tracy ran into the kitchen to get the first-aid supplies. Without another word and only fleeting eye contact, she got busy untying the blood-soaked bandanna and cleaning the cut on Bull's arm. She'd finally pulled her act together by the time she was winding an elastic ban-dage around the middle of his forearm to anchor the medicated gauze pad into place. She could even manage a teasing remark. "It doesn't look too deep. Probably still wouldn't hurt to have a doctor look at it. Bet it leaves a nifty scar, though."

"You do good work. Thanks."

With a nod, Tracy put away the scissors she'd used and tossed the soiled gauze, wrappings and bandanna into the trash. She lifted the hem of her blouse and inspected the damage there. "I'd better go clean up and change my clothes."

Bull was flexing his fingers to ensure the wrapping wasn't too tight, his focus thankfully shifted from the almost-kiss that would have played havoc with their best-bud status. He pulled his cell phone from his pocket. "Take your time, I need to call Wyatt and let him know what's happened."

Tracy could hear Bull deep in a conversation with his brother in her living room when she peeked out of her bedroom and dashed across the hall to the bathroom to rinse out her blouse and wash the streaks of his blood from the right side of her rib cage before pulling on a clean T-shirt. With the door cracked open behind her, she could still hear his deep-pitched voice booming through her apartment. Tracy grinned. Subtlety would never be one of Bull McCabe's finer traits. He was honest to a fault, dove into trouble with both feetfirst, apologized after the fact rather than ask for permission beforehand, and he guarded his heart as fiercely as he defended underdogs and baby sisters and a friend who thought she might actually be able to get answers from a pair of dangerous men.

Why would she ever think Bull might have been hiding tender feelings for the grown-up tomboy staring back at her from the mirror the way she'd been hiding feelings from him all these years?

Tracy picked up a brush and tried to tame her hair into a neat ponytail. But some things, no matter how badly she wanted them, just weren't going to happen. They hadn't happened ten years ago, and they weren't going to happen now.

But they had shared a real kiss once.

Big, rough-and-tough Bull McCabe—most folks around Serpentine thought his only talents were taming rodeo bulls, winning fights and standing up to his hard-nosed father—had a secret gooey center that only a few lucky people ever got to see. She knew he was sensitive to the teasing he feared he'd get over his old-fashioned name. It had annoyed him that his classmates didn't give him credit for being as smart as he was. He'd ached with the need to measure up to his father's standards.

And when he'd shown up at her father's barn one afternoon, with blood at the corner of his mouth and anger and hurt streaming out of every pore, she'd known Justice had lashed out at him again. Tracy had saddled up Lady and ridden down into the rocky valley near Homestead Creek with Bull that day. She'd listened for hours and wiped away the tears he'd shed, swearing that she'd never tell another living soul that Bull McCabe cried.

They were sitting on a flat rock, overlooking the trickle of the summer creek when he'd pulled her into his arms and hugged her tight. Much like he had a few minutes ago in her kitchen.

Only, at age seventeen, that thank-you, that shared closeness of bared souls, had turned into something more. With no kidnapped sister or seeping wound to distract him, with adolescent urges raging through their veins, Bull had kissed her. He'd pulled her onto his lap, knocked her hat off into the dust, tunneled his fingers into her hair and kissed her. And just as the shock wore off, just as she realized how much she liked his hand on her bottom and his tongue in her mouth—just as she decided she was in love with the boy next door—Bull had ended the kiss.

He had set her aside on the hard, sun-warmed rock. He'd raked his fingers through his hair and glanced at her with a red-faced grin.

"Was that weird?" he asked.

Before she could answer how special her first kiss had been, how unexpectedly perfect it had been to share that first kiss with Virgil McCabe, he was pushing to his feet, checking on his horse. "That was weird. I'm sorry, Trace. I just... I wasn't thinking. We're still cool, right? I mean, that won't happen again. I promise."

He seemed to be holding his breath, waiting for her answer as though he was afraid that kiss had somehow altered the friendship they'd always shared—that she'd be dumb enough to think he'd want something more from her. But she wasn't dumb. "We're cool."

Swallowing the lump of hope and longing in her throat, Tracy picked up her hat and untethered Lady. If kissing her felt weird to Bull, then clearly, whatever feelings had suddenly sprung up inside her weren't mutual. And wasting another moment lusting after her best bud wasn't going to help either one of them. "The sun will be setting soon." She offered the easiest reason to end the conversation and put some much-needed distance between them. "I'd better head back home." She mounted up into the pinto's saddle. "You coming?"

He shook his head. *"I want to hang out here a little longer. The quiet is something I don't get much of at home."*

"Are you gonna be okay?"

"Yeah. Thanks for listening." He winked, resuming the familiar persona of the friends they were.

"See you at school tomorrow, Bull."

"See ya, Trace."

She nudged her heels into her horse's sides and took off at a canter. Tracy made it all the way to the arroyo that split the Mc-Cabes' land from her father's before the embarrassment of forgetting she was just one of the guys, and the what-ifs of feelings that would never be, brimmed over into tears.

"Tracy?"

Her hairbrush clattered into the sink as the knock on the open bathroom door startled her back to the present.

Bull's eyes narrowed as they caught her gaze in the mirror. "You okay?"

Oh, great. Her eyes felt gritty, as though she was going to give in to those adolescent tears again. Needing to hide those raw feelings now as she had back then, Tracy quickly turned on the faucet and splashed cool water on her face. "Yes. I'm fine." She grabbed a towel to dry her skin and turned once she felt she could look him in the eye without giving anything away. But all those silly self-doubts vanished when she saw the tension lining his rugged face. Fear tightened her belly. "Is something wrong?"

He held up his phone. "There's been another message from Calderón."

Chapter Three

"Good ID, Tracy." Wyatt pocketed his smart phone after pulling up some suspect photos that matched her description of the men in the alley the night before. Looking far more authoritative than the kid brother he'd grown up with, Sheriff McCabe confirmed Bull's suspicions. "Sol Garcia and Manuel Ortiz. Intimidating and eliminating their enemies is just the kind of work Calderón hires them to do. They may have been in town, scouting out our actions—finding out if Justice has talked to a lawyer about deeding over the land rights down by the river, or if we'd brought in reinforcements to go up against the *Los Jaguares*."

Bull felt his brother's gaze slide across Justice's office to where he stood behind Tracy's chair. *He* was the reinforcement Wyatt was talking about. Morgan, too, if he ever came out of where he was hiding and got his butt here to Texas.

"Garcia and Ortiz have had plenty of time to report in." Wyatt shared the grim news with everyone in the room. "So Calderón knows we're looking for him."

"Are we sure this is Brittany's hair?" Bull asked, handing off the plastic evidence bag to Wyatt. "Is this our proof of life?"

"She'd better still be alive." Justice pounded his fist on top of his desk. "Calderón won't want to mess with me if he harms my daughter."

"Let us handle Calderón, Dad." Wyatt was trying to play peacemaker again. "You'll get your chance with Brittany."

"It sure looks like Brittany's hair. She told me she was growing it out for prom in the spring." Tracy's queasy expression as she watched the long twists of dark blond braids go by seemed more genuinely concerned than his father's outburst had. "Is this my fault? Did I provoke them to hurt Brittany?"

Bull reached over the winged-back chair where she sat to squeeze her shoulder. "If Garcia and Ortiz are the men who delivered this to the house last night, then they already had it on them when we met them."

Wyatt agreed. "Frankly, I like the idea of you getting a few licks in on Calderón's men and throwing them off their scheduled plan. Makes me feel like he's not controlling every move we try to make."

Tracy sat a little taller in her chair. "So making contact with Calderón's men was a good thing?"

"Yeah," Wyatt assured her.

"No." Bull couldn't agree. Sol Garcia's backhand had left a bruise on Tracy's cheekbone. "We've already got a sister in trouble with the *Los Jaguares,* we don't need anyone else to get hurt."

"Bull—"

"I just meant—"

"All of you, shut up!"

For once in his life, Bull didn't snap back at his father's shouted order. Of course, the quick squeeze of Tracy's fingers around his where they fisted on her chair might have something to do with that. Everyone's nerves were on edge this morning.

He opened his hand and squeezed back, thanking her for her calming influence before pulling away and crossing to the window to gaze out over the east paddock and the mares and colts there. The flies must be bad today. The horses seemed to be a little skittish, dancing around like that instead of quietly grazing. Bull wasn't feeling quite like he belonged inside his own skin today, either. A reassuring touch from an old friend shouldn't make his pulse leap like that.

He'd like to attribute this whole weird vibe with Tracy to fatigue and stress. It had been a long night with little sleep, thanks to the bittersweet memories he had of bunking in his old bedroom on the second floor and to the fitful dreams he'd had about Tracy herself.

The trouble was, he didn't know which was more unsettling—

images of Tracy being beaten or cut by a pair of *Los Jaguares* gang members, or the erotic visions he'd had of sharing that bed with her. Somehow, the long, friendly hug he remembered from Tracy's apartment had become her soft skin and lean curves pressed against his naked body. And there were no teasing remarks or words of solace. There'd been moans and sighs and that wild chestnut hair falling all around him until he'd sat bolt upright in bed—wide-awake, hot with sweat and wanting.

A cold shower and a silent breakfast with Justice this morning had convinced Bull that it was just wishful thinking to believe something had changed between him and Tracy over the years. She'd been a rock of caring and common sense to him growing up, and he needed her to be that for him now. He wouldn't chase away her support by acting on that latent attraction he felt for her. Nor would he mislead her into thinking he had any intentions of staying in Serpentine once Brittany Means was safely back at the J-Bar-J.

"The longer Brittany's away from us, the harder it will be to get her home unharmed." Justice's sharp voice intruded on Bull's thoughts and pulled his attention away from the horses outside. "That's what this latest threat means, isn't it?"

"May I?" Tracy reached for the sealed note Justice handed across the desk. *"I don't think you believe we mean business, Mr. McCabe. Here is your daughter's hair. Next time it will be a slice out of that pretty face of hers. 12 a.m. Christmas Eve— your land, or your daughter's life."*

"There has to be something more we can do than sit here and listen to the clock ticking. She's only seventeen. Brittany thinks she's all alone in this world. She may not even believe this new family of hers is looking for her. Missing her." Tracy's soft gasp of anger and despair punched Bull right in the gut. His instinct was to reach for her, to soothe her raw emotions. He curled his fingers around the window sill, instead, and watched her scoot to the edge of the leather chair, pleading with Justice. "I can't imagine how frightened she must be. We need to do whatever it takes to get her home safely before Calderón makes good on these threats. Can't you talk to him? Make some kind of deal with him so we can at least speak to her and reassure her?"

"If I give him access to that part of the ranch to smuggle his drugs, who knows what he'll want next? And who knows what he'll do or who he'll hurt to get it?" Justice shook his head, denying Tracy's request. "I can't stand the thought of him touching Brittany—much less hurting her. But I have to protect my family and their future. I don't want Javier Calderón to think that he can come after me again and win."

"Then we have to rescue her," Bull stated plainly, striding back to his father's desk. Justice might put his principles above people's lives and feelings, but Bull wouldn't. "We have to take away his bargaining chip."

"We have to *find* Brittany first," Wyatt reminded him.

Tracy turned those sweet blue eyes, bright with hope, up to him, reminding Bull to start thinking like the detective he was. "Let's track them down. There has to be some lead as to where he would take her."

Wyatt shook his head. "You think I haven't tried? Calderón's not a man who leaves loose ends."

"Wait a minute." Tracy picked up her purse from the floor beside her chair and pulled out a folded-up piece of paper. "I don't know if this would be any help, but I looked up the names of other students who missed the same three days of school before Christmas vacation that Brittany did."

She unfolded the paper as she stood and handed it to Bull.

Wyatt circled the desk to look around Bull's shoulder and read the list of names with him. "What do the X's mean?" he asked.

"I double-checked against the principal's truancy list and crossed off the students who had excused absences because of illness or family travel."

"And the three that are left?" Bull read off the unmarked names. "Marvin Tate, David Echevarria and Julio Rivas?"

"Unaccounted for," Tracy explained. "David and Julio are seniors. Marvin is a sophomore."

Wyatt was typing the names into his smart phone.

These students being absent might be nothing more than a coincidence, but Bull could tell that Tracy believed them to mean something more. "Do you have any reason to suspect that one of those students had something to do with Brittany's kidnapping?"

"No, but Brittany is a young woman with a lot of hurt and anger to work through. One of the causes that she seemed to obsess over was reuniting families who've been separated by immigration laws or divorce or whatever."

"She wanted to make sure that no one was denied her real family the way she was." Bull could understand that sentiment.

"Something like that." Tracy hugged her arms in front of her, clearly uncomfortable with where her suspicions were taking her. "At least two of those boys—David and Julio—still have family down in Mexico. I can see Brittany agreeing to help one of them get back to his family for the holidays."

"Watch your accusations, son." Justice rolled back his chair and stood. "I didn't deny that girl anything. I respected her mother's wishes. I want my daughter to be a part of this family, even if you don't like it."

"Get off your high horse, Justice." Bull didn't have time to either reason or argue with his father. "This isn't about you. Or me. We're profiling Brittany and her motivations—why she might choose one option or another. See if we can retrace where those options took her. It's called investigative work. It's what I do. And I'm damn good at it, too, if you want to know." He turned from Justice's snarling shock to Wyatt and his phone. "Do either of those boys drive a rusty black farm truck?"

"I'm checking them in the DMV database now to see if we get a match."

"If she drove across the border with one of them, she'd make an easy target for anyone following her." And she'd be a hell of a lot tougher for U.S. authorities to find. But this was McCabe territory, and Bull believed he could find anything—or anyone—here if he put his mind and considerable will to it.

But Wyatt was shaking his head. That search was a bust. "Neither one of them is a registered vehicle owner."

Bull turned the paper back to Tracy. "Are the addresses you have on here current?"

She nodded. "Those are the homes they have listed in their school files."

Bull handed the list off to his brother and picked up his hat. "I'll check out one and you get the other."

Tracy followed Bull out the office door into the main room. "What would Calderón's men do to the boy she was helping?"

Bull took his time settling the black Stetson into place, trying to figure out how to make "Don't ask" sound like a reassuring thing.

But Tracy's fingers had already curled into the tight muscle of his uninjured forearm. The skin beneath that dusting of freckles on her cheeks had paled. She understood that Calderón wasn't the type of man who left innocent witnesses to his activities alive to talk about them. "They're expendable, aren't they? We have to find them and make sure they're okay."

"Easy, sweetheart." Bull couldn't help it if the endearment slipped out. He needed to see a smile on her face again. He at least needed to see a little bit of that lifelong faith in him shining in her eyes. With a gentle fingertip, he caught that long curl that refused to stay in her ponytail and tucked it behind her ear. "I won't let anybody get hurt."

"I know you won't." Despite her fear for her students' safety, Tracy was smart enough to realize the importance of moving quickly on this. She rested her hand at the center of his chest and nudged him toward the hallway. "If Brittany was with one of those boys, then he would have been the last person to see her before the kidnapping."

Bull finished her thought. "And talking to him could put us that much closer to finding her."

"Then you need to hurry. Is there anything I can do to help?"

"Don't set up a clandestine meeting with any drug dealers while I'm gone?"

That triggered a smile. "I won't. How about I wait here and keep an eye on your dad—make sure he stays out of trouble." She nodded toward the Christmas tree at the front end of the room. "Maybe we could string a few more lights on that tree.

Looks like he hasn't quite bought out all of Serpentine's supply of decorations yet."

"Sounds like a plan." And then, because it seemed like the right thing to do, Bull dipped his head and pressed a quick, chaste kiss to her soft smile. But her fingers folded into the placket of his shirt and she stretched up on tiptoe to cling to his mouth for a few seconds more. He inhaled a breath of her clean, citrusy scent. Her other hand came up to cup his jaw and hang on to him. Her mouth opened at the touch of his tongue and her moist heat swept through him. His fingers tunneled under the silky weight of her ponytail as he palmed her nape to anchor her lips beneath his and give full reign to this impromptu kiss.

Wait. He was kissing Tracy Cobb?

Confusion darkened her eyes and ricocheted like a shot inside him when he lifted his head. She'd felt it, too. That zing of rightness. That sudden heat. An undeniable connection between them. Her lips were pink and decadently parted as quick, warm breaths snuck between them and caressed the sensitive skin at the base of his throat. What the hell…?

"Trace?" His uneven breaths mingled with hers. He narrowed his eyes in a frown, trying to make sense of what was happening here. "Was that weird?"

"Virgil McCabe…" Heat instantly dotted her cheeks. She blinked the confusion from her eyes and released his crumpled shirtfront. Was she angry about that kiss? Had he overstepped some line he shouldn't? He knew he tended to be a little impulsive, but she'd been right here in the room with him, kissing him back. "Sometimes you're totally clueless for a detective."

"Tracy—"

"You coming, Bull?" Wyatt came out of the office and strode past them. A chuff on the shoulder reminded Bull that they needed to move.

"Right behind you." Bull spared one more look at Tracy's flushed cheeks and tilted chin before turning to follow his brother. He could still feel those hands on his skin, clutching at him like she meant it.

"Boss!" The screen door slammed back in the kitchen. Maria

squealed and a pan clattered to the floor. "Boss!" Bull exchanged a glance with Wyatt and hurried out to meet the sound of booted feet running across the house's hardwood floors. He reached the hallway and Rusty Fisher plowed into him. He caught the older cowboy by the shoulders, steadying him on his feet before releasing him. Red-faced and panting for breath, Rusty looked from one brother to the other. "Bull? Wyatt?"

"What's wrong?" Bull asked. Did the horses have reason to be restless?

Tracy and his father filled the archway behind them. "What is it, Rusty?" Justice demanded.

"The southwest pasture, down by the river." His chest heaved with one more deep breath. "It's on fire."

INTERVIEWING THE TWO BOYS Brittany might have been helping cross the border had to wait. Steel-gray smoke billowed on the horizon to the south, and the wisps of black curling higher up toward the sky indicated that the fire was spreading, and fast.

A grass fire under these arid conditions, especially when the winds picked up at this time of year, could have devastating consequences. While Wyatt called 911 to report the fire and call for a helicopter to give them eyes on the exact location and dimension of the blaze, Tracy and every able rider on the J-Bar-J hurried to saddle a horse or get behind the wheel of a truck to rescue the livestock who were caught in the fire's path. A couple of the older hands stayed at the house with hoses to water down the grass and roofs of the main house, bunk house and cabin.

Most of a long, hot day later, Tracy's thighs ached from the hours she'd spent in the saddle. And the ball cap she'd borrowed to help ward off the sun had left enough of her face exposed that she could feel the heat of the late afternoon drawing the freckles out across her cheeks.

"Yaw, yaw." She swatted a coiled rope against her leg, using the sound and the movement and a quick turn of the sorrel mare named Lila she was riding to drive the straying Hereford back toward the stone gate to the section where they were moving all the cattle they'd been able to round up. With the cow now trotting after the others who'd already found the new grass to graze on, Tracy nodded to the woman standing ready to close the gate. "Okay, Dakota."

The tall blonde might not be an expert at herding cattle, but every person on the ranch had gone to work, trying to save as much of the livestock as possible. Maria was a mile away, back at the main house, watching over Dakota's son and calling brothers and cousins in the area who could get to the J-Bar-J quickly and help. Even Tracy's dad was out on his horse, moving some of the cattle onto Cobb land, while her mother was fixing coffee and sandwiches to feed the ranch hands and volunteers who had given up their time to help a neighbor save his home and livelihood.

"Hold up!" Bull came loping up to the gate on his big bay with two more steers.

"Yaw, cow!" Justice trotted in on his horse right behind him with two more. Dakota caught the gate and held it open, and as soon as Bull came back out, she closed the steel bars and slid the lever into the stone post to keep it closed.

Horses and riders gathered outside the gate to rest for a few minutes and drink water from the bottles in their saddle bags. Bull's bay rocked him back and forth as he peeled off his black hat and wiped the sweat from his brow with the fresh blue bandanna he pulled from his hip pocket. For a few seconds, Tracy saw a glimpse of the tall boy who'd stolen her teenage heart.

But when he adjusted his Stetson back over his forehead and used its shade to peer off toward the late afternoon sun, she could see he was all man now. It wasn't just the deeper voice and shorter hair. Or the broader shoulders and harder chest that stretched beneath the dusty white shirt he wore. It wasn't the leather holster that crossed his back or the badge clipped to his belt.

Lines of life experience were etched beside his handsome eyes—hopes, regrets, secrets she might never know created complex shadows there. This was the man who had kissed her this morning—seasoned by life, sure of what he wanted. The boy deep inside, beaten down by his father's will and clinging to the familiar security of a lifelong friendship, was the one who had pulled away and questioned why they were so drawn to each other.

Tracy Cobb loved them both—the hurting boy and the mature man. She gripped the saddle horn tight in her leather-gloved hand. A lot more than her leg muscles ached. If only she could convince him that that love was real—and that it was reason enough to stay.

Catching her staring assessment, although misreading its cause, Bull nodded to her. "The wind shifted and it's taking the fire down to the river. It's out in the wilds now and shouldn't come any closer to the house or irrigated land."

"Hopefully, there's enough water in the river and creeks out there to burn the damn thing out." Justice turned to the man with the mustache climbing over the gate. "How many acres do you think we lost?"

Rusty snapped shut the cell phone he'd been talking on and buttoned it into his red shirt pocket before climbing into the saddle of the quarter horse he rode. "Hard to tell right now, boss. But I counted eighty-four head in there." He tapped his pocket. "Mr. Cobb says he's got another twenty up at his place. That leaves another dozen animals we weren't able to find."

Justice swore. "That's a hell of a lot of money to lose. Not to mention the hay I'll have to buy to replace the grass we lost."

"Hell of a way for an animal to die, too." Bull's sarcasm tempered his father's anger.

"Maybe they found some high rock where there's nothing around them that can burn," Tracy suggested.

Not bothering to mask his heavy sigh, Justice looked toward the coming sunset. "It's too late to start another search. I don't want anyone finding a hot pocket still burning and getting trapped. I'll have to hire some extra men to clean up this mess and sort out the herd again."

With the urge to lash out cooling along with his father's, Bull nodded a grudging agreement. "You'd better take these people on up to the house and feed them." He tugged on the reins and turned his horse away from the group. "While there's still some daylight, I want to check out a few things. We're pretty close to the border here."

"Son?"

Bull heard his father's warning. Maybe he even understood a little of the concern that aged Justice's chiseled face. Bull touched the brim of his hat and nodded. "I'll be careful."

Tracy touched her heels to the sorrel's sides and urged her into a trot. "I'm coming with you."

"No."

Ignoring Bull's protest, she reined the mare in to walk beside his taller mount. "It's dangerous to ride out by yourself when there's been a fire. Your father's right—there could be some pockets still burning. Two pair of eyes are better than one. You do your detective work and I'll watch out for everything else." A knowing smile warmed her face. Patience might not be a virtue Bull possessed, but Tracy had had a lot of practice waiting for him to wake up and realize they were made for each other. She could wait a little longer. "Besides, it'll be like old times—you and me riding the hills together."

"You're not still mad at me for kissing you?"

"Maybe it's not the kiss I was mad about." Pulling the ball cap snugly over her hair, Tracy nudged her horse into a canter and took off.

It didn't take long to hear Bull running up behind her.

Forty-five minutes later, at least one fear had been laid to rest. The fire was out.

But something even more troubling left Tracy twisting nearly 360 degrees in her saddle to ensure that she and Bull and their horses were the only things moving around the burnt pines and rocks on the bank leading down to Homestead Creek, a tributary that fed into the Rio Grande less than half a mile away. Bull was kneeling on the ground, holding on to the reins of his horse as he studied the inky-black streaks that were slightly darker than the charred earth around them. He put his gloved fingers to his nose and rubbed the sooty residue between his fingers.

"Is that what I think it is?" Tracy asked.

Bull wiped his hand on his jeans and pushed to his feet. The leather creaked beneath his weight as he swung up into the saddle. Her heart was already beating a little faster before he confirmed her fear. "I don't have a crime lab out here to verify it, but I think this fire was intentionally set. Those look like chemical pour burns to me."

Tracy tried to cool her concern on a deep breath. "Another message from Calderón?"

"Most likely."

"This is the kind of *enforcement* Garcia and Ortiz carry out, isn't it?"

"Uh-huh."

"Poor Brittany." The girl had been Calderón's prisoner for four days now. The drug lord had lopped off her hair and threatened worse. She must be terrified, and feeling so alone and abandoned. And Justice was aging by the minute, it seemed. Tracy remembered him as a force of nature growing up. Last week she'd seen a father, a normal man. Now, as the clock ticked toward the Christmas Eve deadline, the lines of his face grew more deeply etched, and the height and breadth of him seemed to shrink. And, as if abducting his daughter wasn't enough, now the *Los Jaguares* were bringing the threat right to Justice McCabe's back door.

A tight fist of helpless fear and frustration squeezed around Tracy's heart. She couldn't see the purplish and rose hues surrounding the giant orange sun where it set on the horizon. Its beauty was lost in the enormity of the devastation surrounding them—the cruel deaths of innocent animals, both J-Bar-J livestock and wild animals. The destruction of property that would require money and man-hours to rebuild. The unnatural changes in the landscape, with exploded cacti and char marks on the beautifully dramatic rocks. Calderón and his men were responsible for all this waste and intimidation and galling lack of compassion for anyone and anything. All for drugs. All for money.

Tears scratched like grit in her eyes. Such a waste. Such a violent, horrible waste.

"Brittany's a McCabe." Bull tried to reassure her. "She's tough. She'll be okay." Or maybe he was trying to reassure himself. "She's a tough kid in school, right? You said she tries to help others?"

"Yeah." Reaching across the space between their horses, Tracy linked her hand to Bull's, needing some of his strength at that moment. "Now that I think of it—the essays she writes, the way she expresses herself in class—she reminds me a lot of you."

"Smart and good-looking?"

His teasing made her laugh. Tracy returned the favor. "Hard-headed and passionate about the ideas that get stuck in her head."

His laugh was deep and rich and drove away the tears that had tried to spill over.

Then, just as though someone had flipped a switch, the laughter stopped. Bull released her hand and stood up in his stirrups, peering over the top of the creek bank. "What's that?"

"What's what? Bull?"

He was already picking his way down through the charcoal tree stumps and limestone outcroppings by the time Tracy got her horse to high enough ground to see the old dirt supply road that ran parallel to the creek bed. But it wasn't the washed-out road that had caught his eye. It was the burned-out flatbed truck sitting on four melted tires in the middle of that road.

"Oh, my God. You don't think somebody got caught in the fire, do you?" Tracy followed him down and tethered the horses while Bull circled the truck for a closer look. Had the *Los Jaguares's* intimidation tactics turned to murder? Had the fire been set to get rid of the truck? Or its contents? "Brittany?"

"Stay there." Metal screeched across metal as Bull pried the blackened passenger door open. "There's no driver. No body. She's not here."

Tracy's breath rushed out in a gasp of relief. "Thank God."

With a grunt of steely determination, he forced the glove compartment door open. It snapped off in his hand and Bull dug through the debris inside. "Whatever identification was in here is burned to a crisp. Let's hope the thing has plates."

As Bull inspected the rest of the abandoned vehicle, Tracy evaluated the skeletal remains of the truck's shape. "Do you think that's the farm truck Brittany got into at school?"

"With this location and the destruction of evidence?" Bull circled the truck, scanning up and down the creek bed. "I'd bet my badge on it. Hold on."

"What is it?"

He pulled out a pocketknife and pried a sticky tar-like substance off the bed of the truck. He sniffed it, then nodded. "I've seen this before, when drug dealers burn their cocaine stash. Somebody was using this truck to run drugs." He knelt down to clean the substance off his knife. "It'd be easy enough to hide a kilo or two inside the middle of a hay bale. I'll call Wyatt, see if he knows who some of Calderón's drivers are. Maybe one of them picked up Brittany."

"I don't think she'd get into a truck with a total stranger. It'd have to be someone she—"

"Miss Cobb?" a raspy voice croaked from the rocks behind Tracy. The horses shifted. A bloody, soot-stained hand clamped over her shoulder and Tracy screamed.

Chapter Four

Bull flew around the truck. "Tracy!"

A man had staggered out from the rocks and grabbed her. Bull pulled his gun as the man dragged Tracy down to the ground.

"Police! Stop or I'll... Damn it, Trace."

The man wasn't attacking her. He was collapsing. Streaked with soot and mud, with dirty red smears on his face and hands that had to be blood, the man was falling. And instead of protecting herself, Tracy was turning him in her arms, trying to catch him.

They were both on the ground by the time Bull had scooted the horses aside and knelt beside them. "He could be armed or booby-trapped—"

"Bull, help me. It's Julio Rivas." She pulled the man's head into her lap. "One of my missing students."

"Miss Cobb..." *Mees* Cobb. Not a man at all. A lean, lanky teenage boy with filthy clothes, a thick accent and an unfocused look in his eyes that indicated shock or dehydration. "We have to save Brittany."

Even if he wasn't friendly, the young man was too injured or exhausted or both to be much of a threat. Bull holstered his weapon and gently lifted him so that Tracy could pull her arm from underneath him. Then he turned the boy and together they laid him on the burnt grass and gravelly soil in a more comfortable position. Bull took a closer look at a mat of sticky black hair and the puffy swelling at the boy's left temple. A quick inspection beneath his damp, mud-caked T-shirt confirmed Bull's suspicions. Julio Rivas had been hurt in ways that didn't look like the results of a truck wreck or burns.

"Shh, Julio. Don't try to talk." Tracy's comforting tone for the teen turned into a command for Bull. "He needs water."

With a nod, Bull got up and pulled a water bottle from his saddle bag. He wet down the bandanna from his back pocket and handed it to Tracy while he took over holding up the teen's head and helping him drink several swallows of the warm water.

"Son? I'm Detective McCabe. Who hurt you?" He waited for Tracy to wipe some of the grime from the boy's nose and mouth before he offered him another drink. "Julio? Who did this to you?"

The dark brown eyes blinked, his focus improving a little bit each time. Exhaustion, blood loss, and potential internal injuries like a cracked rib or bruised kidney were still a concern, but Julio was breathing more deeply now, even though he winced at the pain. "Two men. A big man with a white bandage on his nose and bruised eyes. And a skinny guy. He was meaner."

Bull didn't need a police blotter to make the identification from that description. "Manny Ortiz and Sol Garcia."

He handed the water bottle off to Tracy and let her continue cleaning the scrapes and minor burns the teen had sustained on his face and hands while Bull pulled out his cell phone to report in to Wyatt. He climbed back up to the top of the bank, but it didn't make any difference.

"No damn reception out here." He looked up and down the creek bed and back across the rising flatland from where they'd come. A quick assessment of the situation and some quicker decisions had to be made. They were alone out here, although what little sunlight remained made it difficult to see for more than a couple of miles in any direction. Although they were still on J-Bar-J land here by the creek, they were closer to the Mexican border than to the main house or any paved road. And Julio was a long way from even being able to climb up the rocky creek bank, so a long hike or fast ride back to civilization would be out of the question. And Bull's teenage sister was about to spend another night held hostage by a dangerous drug lord. Snapping the phone shut, he tucked it into his pocket and slipped back down through the steep rocks to rejoin them. "Is that your truck, Julio?"

"I was driving it."

Tracy poured a little more water on the bandanna to tend to the boy's scraped knuckles and burned fingers. "How did you escape the fire?"

"When I came to in the truck, the fire was already coming over the hill. I lay down in the creek water." Other than the singe marks on the hem of his jeans and boots, the trick had worked. The kid must have crawled out of the water and either hid or passed out amongst the rocks afterward. That was soot and mud on the surface of his clothes, not burnt material.

"That was smart." Bull cooed to the horses to keep them calm as he checked both saddles for the gear they had on hand. "There's no place between here and the Rio Grande where you could have escaped until the fire burned itself out."

"Was Brittany with you?" Tracy asked.

"No. The *Los Jaguares* have her. Señor Calderón—he made me...I am sorry, Miss Cobb. My family owes him a debt." The boy's voice was raw from smoke or emotion or lack of water, but the energy behind it was a little stronger. "He would hurt my grandmother if I did not help."

"Julio. We're not placing blame right now. We just need to find answers." Tracy's tone was soft and solicitous, but her words were to the point. "Did you take Brittany from school?"

"I did not know they would... Señor Calderón said to bring the girl when I drove the truck—that it would look more like we were going on a date to visit my uncle. No one would ask us questions."

Tracy whispered a curse through tight lips. "He was taking advantage of how young you are."

"They met us for lunch. And Brittany got so sleepy. They had a place where she could nap."

Bull's fists clenched around the leather ties binding the rolled-up blanket to his saddle. "They doped her up."

"I was going back to find her," Julio insisted. "But the men. They said it was not my business. They took Brittany to his hacienda."

"Calderón's?" Bull stroked Jericho's withers, silently apologizing for the tension the animal could sense, and telling the horse there'd be no comfy stall or grain tonight.

"*Sí.* Yes." Bull went back to Tracy and stood over both of them to hear the rest of Julio's story. "I went to see my grandmother, to tell her she would be fine. And then I was coming back to Serpentine. Go south with a load of hay and the girl. Come back with—"

"Drugs hidden in the hay bales?"

"Yes. But Brittany was friendly at school when I started hitting on her, talking her into going. And then she said she'd help me see my grandmother for Christmas. She wanted to help me. And she is so pretty. And so funny." Julio turned his cheek into the charred dirt where he lay. "We kissed. I did not want to leave her."

Bull propped his hands at his hips. Spare him the teenage angst. He needed a few more facts. "Okay, Romeo. So you decided you liked my sister, after all, and went back to Calderón's hacienda to bring her home?"

Julio swung his gaze back up to Bull. "Brittany is your sister? I am so sorry, *señor.*"

"Apologize later." Bull knelt down, eliminating some of the distance—and intimidation—between him and the lead he'd been looking for. "Did you see Brittany when you went back to the hacienda?"

Shaking his head, Julio struggled to push himself up onto his elbows. "Señor Calderón was angry that I had returned. Angry that I did not deliver the hay and return the truck to his associate in Serpentine." Tracy shifted to get behind Julio's shoulders and help him sit up. "I did not know about the drugs. I swear it."

Bull picked up a palmful of burnt grass and dirt and crushed it in his fist. "But you're willing to kidnap an innocent girl?"

The daggers in Tracy's eyes warned him to keep his emotions in check. "So Calderón was angry with you." She gently dabbed at the wound on the side of Julio's head, calmly taking over the interrogation. "And he had his men do this to you?"

"I tried to fight." Bull was twice as big as this kid, and far better trained, and it had taken everything he had to get rid of Garcia and Ortiz. "Then, I hit my head."

"More likely someone hit you." Julio hissed when Bull pulled aside his shaggy mat of hair to inspect the wound. "Looks like the shape of a gun butt to me."

The boy sucked in a steadying breath and continued. "When I woke up, I was in the truck. Everything was on fire."

Bull squeezed the teen's arm, thanking him for keeping it together and answering their questions. "Do you know where this hacienda is? Can you take me there?"

"Bull," Tracy warned him. "Julio needs to rest. He needs a hospital."

But the boy had some grit in him that Bull admired. He pushed himself away from Tracy and sat up under his own power. "I know this hacienda. I will take you." He poked his thumb over his shoulder. "But my truck? It is too far to walk."

"You can ride double behind me or Tracy…Miss Cobb." Bull looked beyond the wreckage of the truck to the graying twilight sky. "But the horses need rest." And despite his dogged determination to rescue Brittany, so did the boy. Getting lost out in the south Texas badlands at night wasn't a real brilliant idea, anyway. Not with drug runners and coyotes and rocky drop-offs and arroyos hiding in the shadows. First light would be soon enough. Bull nodded, talking to Julio as one man to another. "Let's make camp on the other side of the creek. There's grass there for the horses to graze on. We'll get some food in our bellies and a little sleep, and we'll head out in the morning." Bull patted Julio's shoulder before pushing to his feet. "You rest here for a few minutes while I set up camp and hobble the horses. Then I'll come back and help you across the creek."

With a grateful nod, Julio stayed where he was. His shoulders hunched with fatigue and he stretched back out on the ground as soon as Bull moved away. But Tracy shot to her feet, taking the mare's reins from his hand and falling into step beside him as he led Jericho down into the creek's shallow current.

"Thank you," she whispered, glancing back at Julio. "You could have really come down hard on him. He and Brittany both made some stupid choices. And if she's being treated anything like he was…"

The water swirled around Bull's ankles as he stopped midstride. "My plan isn't just about taking care of Julio. We could lose a lot of time returning to the ranch house and coming back this way tomorrow. Besides, once we take this kid into Serpentine, Wyatt's probably going to want to book him for drug smuggling, aiding and abetting and who knows what else?"

"But his grandmother…"

"Even if charges are dismissed due to extenuating circumstances, that'll all take time Brittany may not have."

Tracy's clear blue eyes darkened with suspicion. "What are you planning, Bull?"

"With Garcia and Ortiz around, and who knows who else, Calderón's got ears in Serpentine." He tipped his gaze up over the rocks at the top of the creek bank. "This may be the only chance anyone has to get to Calderón and rescue Brittany without them knowing we're coming."

She locked her fingers around his wrist, her gaze purposely dropping to the wound she'd bandaged there. "Don't you need to call for backup on something like that? Look at what the *Los Jaguares* have already done to you and Julio. You don't even know how many men you'd be going up against."

"Easy, blue eyes." Bull touched his gloved finger to her sun-kissed cheek and curled that independent lock of sorrel-colored hair around his fingertip. "I'm not going on any suicide mission." He tucked the curl behind her ear and cupped her jaw, angling her face fully up to his. "I am going in. I'll scout the place out—get Brittany's location, where Calderón's men are stationed. Find out what kind of firepower they have. He has to have cell reception there because he called my father with the ransom demand—and Brittany was with him to deliver the message. I'll call for backup then."

"What if something happens? What if you get hurt?" Her hand moved to the middle of his chest, her fingers curling beneath the buttons of his shirt. He liked how she didn't just touch him. She held on. He liked her holding on to him a whole lot. "Julio is already injured and I'm willing to help, but I'm not a detective. I don't even have Dad's hunting rifle with me to help you."

"I won't get hurt. And I won't let anybody else get hurt." He stroked his thumb across the curve of her bottom lip, soothing her worry. Going after the bad guys was his job. It was his duty as a cop, even if he was more than a thousand miles away from the city stamped on his badge. It was his duty as a McCabe to help bring his sister home. "I promise."

"Bull..." Her grip tightened in the front of his shirt.

He shushed her concern by lowering his head and pressing his lips against hers. Those urgent fingers clung to the skin and muscle beneath the cotton he wore, and she pulled herself up to deepen the kiss. Her lips softened beneath his. Their tongues touched and danced. The contact was quick. It was deep. It was right. And this time he didn't question why he'd kissed her. Tomboy Tracy Cobb was his best friend. She always had been. He hoped she always would be.

But he was finally beginning to get it through his hard head that she was also something more.

When he pulled away, Tracy nodded, agreeing to his plan. "Let's make camp."

Chapter Five

Tracy's eyes drifted open to the first glimmer of sunrise peeking over the lip of the rocky bank on the far side of the creek. She should be cold and achy from a night on the hard ground with nothing but a saddle blanket to sleep on, and one to curl up under.

Instead, she was deliciously warm. The backside of her was, anyway, as were her legs and stomach. She tugged the blanket more snugly around the front of her body, nestled her head against its hard pillow, and let her eyes blink shut again.

There hadn't been enough usable wood to build a fire last night, so they'd dined on energy bars, dried fruit and water, taken care of the horses and let exhaustion carry them off to sleep. Well, Julio's eyes had closed as soon as he'd wrapped up in his blanket. And though she'd valiantly attempted to wait up until Bull had finished circling the camp, checking the horses, checking the weather, checking for any signs of unwanted company, sleep had claimed her before she could convince Bull that he needed to be rested and alert even more than she did.

Had Bull slept at all? Had he taken her up on her offer to share the second blanket? Tracy stretched her legs, frowning as conscious thought pushed aside memories from the night before. Had he done something dumb and selfish and heroic and wonderful like stay up all night keeping watch over them?

"Shh, blue eyes." The blanket around her waist tightened as Bull's deep, drowsy voice whispered against her ear. "I need five more minutes of quiet before I'm ready to do this today."

Tracy's eyes popped wide open. With every suddenly rapid heartbeat, a new level of awareness assailed her. The delicious warmth was Bull spooning against her back. The blanket at her waist was his arm cinched around her, her pillow was his strong biceps. Their legs were tangled where they lay on Jericho's blanket, facing the sunrise. The cover she'd tugged up higher was Bull's hand, splayed possessively across her torso, his thumb and fingers nestled beneath the weight of her breasts. His lips, when he spoke, danced against the tender skin of her neck while his warm breath teased the shell of her ear.

He lay behind her, encircling her with his strength and heat. His breathing moved in sync with hers. And his lips weren't just moving against her skin—they were kissing her, seducing her. "I could wake up like this every morning. Quiet breeze. Fresh air. You."

"Bull." She didn't know whether to protest or make a joke or let the melody singing in her heart drive away the cautionary logic of that seventeen-year-old girl who still lingered inside her. "I see you took me up on my offer to share the blanket."

"Funny." His teeth excited a sensitive bundle of nerves beneath the neckline of her shirt and she didn't feel like laughing at all. He shifted behind her, perhaps easing some space between them, perhaps simply giving his hand easier access to the snap of her jeans. "Do you know you have the prettiest, most perfectly shaped bottom I've ever seen fill a pair of jeans?"

Bull splayed his hand over her abdomen and pulled her back, snug against the cup of his pelvis. Tracy gasped at the evidence of what he was feeling pressed against that perfectly shaped bottom. Tracy felt her face heating at the compliment. Other things were warming up, too, and she didn't seem to be making any effort to stop what was happening to her. "Is this what you meant when you said you needed five more minutes of quiet?"

"Don't argue semantics with me, Miss Cobb," he teased. "I'm just going where the morning takes me. Unless you want me to stop?"

Shaking her head, Tracy lay her hand over his and guided it back down her belly.

Without another word, he rolled her over and moved partially on top of her, his heavier weight sinking down around her yielding body, reminding her that he was every inch a rugged, powerful man. And yet he was being so careful with her, careful not to crush the breath out of her, careful not to let the calloused hand that slid beneath her blouse be too rough against her skin or too needy when he squeezed her breast in his palm and rolled the hard, achy tip between his fingers.

Despite the moan of secret pleasure she trapped in her throat, Tracy locked her eyes onto the beautiful gray eyes above her and whispered, "Did you know you were my first kiss back in high school?"

"Hadn't thought about it. But I'm glad. I like the practice we've been getting lately, too."

Tracy gasped at the shards of pleasure tingling in her and shooting down through her womb, making her feel heavy and tight. Taking his own sweet time, Bull slid his hand down inside her jeans, and she squeezed her thighs around him, eager to relieve the pressure building there. "Easy." But his chest was expanding and pushing against hers with the same excited rhythm consuming her. "Five minutes of quiet, remember?"

He slipped a finger inside her, pushing against that most sensitive nub. "Not fair," she gasped, urging the buttons of his shirt open, eager to take some of the same liberties he was.

"Shh. Just let me." It was getting harder to keep her eyes open, harder to remember that they weren't alone, hard to remember those five minutes of quiet he wanted when he was priming her to cry out his name.

"And did you know…" She didn't think she could take much more of the slow, wicked massage of his fingers. She wanted… she needed… "I've never been…" The pent-up release of her body spasming against his hand came out in a long, voiceless gasp from her throat. "…with anyone else."

"What?" Bull was breathing just as hard as she was. But the handsome grin faded before her eyes. "You saved yourself for me?"

Aftershocks still made her body weak when he pulled his hand from her jeans and looked down into her eyes. Propping himself up on an elbow, he shifted his weight off her. He glanced over to ensure Julio was still snoring away. But suddenly Tracy felt as though a clock had started ticking down some sort of countdown again. "Well, technically, we still haven't done it."

"Tracy…" Bull opened his mouth to speak, then dropped his head to brand her lips with his. It was a quick, hard kiss, hinting at something more before he pulled away. "You should have told me."

She reached up to stroke the worry lines from beside his eyes. "Like we ever had a conversation where the topic came up? In fact, I thought with what was happening, it was exactly the right time to mention it."

He shook his head. Glanced over at Julio's sleeping form. Shook his head again. "I don't have time to do this right this morning. And it needs to be right. But I want to do it. I want to be with you."

"Bull, I—"

"Uh-uh." He swept aside the hair that had fallen across her face. "When we're this close and you're looking at me like that—a conversation like this?—you call me Virgil."

"Virgil." It felt like saying yes to him. Using his given name felt like she was special to him. She wanted to be special to Virgil McCabe. "Please don't tell me you think this is weird. I can't tell you how much I hate when you use that word. I've waited a long time for you to want me the way I want you."

"I can't tell you how much I do." He wound his finger into that stubborn tendril of hair that refused to be contained. He pulled it to his lips and kissed it before tucking it gently, albeit futilely, behind her ear. "I'm still having a hard time wrapping my head around the idea that Tomboy Tracy and you are the same woman. The only thing *weird* is how thickheaded I've been about us. I never even considered staying in Texas. I just knew I had to get away. Now I've been gone so long. And my timing is as bad as ever. I still don't know if I can stay with Justice around. And you deserve someone who'll stay. Plus, there's my job in Chicago. And Brittany. If I'd had a lick of sense any sooner… And now the clock's ticking—"

She pressed her finger against his mouth, silencing his apology. "Our time will come. If it's meant to be, and you're willing to give us a chance to be more than friends, it'll happen. I'll wait for you to come home for however long it takes you to be ready, Virgil. Trust me, I'm a patient woman."

"I don't deserve you."

"I know. But I love you, anyway."

They both smiled. He kissed her one more time, giving her comfort, giving her hope. Then he rolled off her and stood, grabbing Tracy's hand and pulling her to her feet in front of him. "Then let's go get my sister. We've got a lot of talking to do."

"THERE'S NOBODY HERE." Bull paced off the dusty length of the short adobe wall that surrounded the hacienda's front yard. The cell reception was better out here than it had been inside the house. Squinting, he tipped his face up toward the sun burning high in the sky. Judging by the food still sitting on the plates inside on the long kitchen table, and the multiple tire tracks that hadn't yet blown off the dusty gravel road, the people who'd been at Calderón's hacienda had left fast, and not all that long ago.

"How hard is it to find?" Wyatt asked.

"It's in the middle of nowhere," Bull answered. "There are no alpacas grazing, and no coca plants that I can see. It's like a weigh station. Julio Rivas said Calderón has a bunch of these hidey-holes around the area. It's situated on high ground. Everything's beige and dusty. But he must have an underground sprinkler system here. If you're in the air, there's no way you'd miss the green grass." With a nod to Julio, who was watering the horses at a shade-covered trough just outside the fence, Bull turned and strode back toward the house. "Use GPS to mark this spot. It may be a wild goose chase to misdirect us, but if you can get the authorities to cooperate, there's got to be some evidence you can process here."

"Bull?" Tracy called to him from the front door and waved him inside. "She was here."

"Hold on, Wyatt. I think Tracy found something." The temperature dropped a good twenty degrees as he hopped onto the porch and stepped inside the hacienda's thick clay walls. His eyes

immediately went to the lime-green-flowered backpack Tracy
was sorting through.

"I found this in that little building out back—probably the
old summer kitchen from when this place was first built." She
pulled out a crumpled spiral notebook with green and purple ink
doodles all over the cover. "This is her class journal. She always
has it with her."

"Show me." Bull followed her through the house and out the
back door to the crumbling summer kitchen. Inside, he found
an empty roll of duct tape and the stinky odor of dried vomit.
Glancing at the rope bed with its straw mattress and evidence of
it being used, Bull muttered a curse and turned his attention back
to his brother. "She was definitely being held here. I'm not sure
for how long." He touched the sticky, splintered spot on one of
the bedposts where some of that duct tape had anchored something, or someone. "But they've moved her."

"Got any idea where they went?"

"I'll look around. But the horses—and Julio, too—are going
to need to get back and get some rest."

Off in the distance, Bull heard the horses whinnying and
shuffling about. Something had Jericho and Lila agitated. Julio
shouted something in Spanish.

Bull pulled the phone from his ear. "What did he say?"

Tracy handed him the notebook and backed out the door. "I
couldn't make it out, either. Finish your conversation. I want
help here as soon as we can get it. I'll check it out." She spun
around and broke into a jog. "I have no idea how experienced
he is with horses."

Wyatt was still talking when Bull put the phone back to his
ear and followed. "...worry about preserving any of the evidence.
I'll see about getting a task force helicopter there ASAP. Can you
make it back to J-Bar-J land all right?"

"Yup. I'll get everybody home."

He heard a gunshot and a scream and a galloping horse. Bull's
heart sank and his entire body tensed. *Tracy.* "Get your backup
here now! I've got company."

He snapped the phone shut, exchanging it for his Smith &

Wesson as he approached the front door. Pressing his back against the wall, he angled his head to get a visual on whatever was happening out front. A plume of dust masked most of what he needed to see, but he could make out Jericho, ears pricked and tail nervously erect, trotting down the road after the bolting mare.

"Señor McCabe!" Bull's blood turned to ice in his veins at the familiar thick Latin accent. "You come out, detective. I have your woman and the boy."

"Bull?" Tracy called out. "They shot Julio."

"Silencio!"

"Tracy!" That bastard had hit her again. But she was alive. He could work with that. Bull put his hands in the air and moved to the open doorway. "I'm coming out."

Cautiously, he stepped onto the porch, making a big, bad target of himself and hopefully taking Sol Garcia's focus off Tracy. But his patience stuck in his throat when he saw Garcia standing in the middle of the gravel road beyond the adobe fence. Tracy knelt beside Julio, who lay in the dust. Garcia had a handful of Tracy's hair clenched in his fist, pulling her head back so he could press his Glock 9 mil into her temple.

"Out here," Garcia ordered. "Put down your weapon."

Holding his hands high in the air, Bull stepped down to the grass. His gaze darted from Tracy to Garcia and back again— reassuring, condemning, reassuring again. Tracy was breathing hard, her eyes were afraid, but she wasn't hurt. Julio, on the other hand was bleeding between the fingers he clutched over his upper arm. And the horses had charged off to who knew where?

Everything inside Bull twisted up with the need to go to Tracy. But she needed him to harness his impulsiveness and be patient. For her. "You hurt her, you son of a bitch, and I will kill you."

"My employer, Señor Calderón, said to kill the boy before he talks. But I see he has nine lives, and that he already has told the authorities about the girl. Calderón is tired of your interference. And so am I."

"Where's Brittany?" Bull demanded. "Where's my sister?"

"Your sister? Ah, no wonder you are so relentless in pursuing us." Garcia's teeth shone white against his tanned skin as he laughed. "She is someplace safe with Calderón himself. He will convince your father to grant him the land he needs. You cannot stop him." The sick white smile vanished. "You should be worried about the problem here, *señor*. Now put down your gun, before I shoot your woman."

His woman. Damn straight, Tracy Cobb was his. Always had been but he'd been too caught up in the idea that nothing ever changed with Justice, the J-Bar-J or Serpentine. But *he'd* changed. Tracy had changed. Their relationship had changed. And no smiling son of a bitch with a gun and a knife was going to take Tracy from him before he could tell her just how much being with her these past couple of days had changed him—and how he was willing to put up with Justice and wrestle with the demons from his past if she'd give them the chance to be together.

He flashed his gaze over Tracy, hoping they were still in tune enough for her to read how much he loved her.

Then he set down his gun in the grass, never taking his eyes off Garcia's. This standoff was a little unbalanced. Bull against one man? Even if he was unarmed, men like Sol Garcia liked to have a little insurance. "Where's the big guy?"

Tracy's blue eyes darted to his right. At her warning glance, Bull turned to see Manuel Ortiz charging from the corner of the house. Why the big man didn't use the gun in his hand to shoot him instead, Bull would never know. When the gun came swinging at his head, Bull ducked and rammed his shoulder into Ortiz's gut. They hit the ground hard and rolled. The gun got kicked underneath the porch as the two men traded blows.

Bull took a punch to the gut and a crueler blow to his injured forearm. But his attacker lacked Bull's motivation to end the fight sooner rather than later. Howling with pain and the adrenaline pouring through his system, Bull planted his fist in the middle of Ortiz's broken face, knocking the man out cold. Then, breathing hard, not wanting to risk any more surprise attacks, Bull pulled his handcuffs off his belt and slapped them around Ortiz's wrists. "You're next, Garcia."

"Enough, detective!" Bull pushed himself up onto his knees and froze. He'd forgotten about patience. "Calderón said someone would be coming. That we should stop them and send a message back to Justice McCabe." Garcia had tucked the gun into his belt, yanked Tracy to her feet and now held that damned stiletto to her throat. A tiny drip of blood trickled down Tracy's smooth throat from where the blade pricked her skin. "I know how to get your attention, don't I, detective?"

"Virgil?" She clawed at Garcia's wrist.

"Here's your message."

The seconds ticked off like eons frozen in time. Bull dove for his gun. He came up with the weapon in his hands. The knife moved. He planted his knee. Aimed.

Bang.

Garcia's head jerked back. Forget negotiating with the bastard. Garcia crumpled to the ground, taking Tracy with him.

"Tracy!" Bull ran to pry her from the dead man's grasp. "Are you hurt? How bad is it?"

She scrambled to her knees and flung her arms around his neck, clinging to him like a life preserver. Bull lifted her with one arm behind her back, turning her face away from the blood pooling beneath Garcia's head. He kicked away the knife and stepped over the body to check on Julio. "You okay, kid?"

The boy still clutched his arm, but nodded. "Miss Cobb?"

Bull set her feet on the ground, okayed the color in her cheeks and the beautiful clarity of her eyes before planting a kiss on her mouth. "She'll be okay."

Tracy's hands were moving over him, touching the abrasion on his chin, muttering a sweet little curse as she pulled his arms between them. "You're bleeding again."

"I'll live."

She wrapped her hand around his neck and stretched up on tiptoe to return the same quick, needy kiss he'd given her. "You'd better."

And then she was on the ground, rolling Julio onto his back and checking the bullet graze on his arm. "I came out and saw Sol Garcia had dragged him into the road. I spooked the horses. They knocked Garcia out of the way so I could get to him."

Bull holstered his gun and knelt down to give Julio's good

arm a reassuring squeeze. Thank God the kid was still breathing. There was something tough and tenacious about this young man that Bull was learning to admire.

"Garcia shot him. I never saw Ortiz. They must have parked away from here and walked up."

"The shot just winged him. He'll be fine."

"But he's been through so much. Too much. He's just a boy."

Bull reached over and brushed that sexy little twist of hair off her forehead, calming her the way she always did him. "He's gonna be okay. Get some water from the house and anything you can tear up to use as a bandage."

"I'll find one for your arm, too."

Stubborn woman. He allowed himself a brief moment of indulgence to watch her run back into the house before pulling out his phone and punching in Wyatt's number. "Put a paramedic on that chopper," he advised his brother after giving a concise report on the two *Los Jaguares* he'd put out of commission. "Better send a horse trailer, too."

Bull spotted Jericho, grazing off some of that pristine grass Calderón had planted. The big horse let Bull tether him up. Hopefully, Tracy's mount would calm down and rejoin them, too, before she ran herself all the way home.

"Señor McCabe…" Julio had managed to get himself up to a sitting position, and was leaning back against the low adobe wall by the time Bull came back. "Are they dead?"

"Garcia is. Neither one is coming after you again."

"But others will?"

"I think so. As long as Calderón thinks you can tell the authorities about his organization, you're a threat to him."

"If I tell the authorities what I know, will they still arrest me?"

Bull knelt down to the teenager's level. "I can't say for sure. But I do know that telling us everything you know will help us learn more about Calderón and his operation. And that kind of knowledge may be what helps us bring Brittany home before Christmas."

The boy nodded resolutely, despite a grimace of pain. "Then I will tell all I know. For Brittany."

"I think you'd better start calling me Bull. I have a feeling you and I are going to be spending a lot of time together."

"What about Miss Cobb?"

"Oh, I intend to spend a lot of time with her, too."

Chapter Six

"He'll be safe here." Justice crossed his office to the wet bar in the corner and uncorked the bottle of whiskey.

Bull rose from the wing chair where he'd been sitting. "Dakota and Cody are helping Julio get settled in the studio apartment on the second floor of their cabin. Now that he's all stitched up and shot full of antibiotics, the main thing he needs is a good night's sleep."

Nearly every light in the main house was blazing, from the decorations on the tree at the front window to the security lanterns on the front porch. Justice lifted the bottle from which he'd just poured himself a second shot, but Bull shook his head at the offer of a refill. He needed to keep his senses clear if he was going to run the security here on the J-Bar-J.

Looking more like a weary father, and less like the tyrant Bull remembered, Justice downed the shot and set the glass in the sink before coming back to sit at the corner of the desk, facing his middle son. "Wyatt promised to come by as often as he can. And as long as you're here, that'll put a guardian on the ranch 24/7."

"We need to keep it hushed up that he's here, too. Shouldn't be a problem as long as school is on break." Bull scrubbed his hand over the late-night stubble shading his jaw. Even by helicopter, it had been a long trip back from the hacienda. And Bull had a feeling the days were going to be a hell of a lot longer in the week between now and Christmas—until they brought Brittany home. "Calderón seems to have a way of getting wind of things he shouldn't, so we need to be careful."

"Maria and Dakota know, of course, but I'll try to keep the ranch hands in the dark about our guest for as long as possible, too." With a firm nod, Justice rose and headed out to the main room. "I'd better go check on Mr. Rivas. I'm not too sure I like having a kidnapper under my roof. But I understand that he may still have information we need. And that we have to protect him until we get it."

"Don't be too hard on him, Justice." Bull followed him out, stopping when they reached the hallway. "He's full of regret, and pretty beat-up besides. He was just trying to help his family."

"By putting my daughter in danger?"

"Calderón doesn't discriminate when it comes to using or hurting anyone." Bull shoved his hands into the pockets of his jeans. The last time he'd tried to give his father advice, the conversation had ended with Bull running off to college and never looking back. He was done running from this man. "Try talking to him, Justice. Ask him to tell you about Brittany. You might learn something by doing a little bit of listening."

"Listening isn't my best thing."

"I know." He glanced up the stairs where he could hear the shower running. Tracy was up there, washing up after their overnight ride down to Mexico. After their run-ins with the *Los Jaguares,* he didn't trust that she'd be safe alone in her apartment. "It's a skill I'm learning to get better at myself."

"I'll try," Justice conceded. "It's not easy for an old dog to learn a new trick, but I'll try."

Bull saw the opening to say something to his father. Maybe he was getting some age himself. Or maybe Tracy's and Wyatt's insistence that their father was a changed man was starting to make sense. After nearly losing Tracy to the *Los Jaguares,* he had an idea of just how bad a man's heart could break if he lost the woman he loved—giving him a tad of insight into his father going off the deep end after his mother's death.

Still, the idea of sharing a civil, meaningful conversation with his father felt about as comfortable as breaking in a new pair of boots. But after ten years, maybe it was time one of them tried. "Wyatt's got a lead on Morgan. He's flying in from wherever he is. Rusty rounded up Jericho and Lila, and is driving them back from Calderón's hacienda. In the meantime, I'm locking down this ranch. No one is going to hurt this family or the people we care about again."

"No, son. They're not. I'm glad you're home to help me." Justice raised his silvering head. His mouth curved into an unfamiliar smile. "I'll see to the boy, and…I promise just to talk." Bull was halfway to the second floor when Justice came back to stand beside the newel post at the foot of the stairs. "You *are* staying, aren't you? At least until we get your sister back home?"

An uneasy alliance had been formed. Circumstances were forcing Bull to team up with his father to protect their family. And, possibly, the beginnings of trust between them was being rekindled. "Yes, sir." But they weren't going to hug and say Merry Christmas just yet. Bull tilted his head up the stairs. The running water had stopped. "If you don't mind, I'm a little beat-up myself. I'm heading upstairs."

"Good night, son."

"Good night."

Bull opened the door of his bedroom in time to see Tracy pulling one of his old T-shirts on over the panties she wore.

She turned around, reprimanding him with those beautiful eyes as she pulled her damp hair out from beneath the collar and shook it loose down her back. Yep, he had it bad for this one. "Don't you knock?"

"My bedroom," he reminded her, shrugging out of his holster and laying his gun out of the way on the dresser. He set his badge down next to it and untucked the tails of his shirt.

"Oh." She gathered up her wet towel and dirty clothes. "Justice sent me up to this room to change. I guess he thought we…" Her skin blushed pink around the bruise on her cheek and the bandage on her neck. "I remember where the guest room is. End of the hall, right?"

Bull caught her with one arm as she made a beeline for the door. "You're bunking here tonight."

Without further discussion, he scooped her up and carried her to the bed, dumping the laundry on the floor and sitting beside her to pull his boots off his feet. One hit the floor, then the other. He stood to unbutton his shirt and peel it off over his re-bandaged arm.

"Virgil?" She curled her knees beneath her and sat up. "What are you doing?"

The shirt joined his boots and he crawled into bed beside her. He wrapped her in his arms and pulled her soft warmth close to his chest. "Even if all we do is sleep, blue eyes, I'm going to hold you in my arms tonight."

Those blue eyes sought out his. "Why?"

"Because I need to. Because I love you. Because leaving the J-Bar-J—and you—behind in Texas was the dumbest thing I've ever done. And this teacher I know taught me to be a smarter man."

Tracy smiled, winding her arm around his waist and holding on like she meant it. "Are you finally coming home to me—to where you belong, Virgil McCabe?"

With a slow nod, he sealed her in his arms, holding on just as tight. "I'm coming home."

* * * * *

DANA MARTON
MORGAN

CAST OF CHARACTERS

Morgan McCabe—Commando soldier who spends his life overseas on missions. When he is called back to the family ranch to rescue a half sister he's never known about, he espects having to face his shaky family past. He doesn't expects to be confronted by the only woman he's ever loved on the first day of his arrival. Years ago she chose someone else over him. Has he built too many walls around his heart to take advantage of a second chance?

Dakota Dayton—Raising her son, Cody, alone, Dakota found sanctuary and a job on the McCabe Ranch. But the careful balance in her life is shaken up when Morgan McCabe returns home. He has plenty of secrets. His job is a mystery. But when dangers surround her and her son, he is the man she can trust to save them.

Brittany Means—The half sister the McCabe brothers never knew they had.

Justice McCabe—Wyatt's rancher father hasn't always been the best of fathers. But how far will he be willing to go to save his daughter?

Javier Calderón—The drug lord needs access to McCabe land for trouble-free access to a coast-to-coast highway that will greatly expand his drug trafficking business. But will he let his personal vendetta against Agent Elena Vargas get in the way of his pragmatic concerns?

Los Jaguares—Calderón's vicious enforcers spread fear and terror throughout the small towns of the Texas/Mexico border. But are they completely loyal to Calderón?

Rusty Fisher—He has worked at the ranch most of his life. Yet when the past reaches out to pull him down, will he able to resist? He's not the only man at the ranch with secrets. Is he a family friend or the man lurking in the shadows to harm them?

Virgil "Bull" McCabe—It took the kidnapping of the half sister he didn't know he had to bring the cop back home to Texas. Does he have it in his heart to forgive his difficult father?

Wyatt McCabe—Morgan's youngest brother, the Serpentine, Texas, sheriff will do anything it takes to help bring their sister home.

To Julie and Paula

Chapter One

If they caught him, he was going to say he had a question about his pay. As good an excuse as any, since Dakota handled the payroll. The man looked around to make sure nobody watched, then ducked into the old cabin, built back when Texas had been a wild frontier. The small entry hall, hung with Christmas garlands, was just enough for a person to kick his boots off. He kept his on, reaching for his weapon.

He hadn't come for a social visit.

To his left stood a door to the ground floor living quarters, ahead of him, up at the top of the stairs was another door, which led to the small apartment that had been added when the cabin had been updated. One of those two doors hid his target.

Blood drummed in his ears, the collar of his shirt feeling too tight all of a sudden. He rolled his shoulders and shut down all emotion, steeled himself. He'd killed before; he could do it again. And this would be the last time. With this, his debt to *Los Jaguares* would be erased.

He stepped toward the downstairs door that led to the two-bedroom living quarters Dakota Dayton and her son occupied. She was the boss's pet. She would hide Julio at her place in a blink of an eye if Justice had asked her.

She and her kid should be at dinner by now at the main house, the best time to catch Julio alone. He listened for a moment, but couldn't hear anything from inside. He reached for the door.

The doorknob wouldn't turn. He shoved the gun into his waistband in the front where he could easily reach it, and pulled the picks from his pocket. Fumbled.

Getting rusty from too many years of honest work. Except for a few small jobs for *Los Jaguares,* he had been on the straight and narrow. But he *had* started his career as a petty thief.

Today he was an assassin. His third hit over the years, not that experience made the task more pleasant. Still, he would do what he was told. *Los Jaguares* didn't take no for an answer.

This one last job, then he would be free.

The lock clicked. The door moved silently, inch by inch.

Dakota's three-year-old sat in the middle of the living room, bent over a coloring book, too busy to notice the intruder. The shower was running in the bathroom in the back, the muffled sound of the water unmistakable.

What the hell were they still doing here? Justice always had them up at the house for dinner.

His palms began to sweat.

He scanned the room with a quick glance. Only Dakota's hat hung on the peg by the door, and the kid's smaller one. No men's boots on the shoe rack, nothing to indicate that they were hiding Julio here.

He backed out quietly and closed the door behind him, drew a steadying breath. Swore as he looked up to the door at the top of the stairs. He didn't like doing the job with those two downstairs, but he could. The gun Calderón had sent him—serial number carefully filed off—had a silencer.

Sweat was rolling off his forehead by the time he reached the top, one careful step at a time. He tested the door. Locked like the first one. Good thing he'd brought the picks.

He almost conquered this lock, too, when the downstairs door opened. He moved his right hand near the weapon hidden under his shirt and held his breath.

The little boy bounded out, carrying his mini cowboy boots, sat on the bottom step and yanked them on, then ran outside without once looking up.

The man waited a few seconds as he swore under his breath. Where the kid went, the mother would soon follow. He hurried down the stairs, then looked outside through the front door the kid left open. The boy was scampering toward the corrals.

He ducked out and hurried off in the opposite direction. He'd come back for Julio later. The first try was a bust, but at least nobody saw him.

"I DON'T NEED MEDICAL LEAVE," Morgan McCabe told his superior officer over the phone as his rental SUV rolled forward on the dusty private road toward the ranch buildings. He watched the retreating back of a ranch hand as the guy hurried away from the old cabin across the yard from the main ranch house. Something about the way the man walked, his neck tucked in, his hat pulled into his face, pricked Morgan's instincts.

He shook it off. He wasn't on the battlefield. Better get used to civilian life while he was here.

Man, it sucked to have to be back.

"Medical leave and a psych evaluation before you are returned to active duty. You've been through hell," the officer snapped.

"And made it through."

The man on the other end went on about the importance of safety measures and the like.

Morgan parked the SUV in front of the ranch house, but felt none of the fuzzy warmth a person was supposed to when returning home after a decade. He didn't recognize any of the ranch hands going about their business between the stables and the outbuildings, all jeans and cowboy boots and Stetsons. He got out, stretched his legs and looked down at his clothes. In his combat boots and black cargo pants, he stuck out like a sore thumb.

Not that he couldn't blend in, if he wanted to. He'd worked undercover commando missions long enough to be able to adapt to any surroundings, disappear into any culture, be an invisible part of any crowd. He simply hadn't cared to change his clothes. He wasn't here to play masquerade. He was here to rescue Brittany, the stepsister he'd never met, then get the hell out of the place as fast as possible.

"I'll see you when you have your return paperwork in order," his superior officer finished at last. "If you think you're too macho to go on medical leave, consider it a vacation. You deserve a break. Give me a call after the new year."

He tamped down his frustration. "Yes, sir." Then he ended the connection.

As he pulled his earpiece off, his gaze caught on the burned fields and he scowled. A faint scent of smoke still lingered in the air. The wildfire had reached dangerously close to the buildings. It was good to see the house and barns and all the outbuildings still standing. He didn't hate the place. He just didn't like it.

The main house stood in the middle, as proud as ever, miles of Christmas garlands wrapped around it. He could make out the outline of a large Christmas tree through the big window. His mother used to do all that when she'd been alive. Who played Santa's elf now?

"Not the old man," he said under his breath as he considered his situation.

He had no intention of sticking around the family ranch for the holidays. He'd help them rescue Brittany, then go back on active duty. Preferably by the end of the week. He would play his short stay here the same way he played his missions: in and out as fast as possible, no mistakes.

He knew the doc who did the psych evaluations. In fact, the man owed him a favor. The thought cheered him more than a little.

He was reaching for his duffel bag in the back when the horses whinnied and drew his attention to the nearest corral. His instincts kicked in. He narrowed his eyes against the sun, and spotted a little boy among the nervously prancing mares just as one of the massive quarter horses reared up.

If those sharp hooves came down on the kid... But the boy seemed oblivious to danger, and Morgan didn't dare shout.

He ran.

Two hundred feet between them.

One hundred.

"Ho." He vaulted over the side of the corral.

Calm now. He slowed, eased toward the horse that seemed most bothered by the kid. Some horses, especially ones who'd been spooked by coyotes in the far pastures before, were skittish of small things approaching.

"Ho." He put himself between the agitated animal and the boy.

The horse danced back and snorted at him angrily, head high, black mane flying in the wind. A beautiful sight, but dangerous. The animal, already in a bad mood, didn't know him, didn't like him in her space.

"Hang on, buddy." Morgan snatched up the kid and dove through the wooden bars of the fence as the horse charged.

Umph. He hit the ground hard, keeping the kid safe even as pain shot through his cracked ribs that had barely started healing. He would have broken them this time, if not for the layers of Ace bandages under his shirt.

"Do it again!" The boy laughed, his face lit with delight as he sat on top of him. "I want to fly through the air!"

"You should never go into the corrals without an adult." Morgan kept his voice calm but firm.

His first instinct was to threaten to tan the boy's hide if he ever did anything this stupid again, the same thing his father would have done. But he wasn't his father, he reminded himself. And the wide-eyed toddler wasn't his son. And spanking kids for bad behavior had gone out of fashion since he'd been this size, from what he'd heard.

Except, with that option crossed out, he was out of ideas. He sucked with kids.

"I'm Cody," this one said, looking more entertained than shaken up. "Who are you?"

"I'm Morgan. And I want you to stay away from those horses. I mean it."

"Wyatt says I was born to ride. I'm very good at it." The boy wiggled as if riding, caring nothing for the cracked ribs.

"Easy, cowboy." Morgan sat up and set the kid aside with care as he looked around. The little bundle of terror had to have a mother. Where was she?

"Cody?" Dakota peeked into the kitchen, running her fingers through her wet hair. "Where are you, honey?" She padded over to her son's horse-themed bedroom, toys all over the rug, books laid out on the floor, but couldn't see the little boy in there, either.

"Are we playing hide and seek?" She smiled and jumped in front of the gap between the wardrobe and the wall, but Cody wasn't there.

Her bedroom came next. She didn't find him under the bed.

The kitchen cabinets. She went back that way. Cody loved hiding in the corner cabinet among the Tupperware.

"Where could he be?" she asked in a dramatic tone, her hand on the knob. "Right here!" she yelled as she yanked the door open.

But she saw nothing save plastic containers.

Unease crawled up her spine, her tone changing from playful to serious as she asked, "Cody, honey?"

She stepped back into the living room, even looked behind the Christmas tree. "Cody!"

And then she saw the front door standing open a crack. She could have sworn she had locked that before heading into the bathroom to take a shower.

She rushed outside, her heart in her throat, stumbling in her house slippers, her bathrobe tangling around her legs. She brushed her wet hair out of her face as she looked around for her son. A working ranch hid too many dangers for an unsupervised three-year-old. "Cody!"

The kid's favorite rocking chair on the porch of the big house stood empty. She swung the other way.

And saw her little boy on the ground with a strange man, the man's hands on him. She charged forward.

Then noticed that Cody was smiling, happy as anything. *Okay. Okay.* She fought back the sudden panic that had squeezed her lungs way too tight.

Then the stranger spotted her, and the next second he was looking at her as if a horse had just kicked him in the head. Which very well could have been what had happened. Dust smears covered his face. Was he the latest ranch hand Justice hired to help with the cleanup after the wildfire?

She snatched up Cody and stepped back, the question, "Who are you?" on her tongue, but then the man stood and she recognized the way he moved, recognized those gunmetal-gray eyes at last and her heart gave a quick, hard thud in her chest.

"You came." The words tumbled forth before she could have checked them.

An annoyed frown drew lines on his forehead as he dusted off his pants. He was just as lean as the last time she'd seen him, but he'd packed on muscle since and developed some seriously hard edges. The boyishly handsome look was gone. He looked rough and tough and aggravated.

"He got under the horses."

Her heart stopped all over again as she looked Cody over. "Are you okay?" She hugged him to her tightly.

"You should watch him better," Morgan said.

And before she could protest that she *had* locked the door, he'd already turned on the heels of his boots and was striding away from her, without even giving her a proper greeting, without a "How have you been?"

She stared after him, her gaze slipping for a moment to his cargo pants that stretched in very interesting places. Well, that looked… She made herself snap out of it. "Morgan?"

He didn't look back. Maybe he didn't hear her. He grabbed a duffel bag from the backseat of his SUV, then headed straight to the house, his shoulders stiff, his stride a little hurried.

He couldn't still be mad at her after all these years, could he?

Of course not. He hadn't asked how she was, because he didn't care how she was. Why should he? They were strangers now, after all these years.

She swallowed hard. The thought hurt.

Could be he didn't even recognize her—he hadn't said her name. She'd filled out since the last time they'd seen each other, still carried some of the baby weight from the pregnancy. Her hair was shorter, too, she thought, and reached up to tug on a strand. Water dripped onto her fingers.

Oh, God. "I look like a drowned rat in house slippers, don't I?" She spun around and hurried toward the cabin with Cody.

The little gentleman that he was, Cody held his silence, his attention back on the horses.

"How on earth did you get out?" She closed the front door behind them.

Cody squirmed to the floor, pouting. "I wanted to ride."

The thought of what could have happened to him tightened her throat. "You can only ride with me, honey. That's our deal, right? And you're not supposed to go outside without asking me first."

This time when she locked the door to their downstairs kingdom behind them, she also flipped the dead bolt that was too high for Cody to reach. "I don't want you to mess with these locks, okay?"

"Okay." He was already diving for the remote. "Can I watch TV?"

"While I get ready. Then we're going over for dinner." Dinner ran late today because Miguel, the cook, had a doctor's appointment in the city.

Morgan would be sitting at the table tonight, too. The thought popped into her head unbidden and stole her breath away.

She'd known he would come at some point, had prepared herself. Or tried. Turned out she could prepare herself for Morgan about as well as one could for a wildfire.

"I need you to pick up your toys while you're watching TV," she called back to Cody, and tried to push the image of the new and hard-edged Morgan out of her mind as she walked to the bathroom. She didn't succeed. "And when we get back from dinner, we'll clean up your room together."

Dinner with Morgan.

He'd been her best friend once. Then her first love. The first man to take her to bed. *Closet,* really. He'd charmed her out of her pants in the upstairs hall closet of the main ranch house one day when she'd come over to go riding together. They'd been kissing in the hallway and when they'd heard his father coming up the stairs, Morgan pulled her out of sight.

The memory flooded her with heat. And need. And feelings long forgotten. She pushed all that away. They were nothing to each other now. She had chosen another man. When she'd told him, all those years ago, that Billy had proposed, Morgan never even bothered to fight for her. He had left and never come back.

Until now.

She grabbed the comb and attacked her tangles, staring at herself in the mirror, yet seeing him, the schooled look on his face, his sharp gaze.

She still dreamed about him sometimes.

He wasn't going to find out about *that*.

She was a widow. A respectable widow, surrounded by dozens of ranch hands who sniffed after every skirt. She didn't fraternize with the other employees, *or* the owners.

And Morgan was… He was barely here at all. He would help his brothers with the search then he would leave. After all, leaving was what he did best. If she ever let herself fall for anyone again, it would be someone who'd make a great father for Cody, not an emotionally unavailable commando soldier.

Chapter Two

Entering the house was like stepping back in time. Morgan slowed in the entryway. Hell, his old hat still hung on the peg with the others. He couldn't imagine why. Justice had never been the sentimental type.

Garlands draped around the pegboard that held gloves and hats and even a pair of old spurs. Someone had decorated the side table below the pegboard with a holiday floral arrangement—all weirdly homey, as if a normal family lived here.

He walked past it all, toward the voices coming from the living room. Stopped in the doorway. Took in the three men.

Wyatt laughed at something, all grown-up. Man, that was weird. He looked a lot less nerdy than he used to, every inch a cowboy now.

Virgil had put on some bulk. Mostly muscle. He had an I-mean-business look to him. He'd definitely hardened over the years, making his nickname, Bull, even more suitable.

Their father had aged the most, seemed smaller somehow. Not quite as hard-edged as Morgan remembered. He was the first to notice the new arrival. He pushed away from the back window where he'd been standing.

"Son." He walked forward.

Morgan dropped the bag at his feet and stayed where he was. "Justice."

The older man stopped. "Glad to have you home."

Bull got up, too, looking half happy, half annoyed. "What took you so long?"

"I could tell you, but…" he deadpanned.

Wyatt wasn't as subdued as the other two. He strode right over, pumped his hand, pulled him into a brotherly hug, the works. "It's been way too long." Nothing but smiles and open acceptance on his face.

"Any news since we've talked?" He'd called the ranch when he'd gotten off the plane in San Antonio. Wyatt had filled him in on the details. None of them good.

"Nothing," he said now.

"I got a few things in progress," Bull put in. "We should have her cell phone log soon. Something might pop there."

Justice bent to the small table by the sofa and scooped up a picture, handing it over. "That's her."

Morgan grabbed the edge of the photograph. *Brittany Means*. God, she was young. His sister. Half sister. Whatever. Black hair, full lips. Not much McCabe about her. Maybe her gray eyes. Okay, she definitely had that.

"Any reason the law is not handling this?"

Justice's back stiffened. "They're handling it, but we'll handle it better and quicker. McCabes take care of their own business."

He handed back the picture, then looked at Bull. "You shouldn't have gone to Mexico without me."

The muscles around Bull's jaw tightened. "You should have come home sooner."

"I'm here now. I'm going to work out a comprehensive plan of attack, and then we're going to execute it to the letter."

A short Mexican guy in his twenties appeared in the doorway, probably the new cook, judging by his stained apron. Morgan wondered what had happened to the old cowboy he remembered, Hiram. He'd made campfire biscuits with bacon grease that made a man's mouth water.

"We'll plan after dinner." Justice moved forward. "Morgan is my oldest," he said in the way of introduction. "Miguel helps out around the house."

What, not some young woman he could grab and get with, maybe produce another bastard? the mean, dark part inside Morgan wanted to ask. He slapped the old resentment back, and simply nodded. His grouchy mood wasn't entirely Justice's fault. "I'm going to pop upstairs and wash up."

He needed a little space.

"Your old room is set up for you," Wyatt said with an easy smile, looking as happy as a kid. "It's good to have the family together."

Did Wyatt miss the old days? A vague sense of guilt touched Morgan. For the most part, he didn't think too much about the old homestead. Fighting terrorists on a daily basis kept him pretty busy. Just the way he liked it.

He picked up his duffel bag and walked away.

Up the stairs, the pictures he remembered still hung in the same spot. The sight of his mother laughing into the sun cut into his heart. He didn't slow. His mother's memory and the pain was a weakness, and he didn't allow weaknesses. Couldn't afford them in his job.

He stopped in front of his old room, looked to the end of the hallway, at *the* closet—another memory that would weaken him if he gave it half a chance. He wasn't going to let that happen.

Dakota… The sight of her in the yard had knocked the air from his lungs as hard as the vault had from the corral with her son. She was even more beautiful than the last time he'd seen her and… He shoved her picture out of his mind. He wasn't going to go there. No way.

He pushed into his room and glanced around, cataloguing the old and the new methodically. The room, too, seemed smaller than he remembered. Not much had changed here, either. The quilt his mother had made him covered the bed; the old lasso his grandfather had given him still hung on the wall.

More memories bubbled up. He kept moving, refusing to let the past touch him. He dropped his bag and pulled out a clean shirt. He'd barely unbuttoned the one he had on when Wyatt strode in.

"Need help unpacking, big brother?"

He'd always followed him and Bull around, even when they'd been kids.

"I'll be down in a minute," Morgan said, more brusquely than he'd meant. He needed a minute to adjust to being surrounded by them. Yesterday this time he'd been holed up in the Pashtun mountains, trying to save his best friend from bleeding out before their evac chopper showed up.

But Ricky didn't make it.

He pushed that thought aside. Compartmentalization was the name of the game.

The look on his face must have told Wyatt that he meant to be alone, because his little brother backed out the door. "Sure. I'll see you downstairs." Still smiling. Not a speck of offense taken.

Part of Morgan envied that lightheartedness. He couldn't remember ever having had that.

He shrugged out of his shirt and dropped it in the corner, headed over to the bathroom, washed his face, ran his fingers through his short, commando-cut hair. He wasn't back in his bedroom two minutes before someone was at the door again.

"Ever heard of patience?" he snapped before turning around and finding himself face-to-face with Dakota.

"Sorry." She backed away.

Her blond, shoulder-length hair was dry now and pulled into a ponytail. A dusting of freckles ran across her nose. She'd always hated those freckles. He'd loved them—used to kiss every single one. His gaze fell to her slightly crooked mouth he'd also kissed plenty of times.

"I didn't mean to bother you," she said.

His gaze slid lower on her body.

Her plain T-shirt stretched across breasts he didn't remember being quite that full. He could happily have looked at them for a good long time. He could happily have done a lot more than look.

Instant attraction punched through him, just as it had out in the yard. Over the years, he had somehow convinced himself that he was done with her, that he no longer wanted her. Realizing that the opposite was true took a moment of adjustment. Some invisible force pulled him forward.

Instead of giving in, he turned away and shrugged into his fresh shirt. "What are you doing here?"

"I wanted to thank you for saving Cody. You left so fast—"

"I mean why are you living at the J-Bar-J?" Someone should have definitely told him about that.

"Justice gave me housing with the job. He's really nice. I'm very grateful."

There were so many things wrong with that, he didn't know where to start. The words *Justice, give* and *nice* didn't belong together. All the old man had ever given anyone was grief. "Job?"

"I'm an accountant now." She worried the side seam of her jeans with her slim fingers. "I do the taxes, payroll, pretty much everything that has to do with finance."

That, at least, made sense. Last time he'd seen her, she was studying finance in college on scholarship, over in San Antonio. Where she'd met Billy. He didn't want to think about that. He didn't want to think about a lot of things.

Dakota on the ranch. Just what he didn't need. "Does Billy-boy work here, too?" He couldn't quite manage to keep the bitterness out of his voice.

She shrunk back and folded her arms around herself, covering the enticing view of her breasts. "Billy passed away."

A long moment passed, bringing nothing but conflicting emotions, before he processed the words. "Sorry to hear that."

But was he, really? Last time he'd seen Billy, he'd wanted to kill the bastard. He hadn't taken it well that Dakota had chosen to marry the man.

He shook off whatever feelings were threatening to take hold of him. Whatever had happened, happened. He wasn't going to stick around long enough for any of this to matter. He wasn't here to rekindle anything with Dakota. He was a commando soldier, lone wolf and all that.

HE STOOD LIKE A FORTRESS before her. Of course, he'd always been emotionally distant. Which was mostly the reason why she'd chosen Billy, back when. She'd been young and silly and needed the same wild emotions, and affection, warmth, flowers and holding hands and the rest. Billy had been the great romantic.

And Morgan the stoic one, his true feelings always hidden.

He'd liked to keep things clean, and people—but most especially emotions—at arm's length. She didn't like it, yet she had always accepted it.

But didn't want to anymore, suddenly. He might not have changed much, but she had.

He didn't want emotions. He wanted to shove their shared past under the rug. Tough for him. She, for one, liked to address problems and deal with them. She was a little better prepared for him now than earlier.

"Are you ever going to forgive me?" She wanted to clear the air between them, didn't want everything to be all awkward when they went down to dinner, or for however long he'd be here.

His face remained impassive. "There's nothing to forgive."

Which meant, *no.*

Her gaze dropped to his bandaged ribs. "Are you hurt?"

He buttoned up his shirt. "I'm fine."

He'd always been way too proud for his own good. Another thing that hadn't changed. He'd been a hard youth and he'd grown into an even harder man. Now that she had Cody, she understood the love a son needed. But back when the McCabe boys had still lived at home, Justice hadn't been the most loving of fathers. He'd mellowed some with age.

She felt bad for Morgan. But she didn't feel bad enough to humor him and accept the walls he'd built. "You're not ready to forgive me, and you're in pain. I have some pills at the cabin—"

"No."

She didn't particularly like playing games so she drew a deep breath and went for it. "I've missed you."

He gave a slow blink.

"You've missed me, too." She was trying to help. "We were friends once, remember?"

He shrugged. "A lot has happened since."

"You could give me a chance. We could be friends again." She couldn't handle anything beyond that, but she needed more than his cold distance. "And you should think about forgiving Justice, too. You should give your father a chance."

He scoffed.

"People change." Justice had been good to her, had saved her after Billy's death, given her the job and the cabin to stay in. She wanted Morgan to be nice to him. If she could achieve that, she would be paying Justice back in some small way. "He's a good guy. He's great with Cody."

His eyes flashed, his lips twisting into a sneer. "You're his new bed warmer, is that it? Living right across the yard. How convenient."

Anger flashed through her. Her palm was halfway to his cheek when he caught her wrist, holding it in an iron grip.

And for a second she was horrified and embarrassed. She'd never hit anyone in her life. Had never meant to hit him, but— Nobody but Morgan McCabe could bend her out of shape this badly, this fast. "I'm sorry," she mumbled, tugging, hoping he'd release her.

He didn't. "No. I'm sorry," he said, then yanked her into his arms and kissed her.

Startled shock knocked the air out of her for a second. Then a million memories flooded her next, as she stood in his arms, surrounded by the familiar feel and scent of him. Instant sensory overload. A second longer and she was no longer sure who she was, what she wanted or even what decade they were in.

His lips were punishing on hers. She didn't care. Everything inside her responded to the unbridled hunger. Raw need tore through her.

Her knees went weak and she leaned against him.

If they could turn back time...

But they couldn't. And she wouldn't. She had Cody, who was waiting with Justice and the others downstairs. That thought brought her out of her mental haze and she pulled away—not without reluctance.

"This is not what I came for," she said in a weak whisper.

"Then what are you doing in my bedroom half-naked?"

She glanced down at her jeans, confused for a second.

He gave a startled laugh as he stepped back. "I haven't seen too many women without a burka in the last couple of years. I can see your bra strap through your T-shirt."

She glanced down, more than embarrassed to realize that the T-shirt not only failed to hide the outline of her bra, but also revealed nipples that desire had drawn to sharp points. She crossed her arms, part of her flattered, part of her consternated over the fact that he found her desirable to the point of losing his iron control. *Ditto,* she thought. He affected her plenty. But she wouldn't have admitted it for a million dollars. She grasped for something to distract the both of them.

"Were you in Iraq?"

He strode to the window and looked out. She knew the view from here: her cabin.

"Afghanistan?"

He didn't respond, but he turned back to her. "How did Billy die?"

A long moment passed before she gathered herself. "He was out with his friends."

While Morgan had always been principled and self-disciplined, Billy was all about fun. Which she had truly liked about him, at the beginning. Not until later did she realize that her husband sometimes chased fun to the point of being irresponsible and beyond.

"I'd just told him I was pregnant. His buddies took him out to celebrate. Then they decided to do a little drag racing on the old county road." She didn't want to think about the crash.

Billy left her with a boatload of debt and no health insurance. She had to come begging for a job at the ranch. She'd learned to appreciate responsibility and security in a hurry.

"Bull and I have been out on that road a million times at night." Morgan shook his head, then added, "Billy never saw his boy, then."

"He never saw as much as an ultrasound picture." Her eyes burned suddenly. She missed Billy. She'd missed Morgan, too. She'd been such a child when she'd chosen between them. Nineteen. She hadn't known anything about anything.

"Anyway." She half turned to leave. "I just wanted to thank you for grabbing Cody from those horses. He's getting so independent. I have to watch him like a hawk."

His shoulders relaxed at last, and the tight set of his mouth softened. He was almost the old Morgan. "You should have seen the trouble me and my brothers got into growing up."

"Don't tell me. I might not sleep another night if I know what's waiting for me."

A ghost of a smile played above his lips.

She wanted to step back into his arms, wanted it so bad it scared her.

"Welcome home, Morgan," she said and hurried back downstairs, toward the safety of the kitchen.

MORGAN RAN OUT TO HIS car for his phone charger before joining the others in the kitchen, and saw Rusty Fisher who was heading toward Dakota's place. The old guy was plenty rough around the edges, but Morgan had always liked him. They'd broken in a horse or two together back in the day.

"She's at the house for dinner," he called out to the man who turned his way and watched him for a second before recognizing him.

"Morgan. Good to see you home. Heard you were coming." Rusty smoothed down his handlebar mustache. His shirt revealed a line of tattoos around his neck that had impressed Morgan plenty when he'd been younger. "I was just going to ask her about the kid. Heard he'd gotten under the horses earlier."

"Made it out fine." He took the man's hand as he strode closer for a shake. "Everything's good with you, I hope?"

Rusty shrugged. "Things are as good as you make 'em."

Plenty of truth in that.

"It's good that all you boys came back home," the man said. "Family is important."

They could lift you up or smack you down, that was for sure, Morgan thought, but didn't say it. "I better get back in. They're waiting for me for dinner."

Dakota among them.

He shouldn't have kissed her.

Mistake number one.

And he hadn't even unpacked his bag yet.

He didn't want her to start mattering to him again. He didn't want to want her. But he did, and he always would, he realized now. He swore under his breath.

Ignoring reality didn't pay. On a mission, ignoring reality could kill you faster than just about anything else. So as far as he could see it, there really was only one thing he could do: win Dakota back.

Chapter Three

Morgan couldn't fully concentrate on anything else until Dakota left after dinner. She needed to put Cody to bed. She'd taken Julio's dinner to him, so Julio wouldn't have to leave the cabin. For a moment Morgan hesitated whether to go after her. He wanted more time with her, and had plenty of questions for Julio. But he had plenty of questions for his family, too. He would leave Dakota and Julio for the morning.

The ranch manager—who had joined them at the table, an old custom at the ranch—hesitated in the doorway on his way out, worrying his hat in his knobby old hands, his white hair slicked back. "If you have a minute, Justice."

"Sure thing, Shane." Justice followed him out to the porch.

Morgan walked back to the living room with his brothers and sat on the sofa, ready to tackle the reason for his return. "So all we know for sure is that our rescue target is somewhere in Mexico."

"Her name is Brittany," Wyatt said as he sank into one of the oversize armchairs.

"*Most likely* somewhere in Mexico," Bull corrected. He remained standing. "Calderón could have moved her back across into the U.S., but I don't think it's likely. His main strength is on the other side of the border where he has law enforcement in his pocket."

Morgan considered that for a moment before he nodded. "Agreed." He measured up his brothers. They looked as capable as any of his commando team members. "We're going to get her back."

"Of course we will. She's a *McCabe*." Bull emphasized the last word, as if Morgan needed a reminder. "Somebody messes with a McCabe, he messes with all of us. Although, some of us ride to the rescue a little faster than others, I suppose."

"I was busy."

"All important, hotshot-commando stuff, I'm sure."

Annoyance flashed through him. He didn't owe anyone an explanation. "Carrying my best friend's body out of the Afghan mountains," he said anyway.

Bull didn't have a comeback for that.

"Were you hurt?" Wyatt asked.

Morgan shrugged.

Which snagged Bull's attention. "I want to know what shape the man who's going to have my back is in."

"Better than you are, even with a couple of cracked ribs." Hell, they'd been hurt worse at the junior rodeos they'd attended as kids. All the more to feel guilty about. Ricky had lost his life, while Morgan had walked out without being as much as grazed by a bullet, just the cracked ribs when they'd tumbled down the face of the mountain in the dark. Ricky was dead, and he was alive.

Sheer stupid luck. It could just as easily have been him in that coffin he'd flown back to the States with.

He opened the laptop. "I got some satellite images of the area Calderón controls in Mexico and in the U.S."

Bull nodded, but glanced at the clock on the wall, checking the time from the corner of his eye.

Annoyance shot through Morgan. "Got a hot date?"

Bull gave a cocky grin. "As a matter of fact."

"Tracy Cobb. High school English teacher," Wyatt put in helpfully, then gave a wolfish whistle.

Instead of shutting him up, or at least threatening to shut him up, Bull didn't seem to mind. His cocky grin softened into a goofy smile. It looked a lot like love.

"That bad?" Morgan asked, a little jealous. Bull had that satisfied look of a man who loved and was loved back.

"I think she's the one." Bull spoke the words serious-like, not a hint of mockery. "You ready to settle down yet?"

"No reason to rush."

Bull laughed out loud. "I saw you looking at Dakota over dinner."

He flashed his best *leave-it-alone-or-die* look. "Leave Dakota out of this." He wasn't ready yet to discuss her with his brothers.

"Afraid she'll kick you to the curb for another guy again?"

Morgan was standing before the last word was out, pulling his body to full height. He didn't care one bit that Bull was taller. He had plenty of commando combat tricks up his sleeve to make up for that.

"Not to worry," the idiot kept taunting with a superior grin. "There are other women out there. Could be one even crazy enough to take you on. Your day will come, big brother."

Morgan stepped closer, pretended to pass by Bull and smoothly swiped his brother's feet from under him.

But Bull didn't fall. He shifted his weight toward Morgan, jabbing his elbow between two cracked ribs. Then they did go down, together.

Wyatt whooped and jumped on top of them.

And then it was as if they were little school kids again, rolling in the dust of the backyard. Except with much better fighting skills.

Morgan put Wyatt in a headlock. "Haven't learned anything, have you? When the big boys are fighting, you should stay out of it."

But Wyatt had learned a thing or two over the years, it seemed, because he flipped and somehow managed to switch Bull between them.

Someone knocked over the coffee table.

Then the standing lamp.

Morgan got on top of Bull at last, his elbow in the man's windpipe. "Forfeit."

"Look at that. Must have found some sense of humor overseas. Did you buy it at an Arab bazaar?" Bull struggled to get up and shoved him away. "Hope you didn't spend all your combat pay on it. I'm still funnier."

"But I'm still the best-looking," Wyatt put in, twisting Bull's leg while kicking at Morgan at the same time.

Morgan and Bull exchanged a look and went after him together.

By the time they lay, panting, scattered on the rug, the living room looked as if a Texas tornado had swept through.

Bull rubbed his shoulder. "If Mom was here, she would tan our hides."

"Nah," Wyatt said, grinning. "She would threaten to tan our hides, then try to protect us when Dad actually did it."

Morgan pressed a hand against the pain that pulsed in his ribs. "Better clean up before Justice gets back."

The tension was gone. They were brothers again, triplets of trouble. He might not have missed home over the years, but he'd missed *this,* he realized suddenly. Maybe he wouldn't wait quite so long before he came back home again. For the first time, he actually regretted not coming back sooner.

"You're it." He pointed at Wyatt as he stood. "Cleanup duty."

"Why me?"

"I'm going to set up my laptop so we can start working. Bull is getting us some cold beer from the fridge."

"Only because I want to. Don't think you're the boss." Bull sauntered away.

They had everything back in order and the three of them around the laptop by the time Justice strode back in, his face a shade more somber than when he'd stepped outside.

"Everything okay with Shane?" Wyatt asked.

"He quit. He's moving to San Antonio with his wife to help his daughter. She's expecting twins and her husband just left her."

"She already has two toddlers." Wyatt shook his head. "What a jerk."

"Yeah," Morgan couldn't resist putting in. "It's a shame when fathers have no love for their children." He might have found the old tone with his brothers, but he was far from ready to embrace his father, to forgive and forget.

Tension filled the room all over again. And a long stretch of silence.

"I'm doing the best I can, son. I've made mistakes. I'll be the first to admit that," Justice said at last and without bluster.

Maybe he *had* mellowed.

"Are you hiring a new manager?" Bull asked, probably in an attempt to change the conversation.

Justice nodded. "As soon as I can." He glanced at Wyatt. "I want to help them with the move. And see if we can do something for them financially. The man deserves a parting bonus."

Wyatt nodded, then started talking about ordering more feed for the horses and other ranch business.

Morgan turned from them and brought up the first of the satellite images. The four of them in the same room, working together and talking mission seemed oddly normal. Even borderline comfortable. He wasn't sure how to relate to that.

"So here is the area we're looking for. The size of a small state," he said, bringing everyone's focus to their mission. "We're going to split it up. I'll be going to Mexico. You three are taking this side of the border."

THEY DIDN'T ADJUST TO HIS leadership easily. Morgan stared at the ceiling as he lay awake in bed a couple of hours later. They didn't adjust to his leadership at all, truth be told. Stubborn, every last one of them—a McCabe trait.

But they *would* hang together and do what had to be done, because Brittany, who was one of them, was in danger.

He reached for the glass of water on the nightstand. Empty. He kicked the covers off and headed off toward the bathroom. Slowed in front of the window.

What little moonlight there was illuminated the cabin. The original ranch building had been upgraded and a whole top floor added on, before another McCabe realized it was never going to be big enough for the ever-growing ranch and finally built the main house.

There weren't any lights on in any of the small windows, but he could see the glint of Christmas decorations—Dakota's work, no doubt. She must have decorated the main house as well. She seemed at home here, fit right in at dinner, like family. Hell, she fit in more than he ever had. And her son, too.

Cody had made them all laugh at dinner. It was strange, hearing laughter around the dinner table. When the McCabe brothers were younger, Justice used to use dinnertime to point out all their faults, list all the mistakes they'd made during the day, and discipline them.

Morgan was about to turn from the window when he caught a shadow moving toward the cabin's front door. Boots and a cowboy hat. Could be pretty much anyone at the ranch. Maybe even her lover.

He remembered suddenly the man he'd seen sneaking out of the cabin when he'd arrived, just before Dakota had run outside in nothing but a robe.

He put two and two together at long last and hot jealousy filled his chest.

He shrugged into his jeans and shirt and tugged on his boots. Julio was at the cabin, too. Better check on things. He strode out the door, knowing Julio was just an excuse. Nobody knew that Julio was hiding at the ranch.

He glanced at his gun on the nightstand and left it there. He was home, not in a combat zone. And maybe he didn't trust himself if he found some snot-nosed cowpoke with his hands all over her.

He would just walk by, make sure everything was okay.

He made it down the stairs in complete silence, then out the front door. Outside, he kept to the shadows, his training taking over.

Her light still hadn't come on. Maybe she didn't want to wake Cody. What the cowpoke had come for could be done in the dark. His muscles tightened at the thought. Over his dead body.

The dark taste of jealousy was back in his mouth, the same as when she'd brought Billy home from college. He didn't want to think about that now. He put his hand on the doorknob and pushed it open slowly. He had no idea what he would do once he was inside. He had no right to toss the guy out on his ear. But he wasn't going to let the bastard touch Dakota, either.

Once he was inside, he caught a flash of gunmetal at the top of the stairs, at Julio's door. He couldn't make out the bastard's face in the dark. Morgan acted on pure instinct.

He was on the top landing and on top of the guy in three leaps, the two of them wrestling for control of the weapon.

By chance, the man managed to kick his busted ribs. Morgan ignored the pain that sliced through him. The small landing offered way too little space to maneuver, and the guy had some lean muscle on him, a tough cowboy used to wrestling steers and bar fights, judging by the way he grappled. But Morgan got the better of him, little by little.

The door opened downstairs.

"Julio?" Dakota stuck her head out. She stepped forward, reached for the light switch, but nothing happened when she flipped it on.

"Who's that, Mom?" Behind her, Cody peeked out for a quick look.

"Get back in there and close that door!" Morgan snapped, just as the man—using the distraction—tripped them both over the edge.

The long roll down didn't make his ribs feel any better. He saw stars by the time they'd landed with a loud thump at the bottom. He had a hand on the man's right wrist, his other hand going for the bastard's throat. But then Dakota's door burst open again and whacked him hard enough on the head to jar his teeth.

"Stop!" she yelled, aiming a rifle at nothing in particular in the darkness.

"Don't shoot." No way could she aim in the dark. Morgan shook his head, trying to get rid of his sudden double vision, glancing back, making sure she was moving away.

Instead, she took a big step forward, nearly putting his eye out with her toe. He jerked away.

The momentary advantage was enough for the intruder to get loose and dive through the front door into the moonless night.

"Sorry. Here." She thrust the weapon at Morgan as he pushed to his feet and lurched at the door.

He checked to make sure the rifle was loaded, then stepped outside carefully, barrel first. The few seconds that had passed would have been enough for the man to take cover and pick Morgan off right at the door.

Just because he'd taken one gun off the bastard—which lay somewhere at the top of the stairs—it didn't mean the man didn't have another. He'd come to kill Julio. No assassin worth his salt would walk around without a backup weapon.

Something scraped by the stairs behind him. "He flipped the circuit breakers," Dakota said.

"Leave them." Last thing he wanted was for the light to come on and make them an easy target. "Are you okay?"

"You're the one who crashed down the stairs. I'll call your brothers."

"I can handle one man. Get back inside and lock the door," he said, then moved forward.

He ducked low as soon as he was outside and moved into the darkest shadow. He didn't even breathe as he watched for movement. Nothing. No cars hiding out back, either, just the ranch hands' pickups by the bunkhouses where they'd been earlier.

He snuck forward. Justice had expanded the stables and added on here and there over the years. Back in the day, Morgan could have walked around blindfolded. Not anymore. The assassin probably had a better grip on the place now than he did. He would have bet good money that Calderón's man had himself hired on when Justice had brought in all those temporary workers to help with the cleanup and the recovery of the herds.

He moved to the stables first. The inside seemed deserted. The horses didn't act as if anything was amiss. Then again, they wouldn't if someone familiar was hiding among them.

He checked the place, stall by stall. Nothing.

Of course Bull, Wyatt and even Justice were out there by the time he stepped outside, the three men stalking in the shadows. Dakota must have called them anyway.

Another hour passed before they went through every one of the buildings. But they didn't find anyone out of place. Whoever had been out there had either escaped or made it back to one of the bunkhouses where the ranch hands slept, and was now indistinguishable from the others.

When Morgan turned back toward the cabin, his brothers and

Justice followed. Light came through the windows now. Dakota had turned the power back on.

"I'll check on Julio." Bull headed up the stairs as they walked through the front door.

Better him than Morgan. At least the kid knew Bull.

"Get the gun at the top of the stairs. See if you can avoid getting any of your prints on it," Morgan called after his brother.

"I think I can handle that."

Dakota opened her door before they had a chance to knock. She'd gotten dressed and was wearing jeans and a flannel shirt. "Come in."

Bull banged on the door upstairs.

Morgan handed her the rifle. "Thanks for this."

"It was Billy's. I kept it for Cody for when he grows up."

Billy. He still hated the name, and the very memory of the man. Somehow he didn't think that would ever change.

"You okay?" he asked, his tone brusque, wishing they were alone. He strode in, Justice and Wyatt behind him.

Cody peeked out the bedroom door, holding a bedraggled stuffed horse.

"Back to bed, honey," Dakota said.

"Mo-om."

She just stood there and looked at him while he gave the most crestfallen expression a kid could make. Morgan would have caved.

"Yes'm," Cody said at last, then pulled back.

"What happened?" Justice wanted to know once the door closed behind the kid.

"Got up for water, saw one of the ranch hands sneaking into the cabin," Morgan said. "Came after him. Caught him at Julio's door with a gun. I'm guessing Calderón sent an assassin."

"Who was it?"

Morgan scratched the back of his neck. "Not a clue, unfortunately."

"You didn't see any of his face?"

"He had his hat pulled low, walked in the shadows."

Justice's eyes looked hard again for a moment. "You sure it was one of my men?"

The more Morgan thought about it, the more he was sure. "No strange cars anywhere around. Didn't hear any engines start after he ran off. He disappeared pretty fast when I gave chase. Only place he could have gone is the bunkhouses. We searched those. Found nobody in there but the men that belong. The assassin has to be one of them."

The old man's forehead furrowed. "We'll have a talk with the men in the morning."

"And if he disappears by then?" Dakota asked, her arms wrapped around herself.

"He won't," Morgan reassured her. "He thinks he outsmarted us. And his job is unfinished. Nobody wants to go back to someone like Calderón and tell the man he failed in his mission."

A moment passed while the others digested that.

"You should've woken us when you saw him." Wyatt scowled.

"I thought maybe… I figured Dakota had a…gentleman caller. Didn't want to make a big deal out of it." Even as he said the words, he knew he shouldn't have.

She stared at him, then her cheeks pinked, outrage widening her eyes. "In the middle of the night? Like a thief? With Cody in the house? Seriously?"

Way to go with trying to win her over. He should have shut up right then and there, but for some suicidal reason, he felt the need to explain. "I saw someone, I'm pretty sure the same guy, coming out of the cabin when I drove up earlier. Then you ran out a little later in nothing but a bathrobe…."

She looked like she might smack him. "You thought I was entertaining some guy in here while my son was nearly trampled in the corral. Is that the kind of mother you think I am?"

No, actually. On second thought, he really didn't. He lifted his hand in a defensive motion. "I'm sure you're a great mother."

"Damn right," Justice spoke up suddenly, his tone full of bluster. "I'll not have you insult her on my ranch."

"No insult meant, I just—" Before he could put his other foot into his mouth, Bull came downstairs with Julio, a kid of maybe twenty, with short black hair and sleepy, scared eyes, his clothes wrinkled and looking as if he'd pulled them on in a hurry.

Bull held out the gun, handling it with a piece of plastic he must have picked up in Julio's room. "Beretta with the serial number filed off. Silencer. I'll send it off first thing in the morning for ballistics. Maybe we'll get something there."

Morgan nodded, then looked at the kid. "You didn't come out when you heard the noise at your door. That's good. That was the right thing to do.

Julio shrugged. "Sleep with the iPod."

"You'll be sleeping in the main house from now on," Morgan told him. "And someone will be with you at all times." He looked at his father.

He expected the old man to bristle at the veiled order, but Justice just nodded.

Morgan drew a slow breath. "I'll be staying at the cabin, upstairs, in case our man comes back. I don't want Dakota and Cody out here alone," Morgan said.

"I can stay with you," Wyatt offered immediately.

"Not unless you added a second bedroom upstairs since I've last been up there, and a second bed."

Wyatt looked disappointed. When they'd been kids, he'd always wanted to be in the middle of the action, but, since he was the youngest, had rarely gotten the chance.

"Thanks for the offer, anyway," Morgan told him. "The main house is bigger. Needs more people to cover it. You're needed there."

That seemed to put Wyatt in a better mood.

"Are you okay with this?" Justice asked Dakota. "You could come over to the main house, too, with the boy."

She looked at Justice, then at Morgan, and considered her response for a second. "If Julio is over there, we might be safer staying here."

She was right about that.

DAKOTA WAITED FOR MORGAN until he came back with his duffel bag, after the men had moved Julio over to the main house. In the meantime, she'd checked on Cody, glad that he'd gone back to sleep.

Morgan came to her door instead of going straight upstairs. Good. She wanted to see him. Her heart had about stopped when he'd tumbled down the stairs.

"I want to see your wound," she repeated.

"Next time you hear noise outside your door, I want you to stay inside."

"I want to see your wound."

He scowled at her. "No."

"It's bleeding. I can see the wet spot on your shirt."

"I can take care of myself."

"But it's easier for me, because I will actually be able to see what I'm doing. Plus, I have a fully stocked first-aid kit." She stepped back to reveal the box on her kitchen table. "You come in and sit down right there."

He looked her over and a smile came to play above his lips as he finally did as she asked, "When did you become so tough and bossy?"

"When I became a mother."

He sat at the table and shrugged out of his shirt, revealing the blood-stained bandages that wrapped around his chest. He started unraveling them.

"Let me do it."

But he finished on his own, stubborn as always. She stared at the black and blue marks on his bare skin. But the six-inch gash looked the worst, the stitches torn out, probably from the roll down the stairs.

"You should have this restitched."

He didn't look the least perturbed. "You got any butterfly bandages?"

She nodded. "Dare I ask how you got hurt?"

He didn't answer right away, but then he shrugged and said, "Tribal dagger. Nasty little thing."

"If it went in a few inches higher…" She didn't want to think about that. Until now, his elite commando job seemed a concept. But here, at her kitchen table, reality stared her in the face.

Along with his chest. Oh, dear. He had very nice muscles. A lot of them. The testosterone cloud that came off him messed with her head big time. He was a warrior, a hero, a cowboy, the first man who'd ever made love to her....

Was the kitchen getting hotter?

She pulled her shirt away from her skin a little, then finished removing his torn stitches, cleaned the wound and put on the butterfly strips. "I have clean Ace bandages," she offered, and dug them out of the bag.

Putting them on proved to be trickier than she'd thought. As he held his arms up and out of the way, she had to put her arms completely around his torso, over and over again, as she passed the roll from one hand to the other.

For a second she closed her eyes, but she couldn't close her nose. He smelled like soap and gun oil and Morgan. Oh, God, she was so doomed here.

Mercifully, the roll ended at last, so she could finally secure the end and pull away. Except he wouldn't let her.

He pushed forward in his chair and draped his arms loosely around her waist. "I did miss you."

His low voice tickled something behind her breastbone.

She wasn't sure what was happening between them, only that it was happening too fast. Yet she didn't have it in her to pull away. "Don't kiss me again. It makes me feel weird."

"Me, too." And then he kissed her.

Heat suffused her body at the touch of his lips. When he pulled her onto his lap, she didn't protest. His body was hard and warm around hers, familiar.

Need filled her. Hot hunger.

They'd never had a problem with this part. It was the rest, communication and other pesky things that had been off between them.

"You never wrote," she said when they pulled apart for air.

Confusion crossed his gaze.

"When you went away for basic training." He'd joined the army straight out of high school. Went to college through them.

"I came back to you after. I came here on every single leave I had."

"All we did was have sex."

"Great sex. Lots of it." He leaned forward for another kiss, but she pushed him back.

"Is that all I was to you?"

He stilled. His voice dropped lower as he said, "You were everything to me."

The words sliced through her. Her eyes burned for a second. "You never said it."

He waited a moment as he searched her gaze. "I didn't know how to say it. I was an idiot."

She closed her eyes and leaned against him, surrounded by his strength. "We both were. When you left…the last time…I thought you'd come back now and then."

"I couldn't," was all he said.

"You must have lived in danger every day since. Do you ever regret going away? Joining the military?"

His response was immediate and sure. "No. I've done some things that were important. Things that needed to be done. This is who I am."

They sat in silence.

"Do you ever regret… Billy?" he asked after a while.

"No. He was a good man, for all his faults. I'm not perfect, either. I have Cody because of him."

But Billy was gone now, and Morgan was home, and here she was sitting on his lap in her kitchen.

She lifted her head, her gaze seeking his, not liking how unsure she felt of herself. "Morgan, what are we doing here?"

That smile she loved came to play above his masculine lips. "Catching up. Making up for lost time."

"It can't go anywhere. As soon as you have Brittany back you'll go away."

"I won't stay away again. I can come back, between missions. And this job won't last forever." He gave her a sour smile. "I'm one of the oldest on the team. It's a young man's game."

They were discussing the future. Things were moving so fast her head was spinning.

Yet somehow Morgan in her life seemed inevitable. Hadn't she secretly dreamt of this, of him coming home and this time somehow loving her as much as she had loved him years ago?

Except, it seemed he might have loved her, after all, even back then.

God, she couldn't think about that. They'd been so young. Truly idiots, the both of them.

She slipped off his lap with so much reluctance it was ridiculous. But it had to be done. "I better get to bed. Cody will be up in a couple of hours, expecting his pancakes."

He nodded and stood. "We'll talk about this again."

He dipped his head and kissed her, one last time, so sweetly and full of tenderness that her head was spinning by the time he finished. This time he didn't claim, he didn't take, he gave.

In his old bedroom earlier she'd told him she'd missed him, but she hadn't realized until now just how much. How much she wished…

No. She had a son to think of. "Good night, Morgan."

Her hands shook on the doorknob as she locked the door behind him and listened to his footsteps as he went upstairs to Julio's apartment.

Chapter Four

"Howdy."

Morgan took in Cody, sitting cross-legged at the top of the landing, mini cowboy boots and mini Stetson, worn jeans. If he'd ever thought of kids, he thought of them as strange little people, but he had to admit, Cody had character. He held a plate on his lap with half a pancake and traces of something sticky that looked like it could have been maple syrup at one point.

"Cody."

The kid scrambled to his feet, balancing the half pancake precariously, sticking his tongue out with the effort. "I brought you breakfast." He held out the plate once he was standing. "Mom said I couldn't wake you up because you had a late night. But she said it would be okay to wait for you here."

"Appreciate that." He'd been up for hours, actually, working on his laptop, researching Calderón, calling in favors. He would have come out earlier if he knew the kid was waiting. "Would that be my breakfast?"

"I had some. I had to wait a long time. But I left you plenty." The kid gave an angelic smile.

"No problem, buddy." He took the plate and shoved the half pancake into his mouth on his way down the stairs.

He wore jeans and a worn shirt he'd found in his old room last night, and a cowboy hat. The ranch hands would talk to him more easily if he looked like one of them.

Dakota stuck her head out the door. She was freshly scrubbed, hair in a ponytail, ready for the day.

He licked the syrup from his bottom lip and thought about

how much he wanted to kiss her again. How much he wanted to do more than kiss her. Soon, he promised himself.

She held out her hand for the empty plate, a smile playing on her amazing lips. "Look who found his inner cowboy."

"Thank you for breakfast."

"Can I go over to Maria's with Morgan?" Cody wanted to know.

"Maria is Miguel's wife. She watches Cody sometimes while I work." Dakota adjusted the kid's hat. "I usually walk him over."

"I'm heading that way anyway."

"Thank you." She bent to Cody, gave him a big smacking kiss on the cheek. "You mind Maria. I expect you to be good."

The little boy hugged her back with full enthusiasm, not a drop of awareness yet at that age. The love between the two was palpable, and it set off some strange longing deep inside Morgan.

"I'll come over later and we'll have lunch together." Dakota stood. "You have a fun day. Both of you."

"You be careful to keep your door locked," Morgan said, when all he wanted was a send-off like Cody had gotten. "And you have fun, too," he added.

"Sure." Dakota flashed a half smile as she drew back into her place. "Doing the year-end accounting is usually a laugh riot."

He wanted to stay, to talk with her more, but Cody took his hand and was pulling him forward. "Maria has new kittens behind the kitchen. She lets me feed them." He looked toward the corral. "Will you take me riding later?"

His tone was so full of wistfulness, it made Morgan smile. "We'll have to talk to your mom first about that."

His little hand felt strange hanging on to Morgan's calloused fingers. He wasn't used to being around kids. For the first time in a long time, it made him think of family. He was definitely in the wrong profession for that. Then again, as he'd told Dakota, the job wasn't going to last forever.

"I asked Santa at the feed store for a horse," the boy confided in him, his eyes wide with hope and excitement. "And I've been really good. Brush my teeth every night and every morning. I even comb my hair."

"I'm sure Santa appreciates that," he said, not having any idea what kind of response the kid expected.

"I just don't want the horse to get hurt when Santa drags him down the chimney."

"I'm sure he...uh...has his ways."

"Like magic?"

"Sure."

"Can he shrink a horse?"

"I bet he could."

The kid thought about that for a few seconds. "Can he make it grow back big? If he can't, I'd just have a pony. I want a big horse. I'm a big boy, not a baby."

Sure looked like a baby to him, but Morgan was wise enough not to say that.

"If you see Santa, can you tell him I was good? Really, really good."

He nodded solemnly. "I'll tell him the whole combing and everything."

He delivered Cody to the kitchen where, to his surprise, he got a goodbye hug and kiss on the cheek. And a look full of admiration, as if he was a hero or something.

Immediate, unconditional acceptance and unreserved love. He was humbled, wasn't sure if he deserved the vote of confidence, but it felt incredibly good all the same, after what he'd been through in the last couple of weeks.

He was still thinking about that as he went to find Julio, who wasn't the least excited to see him. They had a long chat. Morgan needed to make sure he knew everything the kid knew, that Julio wasn't hiding anything. At least the assassination attempt the night before spooked the youngster enough so he was fairly forthcoming. Albeit not terribly useful. He knew this and that about Calderón, but nothing about where the man might have moved Brittany. No workable leads.

When Morgan was done with him, he went to find his brothers. He found them on the deck in the back, drinking coffee. Wyatt was cleaning a rifle. They had the door open behind them, with a clean line of sight to the front door. They were positioned so they could keep an eye on both who was coming into the main house, and the cabin, too, at the same time.

Morgan appreciated the guard duty. "Where's Justice?"

"In town picking up medicine for one of the horses."

"Anything serious?"

Bull shrugged. "Didn't sound like it."

On a ranch this size, there were always sick animals, the vet a weekly guest.

"When are you leaving for Mexico?" Wyatt asked.

"We'll see." After he'd gotten up, he'd connected with a friend at his unit. He was expecting close-up footage from a military satellite, information that would narrow his search area on the other side of the border. But after what had gone on last night, he wasn't sure now was the best time for him to leave. "We need to figure out who Calderón's man is on the ranch."

Wyatt pulled some papers from his pocket. "Here is a list of all the employees. The dozen men we hired for the cleanup are in bold." He gave one sheet to Morgan, one to Virgil.

"I'll talk to them." Morgan ran through the names, glanced at the clock. The men would be out and about by now, but he didn't want to wait until they all came in for dinner. He didn't mind driving out. It would give him a chance to see how much damage the fire had done on McCabe land.

Wyatt stood. "I'll drive into town and run background checks from the office."

Bull turned to Morgan. "What do you want me to do?"

"Watch the house and make sure Julio stays alive," Morgan said. "Keep an eye on the cabin, too." Handing that job off cost him. He didn't want to let Dakota and Cody out of his sight, but he trusted Bull. "You're pretty damn quick with a gun, if I remember right."

"We're going to work this as a team."

"Rusty will pop," Wyatt said suddenly. "He has a record."

Morgan almost asked why, then remembered. Rusty used to have a brother. They'd gotten into a ton of trouble when they'd been kids, even went to jail together. Rusty chose the straight and narrow at one point, while the brother headed deeper into bad business. He'd died in a shootout with the cops the year Morgan had left the ranch. He'd forgotten all about that.

Bull's phone rang. He picked it up, listened. "Thanks. I appreciate it."

Wyatt got up. "Anything about Brittany?"

"Her cell was used yesterday in a small village on the other side of the border." Bull looked at Morgan.

Morgan had planned on taking the Mexican side, was planning to head over this morning. But last night had changed things. Until the assassin on the ranch was caught, he wanted to stick around here. "I can take care of background checks. You drive down and see about that phone. If anything pops, if you need me, you give me a call. Wyatt can stay here to watch the ranch."

His brothers exchanged a look then nodded.

Morgan snapped a picture of the list of names with his cell phone and sent it to his connection. That should take care of that. Then he headed off to the bunkhouses while Bull headed to his pickup. Wyatt scowled after them from the door.

The bunkhouses stood empty. Morgan went through the two buildings with care, scanning the men's belongings, looking for anything unusual. Weapons he found aplenty, but there was nothing strange about that around here. They all looked legit, mostly rifles, with a couple of pistols here and there.

The Beretta he'd knocked from the assassin's hand, with its filed-off serial number and the silencer, was in another category. That had been meant for a hit job.

Morgan moved from room to room, making sure he didn't miss anything. Nothing stood out. No expensive stereo or fancy designer boots that would have indicated extra money coming in from Calderón. He spent maybe twenty minutes per building, then jumped into his SUV to head out to the far pastures where most of the new men would be working.

The cattle had been herded together to whatever grass the wildfire had spared. Most of the land stood charred, big sections of the fence missing.

The first man he ran into was Davey Chapman, a new hire, rolling out fresh barbed wire.

"We had a break-in at the cabin last night," Morgan said after he introduced himself. "I'm just checking around to see if anyone might have seen anything."

"Not me." Davey spat dust. "Had some beer with the boys before we called it a day. Slept like a baby."

Morgan's gaze dipped to the man's hand, hardened with calluses. Could Davey have been the man he'd fought on the stairs the night before? Hard to say. "You been a ranch hand long?"

"Since I dropped out of high school," the lanky twenty-something admitted. "Like the open land. Working in a factory or some closed-up office would kill me. Couldn't handle that." He shook his head with a half grin.

"You always worked around this area?"

"At the Kinckner ranch."

"How come you left?"

"Old Kinckner didn't like it that I was sweet on his daughter. I'm trying to save enough money to buy my own spread. Prove to him I can amount to something."

Nothing about his body language said that he was lying. Morgan remembered Kinckner. Ornery old man. Almost as ornery as Justice. The kid didn't sound like prime assassin material. "If you see anyone acting strangely, catch anything out of place, you come to me."

"Sure thing, Mr. McCabe."

He nodded goodbye to Davey and strode back to his car.

Half a dozen men worked at digging posts farther down the line. He drove over to them, introduced himself, made sure he had their names. He didn't expect a full confession just because he'd shown up, but he needed a feel for the men—who was open, who had something to hide, who got nervous at having to talk to him.

He zeroed in on Tom Bellamy pretty quickly. The man was in his midthirties, eyes shifty, shoulders tense. He kept stepping back, as if wanting to be as far from Morgan as possible. His name was bolded on the list, a new hire.

He kept glancing at his truck.

"Didn't I see you outside last night?" Morgan bluffed.

The guy shrugged, looking at his feet. "Not me."

"Maybe you went out to your truck for something."

The man glanced toward his truck again, a beat-up Silverado, his mouth tightening.

"How about we look at that truck?" Morgan suggested in a tone that made it clear he would only accept one answer.

Tension thickened the air. The other men had their loyalty to their buddy, not liking that the boss's son was giving one of them grief.

Bellamy knew it. He looked Morgan over, measured him up. "You got no right doin' nothin' in my truck."

"Someone broke into the cabin last night. I got a right to protect my family. You got something to hide?" He kept his tone cold and his gaze colder. "We can do this now, or we can call the cops. The only thing I'm interested in is who broke into that cabin."

Bellamy shot him a look of dark resentment, but then limped off toward the beaten-up, blue pickup.

"What happened to your leg?"

"When we were rounding up the cattle after the fire, one of the bulls didn't want to come." He stopped by his car and nodded.

Morgan opened the door that had been left unlocked. He looked under the seats, then into the glove compartment, found the bag of weed pretty quickly. He held it up.

"Got banged up on the rodeo circuit. Can't afford the doctors, but I gotta have a little somethin' for the pain now and then. Was getting better before that damn bull knocked me down." Bellamy spit on the ground. "You gonna bust me?"

Morgan tossed the bag back where he'd found it. "I won't call the cops."

He dialed Dakota instead. "I want you to cut a check to Tom Bellamy. Please pay him through the end of the week with another week of severance thrown in. He'll be leaving us. Take the check over to Wyatt when you have it ready. Thanks." He hung up before she could have asked questions.

"Ranch work is too dangerous for someone under the influence. Do yourself a favor and figure out your problems," he told the man. "Take the rest of the day to pack up and move out of the bunkhouse. You can see my brother about your check." If Justice didn't agree with him, they could argue about it later.

He ignored Bellamy's angry scowl, walked to his SUV and moved on, looking for the rest of the men. His phone rang just as he spotted another small herd of cattle in the distance.

"Got those background checks you asked for," Troy, a friend of his, said on the other end. "Rusty Fisher had some brushes with the law a few decades back, but nothing since. Tom Bellamy has been arrested for disorderly conduct a couple of times, drunken fighting at rodeos, and possession. Harlan Bender was charged with manslaughter in 2008 for breaking his old man's neck, but let off after a mistrial. Other than speeding tickets and the like, that's about it."

"Appreciate it. I owe you one."

"Don't think I won't collect." A bark of laughter sounded on the other end before the line went dead.

Morgan kept on going, slowing only when the herd shifted and revealed a new-looking RAM 3500 Laramie Longhorn, one of the finest pickup trucks ever made. With actual longhorn horns attached to the grill. Now that was something you didn't see the average ranch hand drive.

He pulled up next to the sweet-looking pickup and got out, walked up to the man who was putting out feed.

"Not enough grass, huh?"

"If we had some rain it would green back up, but for now, we have to supplement," the man said, knocking his hat back and wiping his forehead with his sleeve. He was about the same age as Morgan, with a lean build, tanned from working outside year round.

"Morgan McCabe."

"Harlan Bender."

Bingo.

"Nice car."

"Seemed like a good idea at the time," Harlan said.

"And now?"

"Might be a little overkill." He gave a wry smile.

Morgan sensed no unease, no hidden signs of aggression, no

secrets behind the guy's frank gaze. "Justice must be paying his ranch hands better now than I remember."

"Hell, no. If anyone knows the value of a dollar, it's the boss. That's why he's been successful over the years, I suppose."

"And you?"

Now the man's gaze narrowed. "And I what?"

"What did you do to become this successful?" Pickups like this ran close to sixty grand.

A defensive look hardened Harlan's face. "Don't see how that's anybody's business."

Morgan watched him. He could have come on hard, but he wasn't interrogating terrorists. The man was one of his father's employees. So he decided to go in mild, toughen up later if he saw a need.

"We had a break-in at the cabin last night." He kept his tone noncommittal.

Only honest shock showed on the man's face. "Dakota or the kid hurt?"

He shook his head. "The guy ran off. Didn't see him well enough in the dark, but it was someone from the ranch."

Now the man laughed. "You think you saw me?"

"I'm not ready to come to conclusions yet."

Harlan rolled his shoulders. "The truck came from money from an inheritance."

"From the father you killed?"

Harlan drew himself taller, set his feet apart as sudden tension filled the air.

He was a hard one to get a feel for. Plenty tough, but not like a hired gun. There was nothing ruthless about him. "The old man had it coming, right?" Morgan tried to poke him to make him reveal more.

"It's not something I'm proud of," he said stiffly.

"He went too far? Tore into you for the last time?"

"He tore into my mother and sister. Smacked my mother down plenty of times when I was growing up. Thought things got better as they grew older. Then I stop in for a visit and she has a black eye and Sis has a split lip, and there he is, drunk again, telling me to get the hell out before I get my licks." His lips flattened into a narrow line. "I should have controlled my temper."

Morgan watched him for a second or two. "Are you likely to lose it again?" He didn't want violent people around Dakota and Cody.

"It was the first time. I reckon it'll be the last."

Morgan believed him. "You see anyone acting strangely, you let me know." He gave the man a parting nod, then walked back to his SUV.

He wasn't one to judge. Growing up, he'd considered raising a hand to Justice plenty of times. There had been times when he'd hated his father. It was strange to come back and see him different. Left him with no place to put all the old anger.

He drove on, met Rusty on one of the dirt roads that could barely be called a road on a good day, and was nothing more now than some tire tracks on the charred ground. They both stopped, going in opposite directions, nodded at each other through the open window.

"Wyatt okay?" Rusty pushed his hat higher on his forehead. "Haven't seen him this morning. He's usually out with the cattle by this time of the day."

"He'll be at the house today. We had a break-in at the cabin last night. Someone from the ranch, most likely. You see anything?"

The man shook his head. "You keep an eye on them young whippersnappers. Don't know half of them. They stick to each other. They're here for the money today, gone tomorrow. Don't care if they do a good job, either."

"Let me know if you notice anything out of place," Morgan said, and Rusty promised he would.

He only caught three more men, old ranch hands he'd known from his childhood, before his stomach began to growl for his missed lunch. He turned the SUV toward the heart of the ranch.

He ran into Dakota in the kitchen.

"How is it going?" She was finishing a tuna fish sandwich and made him one without him having to ask.

"Slowly. It's a lot of land. Where is Cody?"

"Down for his nap on the living room couch. He likes sleeping in here. If I take him back to his room, he's too worried he'll miss something."

"He wants Santa to bring him a horse."

"That's not going to happen." Dakota laughed.

He watched her, drinking in the sound. "What would you like for Christmas?"

She looked at him for a long time, a wistful expression on her face. But at the end she shook her head. "Doesn't matter. It's not going to happen, either."

Morgan felt the muscles in his back stiffen. Was she wishing Billy was still here? Jealousy washed over him. He reached out and took her hand across the table. Felt better when she didn't pull away.

"How are things with Justice?" she asked.

He shrugged.

"I'm not sure where Cody and I would be today without him. Things were rough. I had nothing. He and Wyatt took me to the hospital when Cody was born. They stuck around in the waiting room all night." Her voice thickened. "Your father paid the doctors' bills. I paid him back little by little from my paychecks, but it meant the world to me. Can you maybe give him a little credit, if for nothing else than that?"

And suddenly he found that he could. Because Dakota was important to him. He did appreciate that Justice had done right by her.

"I just wish he'd found his softer side sooner," he said.

"None of us are perfect. I make mistakes every single day with Cody. You'll make mistakes with your kids."

There wasn't a single thing she could have said that would have scared him more than that. Because if he somehow became the luckiest bastard on earth and won her back, Cody would come with her. They were a package deal.

And he didn't want to make mistakes with Cody. But he would. He would make a terrible father. All he knew was what he'd grown up with. And he refused to repeat that.

But without Cody, there was no Dakota. The thought left him poleaxed. Why didn't he think of that sooner? Wanting Dakota was fine and well, but what about Cody? He had no right to mess up the kid's life. Cody deserved better. Cold spread through Morgan's limbs.

Miguel came in, and Dakota withdrew her hand. "I better get back to work."

Not grabbing after her took effort. "Me, too." Morgan stood, wishing for…impossible things. Maybe he should talk to Santa about that. He wondered if he could fit driving over to the feed store into his schedule.

Chapter Five

Morgan was driving the property line, his mood grim at the sight of all the destruction, when Bull called.

"Tracked down the guy who has Brittany's phone. A teenager. He says he found it by the side of the road when his mother sent him to town for medicine."

"When?"

"The day Brittany disappeared."

"Calderón's men could have been driving her through there. They probably took the phone from her and tossed it from the car."

"That's what I figure. No sense trying to follow any trail here. We know they've moved her since. I'm heading home. Any progress there?"

"Not even a small step. See you at dinner."

He hung up and drove east where he could see two men dragging burned brush the wind had blown into a shallow creek. The branches were damming up the water. They were struggling to restore free flow.

He brought the SUV to a halt and jumped out. "Need any help?"

"That would be good about now," the older one said, soaking wet. He'd probably taken a tumble earlier.

"Morgan McCabe."

"Any relation to the boss?"

And still, saying Justice was his father didn't come easily. "I'm Wyatt's brother," he said instead.

"Dick Martinez." The older guy nodded in greeting.

The younger one heaved. "José Delgado."

Morgan kicked off his boots before he waded in and grabbed a tangle of branches, put his weight into the pull. The silt lay slippery under his feet. He made sure to keep his balance. He didn't want to end up in the drink like Dick had.

Clearing the brush took the better part of half an hour. Then they stopped for a break. There was more debris up creek, smaller tangles. The men should be able to handle that without him.

"We had a problem at the cabin last night. I don't suppose either of you seen anything." Morgan threw some cold water from the creek on his face to wash off the sweat.

Dick peeled off his wet shirt. "Like what?"

"Somebody going outside. Walking around."

The man shrugged. "I sleep at night."

José seemed to be hesitating over something, rubbing a hand over his mouth.

"What?"

"I might have seen something," he said with reluctance, looking more away from Morgan than at him. "I thought one of the guys went out."

"Do you know which one?"

"Not sure." He kicked at the mud. "Might have been Alvarez."

"Alvarez?"

"Juan Alvarez."

"What time?"

"Didn't look at the clock. Middle of the night."

"Do you know where Alvarez is working today?"

"Down in the yellow gulley. We found a couple of burned cows there. He's burying them."

As uneven as the road was, an hour passed before Morgan reached the gulley. He probably could have gone faster, but he didn't want to kill his rental. Alvarez was hard at work with a Bobcat, swearing up a storm.

Morgan questioning him didn't cheer him any.

"To hell with José." He spat, chewing tobacco distending his cheek. Flies buzzed all around them.

"You didn't go outside last night?" Morgan held his breath the best he could, wishing those cows had been found a little sooner.

"You say you never left the bunkhouse?" Not that he thought he was on the right track here. Alvarez was shorter than the man he'd grappled with in the dark.

"José wants to mess me up, that's what he wants. Word is they might make one of the temporary jobs permanent. He and me both want it."

Morgan asked a few more questions, then mentally crossed the guy off his list.

He didn't have any better luck with the rest of the new ranch hands, either, although tracking them over hundreds of acres wasted the rest of his day. Which left him with a very uncomfortable thought—that the would-be killer was someone who'd been on the ranch for years, someone they trusted.

Maybe he wouldn't go to Mexico tomorrow, either. He could stick around another day. Now that he knew where to look, he should be able to figure out who the assassin was. He didn't want to leave the ranch while his family and Dakota and Cody were in direct danger.

He had a new idea. Something else they could check.

He reached for his phone, ready to dial his connection. Then thought of his brothers who wanted to work as a team. He had better connections, but maybe he didn't have to rub it in. Brittany was a sister to all of them. They all had equal stake in the game.

He dialed Bull. "You got a quick way to get a few more phone records?"

"Could be."

"Why don't we see if anyone from the ranch has been making calls to one of Calderón's businesses? Check everyone. I don't think our man is one of the new hires."

A moment of silence on the other end, then, "I'll take care of it."

There. They *could* work together in peace.

He drove back and stopped in at the main house to tell Justice and Wyatt what he had so far. Pitifully little. Then he headed over to the cabin in the settling dusk and knocked on Dakota's door.

She was cleaning up the kitchen while Cody watched some cartoon, half-asleep on the couch. Cody, who'd accepted him from the first moment, had taken him at face value. Cody, who trusted him with childish innocence. Which scared the hell out of Morgan.

Who was he kidding? He didn't belong here. He belonged on some secret mission, alone. That was where his expertise lay.

"I don't suppose you have a cup of coffee handy?" He planned on staying up all night and staking out the buildings in case Calderón's men tried to hit again.

She raised a slim eyebrow as she reached for the pot. "You could have gotten coffee from Miguel."

He took off his hat and sat at her kitchen table, feeling right there and more at home than he ever had over at the big house. There was something about her that filled the place and made it nice to be in it. "I like the company better here."

He wanted to at least spend some time with her before he left.

"Flattery might get you coffee, but it won't get you anything more," she warned.

He wanted to pull her onto his lap and kiss her so badly he ached with the need. But Cody was still semi-conscious, and Morgan was covered in dirt from the day.

"Maybe not today." He shot her his cockiest smile. "But I'm a patient man." He played along.

She laughed as she set a mug in front of him. "You're such a liar."

Okay, fine, he wasn't patient. Not when it came to wanting to kiss her again.

"Find anything?"

He drank in silence.

"That bad?"

"I'll have him tomorrow. And you'll be safe tonight. I promise you that."

She nodded. Then stood. Cody had finally passed out. She carried the little boy to bed, murmuring something sweet. The sight touched some deep longing inside Morgan's chest.

He finished his coffee and was standing by the time she came back. She walked over to the door with him so she could lock up behind him. He looked into her eyes. His lips were clean enough, he decided, and leaned in for a kiss.

If he couldn't get all he wanted, at least he would take what he could get.

SHE WAS IN LOVE with Morgan McCabe.

Still, in love. Because if she wanted to be honest—and if you couldn't be honest with yourself in your own bedroom in the middle of the night then when and where could you be—she had to admit that she'd never fallen out of love with him.

How was that possible? Dakota lay in bed and stared at the ceiling, reevaluating everything she knew to be true.

All this time, she'd blamed Morgan for being too withdrawn, blamed him for the breakup of their relationship years ago. But she'd been the one to make that decision.

Had she really chosen Billy because he was more romantic, or because he was safer? Morgan demanded all of her. She could lose herself in Morgan. Which had scared her back then, and still scared her now. With Billy, everything had been more manageable.

Had she told Morgan about Billy back then to make him jealous? So he would declare himself? Instead, he'd taken off.

She'd been so young and stupid.

But what now, that she was marginally smarter?

For starters, she wasn't going to push him away again.

He had his job. He had other things going on in his life. But he cared for her. He wanted her. If there was a chance that he could love her again...

She was a single mom. Ever since Cody had been born, she had always played everything safe. She could do that again. But would she be doing Cody a favor? Would she be doing herself a favor?

She wouldn't, she decided.

Morgan McCabe was worth some risk.

MORGAN WAS AT THE FARTHEST of the outbuildings, the one that housed farm machinery, catching up with the last of the older ranch hands when Bull called. He'd driven into San Antonio that morning to pick up the phone records in person. They wouldn't send it in email. Needed his signature and police ID.

Morgan stifled a yawn. He'd patrolled the grounds all night, but not as much as a stray coyote had stirred.

"I got three guys with frequent calls to Mexico, but Wyatt says they all have girlfriends on the other side."

"We'll check them, anyway."

"That's what I thought."

"You know what's weird? I talked to every one of the men now, and I got no vibes that one of them was a hard core, professional killer." Morgan thought that over. "Maybe I'm looking for the wrong thing."

"How so?"

"Don't know yet. But I'll figure it out."

He glanced toward the buildings that made up the heart of the ranch.

"You think…" Bull was saying, but Morgan barely heard his brother. A plume of smoke rose from the old cabin's roof, snaking to the sky.

He took off running as he yelled into the phone. "Get home now! We got a fire!"

DAKOTA WAS SHOWING Justice the spreadsheets in the living room at the big house. Wyatt had gone off to administer the sick horse his medicine. Cody took a cold soft drink and some hunting magazines up to Julio, who'd been complaining about being stuck upstairs.

"Everything looks good," Justice said. "I appreciate all the hard work you do around here."

"And we appreciate that you've given us a home."

"Even as messed up as it is these days?"

"Family business is always messy." She gave him a half smile. "I'll tidy up these charts, then send them over to you as an email attachment." She headed toward the stairs to say goodbye to Cody for a few more hours and get him back down to Maria in the kitchen.

She looked through the front window completely by chance, and her blood froze for a second. "Fire!"

The cabin was on fire. But she didn't run to save her valuables. She was running up, needing to make sure Cody was okay, that he hadn't somehow gotten outside through the back door and gone home.

Justice was running outside, yelling for Maria in the kitchen to call 911.

She was at the top of the stairs, bursting into Morgan's old room. "Cody!"

He was there. Standing in front of Julio. Rusty Fisher was up there, too, pointing a gun at the two of them.

Which didn't make any sense. Then understanding dawned, and her stomach clenched.

"Mom!"

Fear sliced through her. "I'm here, honey."

"And you'll stay right there, too," Rusty said.

Chapter Six

"Now lock that damn door and toss me the key."

Oh, God. Rusty was the assassin? Her thoughts were a confused jumble, but she did as she was told.

The man pocketed the key and moved to the window. Looked out. He didn't seem to take pleasure in the view. Had he set the fire to distract everyone from the main house?

From where she stood, all she could see was the smoke. "Why are you doing this? You have a good place here. A good job. A home."

Keeping calm was the most difficult thing she'd ever done, but she had to do it for Cody's sake. She didn't want to scare her son more than he already was. He stared at her wide-eyed, fear scrunching up his little face, but he wasn't crying. Yet.

She hoped it would stay that way. Who knew what would set Rusty off. He clearly wasn't the man they'd all thought him to be.

He glanced between them, shifting on his feet, obviously agitated.

Not good. Then again, he hadn't shot anyone yet.

She had to think of something to save them.

Everyone would come for the fire, she thought. The great distraction. But sooner or later someone would notice that she and Cody were missing. Morgan, if nobody else. The only question was how far away was he, and how long would it take him to get back here? Had he gone back to the pasture?

"You two shouldn't have come up," Rusty said. "Should've stayed downstairs with Justice."

"It's not too late. Nobody is hurt yet. Nothing bad has to happen today."

"I didn't mean for nothin' to happen to the kid."

"I believe you, Rusty. Listen, you're a better man than this."

The man gave a sour laugh. "Some of us are born to be bad and there ain't nothin' we can do to climb out of it. I tried. Damned if I didn't."

"Whatever Calderón is paying you, I have some money set aside, too. I can ask Justice for more. He'll give it to me."

"It ain't about the money."

"Then what is it about?"

He shrugged. "Too long a story."

Good. She needed to keep him talking until Morgan got here. And in case he didn't, she needed another plan. She eyed the chair in the corner and shifted toward it. "If we are to die, I think we have the right to hear why."

Rusty glanced out the window again, then back at her. "You know about my brother."

She nodded. "He died in a shootout with the cops ten years ago. You wear his rattler belt and rodeo belt buckle to remember him by." Everyone at the ranch knew that much.

"Buddy and I started out a life of crime together. Some cattle rustling, this and that. First time we got caught, we got tossed in jail." He shook his head. "Scared the spit out of me. Didn't want to go back, no way. Got a job, stayed out of trouble."

"But not your brother?"

"He got in with Calderón's men, running drugs over the border. When the cops shot him, he was bringing in cocaine bricks that got confiscated. Calderón's men came after me. Figured the debt transferred to the family."

"They threatened you. Forced you into doing what?"

He shrugged again. "Whatever needed doing now and then."

"Virgil is a cop. Wyatt is sheriff. They can get you into the witness protection program."

"It ain't about me. Got a mother in a nursing home. Got two sisters. Nephews. Nieces."

"We'll find a way out of this."

"I already did. With this last job, my debt to Calderón will be settled. I'll be done with the man."

Nobody was done with someone like Calderón until Calderón said he was done, but just as she would have told Rusty that, the man put his finger on the trigger, aiming at Julio.

The sudden escalation of tension spooked Cody and he tore away from Julio to run toward his mother. Directly into the path of the bullet.

"No!" She dove that way, but she was too far.

The door flew open at the same time, Morgan diving for her son, putting himself between Cody and the bullet. Justice was right behind him, throwing himself in the middle.

The shot went off.

Her ears rang so hard she didn't even hear herself scream again. For a moment she didn't know who was hit.

Not Morgan, she realized the next second, as Morgan was wrestling with Rusty for the gun. Julio was down, but getting up. He'd probably hit the ground when the weapon discharged.

Cody, half under Justice, scrambled up, too, and ran into her arms. "Thank God." She checked him over twice. "Are you okay, honey?"

"I was scared, Mom."

Her throat burned. "You were very brave."

Morgan subdued Rusty at last and had control of the weapon.

Julio was helping Justice to his feet. The old man held his side, blood seeping through his fingers.

"Justice." She was next to him the next second. "Lie back down. Let me see it."

"Don't make a big fuss over this." He tried to walk forward, but his knees buckled.

Sirens sounded in the distance.

"You lie down on the bed then." She pushed him that way. "Help is coming."

"Hey, who's the boss here?" But he let her push him on top of the covers, his face turning white.

Only when Justice was horizontal did she look back at Morgan, who had Rusty tied up with an old lasso. Morgan's arm was bleeding, too. The bullet that had gone through Justice, must have hit him.

Her heart about stopped. "You, too," she ordered him. "On the bed."

He quirked an eyebrow and shot her a hot grin.

She swallowed. Fine. "On the chair. Sit down, for heaven's sake."

"It's a flesh wound." He smirked. "Let's not get carried away."

She wanted to throw him into a chair and see how bad the shot really was, make sure he was okay. She wanted to kiss him.

Instead, she turned back to Justice and pushed his shirt aside, prepared for the worst. The bullet had only grazed him, tore his flesh, but nothing else.

"It's not too bad," she admitted. "But I still don't want you getting up." She picked up Cody and hurried downstairs with him. Someone had to direct the arriving paramedics and cops.

HE HAD FIVE MINUTES, tops, before the cops would take over.

"Secure the door." Morgan pointed at Julio who still looked pale.

He did move to the door, though, and closed it as best he could against the busted doorjamb, put his back against it.

Morgan put a knee into the middle of Rusty's chest as the man lay on the floor, then aimed the gun at the man's head. He held on to his tenuous control as cold fury coursed through him. The bastard had held Dakota and Cody at gunpoint. "Where's Brittany?"

He squeezed off a shot so close to the man's head, it caught a trail of blood through his ear.

Rusty went white. "You don't know Calderón. He'll kill me when he catches me. He'll kill my whole family."

"I know myself. And I know for sure I *will* shoot you, here and now if you don't tell me where my sister is." He brought his knee up until it pressed against the man's throat.

"Don't," he gasped out the single word. Then, "Okay."

Morgan eased up on the pressure. "Talk." He moved the end of the barrel to the middle of the man's forehead.

"She's… They took her to the packaging factory."

"Where is that?"

"I don't know. Calderón has an alpaca farm. He does his drug packaging there. That's all I know, I swear."

It was enough. Morgan eased back a little. He had a map of the territories Calderón controlled. And he had the military satellite pictures. Now that he knew they were looking for an alpaca farm, they should be able to figure out the rest.

Boots slapped up the stairs outside.

"Police! Drop your weapons and put your hands behind your heads." The first officer up the stairs had his gun aimed at them.

Morgan laid down his gun. "Everything is under control, officer."

THAT NIGHT, THEY ALL SLEPT in the main house. Julio moved into Bull's room with him. Morgan doubled up with Wyatt, sleeping on old blankets on the floor. Dakota and Cody settled into Morgan's room.

Trying to sleep in Morgan's bed was surreal in so many ways. Images of the two of them rolled around in her head until she couldn't take it anymore, and got up to walk to the window while Cody slept peacefully.

Moonlight danced on the charred cabin. Thank God the farmhands were quick to the rescue, and the fire department had gotten there in time. The place would need massive repair, but it was salvageable.

As for her belongings…not so much.

Her clothes were ruined, her furniture as well. Cody's baby picture albums burned, too, but at least she had the digital photos backed up online. And, most important, she had Cody, safe and sound, so she wasn't going to complain about anything else.

She pushed away from the window and looked toward the door. Might as well use the bathroom while she was up. With all the people in the house, who knew how long she'd have to wait in line in the morning.

She opened the door at the same time as Morgan did across the hall. He wore nothing but blue jeans. She wore nothing but one of his T-shirts over her underwear, the shirt's hem coming to the top of her thighs, leaving her legs bare. They both paused for a moment as they looked at each other, then stepped out and closed the door behind them.

"How is your arm?" she asked in a whisper.

"Not worth mentioning."

"Justice?"

"Happy on painkillers the last I saw him."

"And you're going to Mexico tomorrow?"

"All three of us." He shook his head. "Not that I need them."

"Of course not."

"They'll be just in the way."

"Everybody needs backup, Morgan. Everybody needs family."

He said nothing to that, his gaze holding hers.

"I'll take care of Justice," she said after a long moment.

"Much appreciated."

"He took a bullet for you, you know." Even as Morgan had jumped in front of Cody to protect her son, Justice had jumped in front of Morgan.

He shook his head. "It's the strangest thing."

"He cares for you."

He just looked at her for a long second. "I'm planning on talking to him before we head out tomorrow."

"And what happens after you come back with Brittany?"

He glanced at his feet. "Back to work."

She watched him. "Don't you want more?"

"I'm not made for more," he said in a hoarse whisper. "I wouldn't make a good family man."

"Says who?"

"I wouldn't know the first thing about how to be a father."

"You've only been here three days, and you've already acted like a father to Cody. You were a friend to him. You stood ready to sacrifice your life for him. That's what fathers do, they give love and protection."

He stared at her, then slowly he reached out and pulled her to him.

Her world was whole when she was in his arms. She felt right in a way she didn't feel anytime or anywhere else. "Morgan," she whispered.

"I don't want to let you go again," he whispered back as he claimed her lips.

"Then don't." Her heart thrilled. Her body sang.

"You would trust me with your son?"

"Without reservations. I know you, Morgan McCabe." She pressed against him, palms flat against the hard muscles of his chest. As he shifted, his muscles played under her fingertips.

She itched to touch more. He must have felt the same, because he hooked his hands under her bottom and lifted her, his hardness pressed against her core.

She sucked in her breath, then explored him more fully while he deepened the kiss. Her mind was in such a haze, she was surprised she heard the footsteps coming up the stairs.

"Justice?"

"Probably Bull," he whispered back, looking at the door behind him that hid Wyatt, and then the door behind her that hid Cody.

In a few long strides he was at the door of the hall closet in the back, then inside. He held her tight against him in the dark. Memories assailed her, sending heat skittering through her body.

The footsteps came closer. Stopped. A door opened next to them, then indistinct noises came as Bull got ready for bed.

"I think we should..." she started in a whisper, but he claimed her lips again, and this time he deepened the kiss.

He swept inside her mouth and tasted every corner of her, toyed with her, teased her until her brain turned to mush. Desires long suppressed unfurled in a slow awakening. His hands tucked under her T-shirt, his fingers massaging their way up her ribcage until he stopped just under her breasts.

She moaned a protest.

He moved higher, cupping her, pebbled nipples pressing into his warm palms—she had taken off her bra for sleeping. When his hands slid back down to the hem of her shirt and drew the soft material over her head, she didn't protest.

Then they were skin to skin, her aching nipples brushing against his flat chest.

"You drive me crazy." The words came in a raspy whisper next to her ear.

Then his arm moved and a soft click sounded above them, and the closet light came on.

"Morgan!" She jerked up her hands to cover herself. She was a lot older than the last time he'd seen her naked. She'd had a baby since. Had breastfed.

"No way I'm missing this." He wore the devil's own smile as he took her in, gently drew her hands away. "Beautiful."

The awe in his eyes was gratifying, making her forget about her insecurities.

The large closet around them was stuffed with camping gear. A bunch of sleeping bags lay tossed on top of rolled-up tents. He pulled her down on top of those.

"I can't believe we're back here again."

"I want you."

She gave a strangled laugh. "I kind of deduced that from um…"

He reached down and unbuttoned his jeans, gave himself a little room. Grinned. Then grew serious. Took her face into his hands, brushed his lips over hers. "I love you."

Her heart skipped a beat.

"I've always loved you. I was just too stupid to say it. I didn't know how to be romantic. I still don't. But I'm going to try. I don't want to lose you again."

She stared at him. "Wow. That's the longest we've talked about feelings."

"My heart is an open book. Ask me anything."

She leaned forward and brushed her lips over his. "What are you feeling now?"

"A bucket load of horny."

Her hands slipped into the front of his jeans. "And now?"

"Like I'm going to die of frustration if I can't have you in the next two minutes."

She laughed, liking the sense of power.

"I know you're doing this to torture me."

She withdrew. "Sorry. If my touch is torture…"

He took her hand and put it back where it had been a second ago. "Not your touch… I said I loved you and you didn't say anything back."

"I love you, too. That's all that matters, you know. We'll figure out the rest."

With a groan that came straight from his chest he claimed her lips, shedding all restraint. He made her feel alive for the first time in a long time, her body buzzing with pleasure.

"I'm on leave until the New Year. After that… We'll work out the details."

THANKFULLY, THE CAMPING emergency kit had a condom. Morgan didn't question why, he just took the gift.

Dakota's eyes drifting closed and her back arching as he entered her was the most beautiful sight he'd ever seen. He planned on seeing it again and again, as often as possible for the rest of his life.

"I love you," he told her again, and his heart thrilled when she echoed the words.

He made love to her slowly, thoroughly, making up for all those lost years. And when they lay sated in each other's arms, they talked, caught up, laughed.

"I better get back," she said at last. "In case Cody wakes up."

"Is he a light sleeper?"

"Sleeps like a log. I swear he doesn't even twitch."

He helped her dress—any excuse to touch her again. He walked her to her door and kissed her, putting all his heart into the kiss.

Then he snuck into Wyatt's room, making his way to the pile of blankets on the floor in the dark.

"You have a supportive family," Wyatt said without turning. "It's okay to come out of the closet."

Morgan bit back a grin and punched his brother in the shoulder.

Man, it was good to be back.

* * * * *

PAULA GRAVES
WYATT

CAST OF CHARACTERS

Wyatt McCabe—The Serpentine, Texas, sheriff's young half sister has been kidnapped by a ruthless Mexican drug lord who's using her as leverage against his rancher father. He needs the help of ICE agent Elena Vargas, but does Elena have her own agenda?

Elena Vargas—The Immigration and Customs Enforcement agent has been put on mandatory vacation by her boss, who thinks she's too close to the kidnapping case. But she won't let anyone stop her from finding the brutal drug runner who's put a price on her head.

Brittany Means—The half sister the McCabe brothers never knew they had.

Javier Calderón—The drug lord needs access to McCabe land for trouble-free access to a coast-to-coast highway that will greatly expand his drug trafficking business. But will he let his personal vendetta against Agent Elena Vargas get in the way of his pragmatic concerns?

Los Jaguares—Calderón's vicious enforcers spread fear and terror throughout the small towns of the Texas/Mexico border. But are they completely loyal to Calderón?

Clive Howard—Elena's boss at ICE thinks she's letting her personal concerns get in the way of her job. Is he right?

Justice McCabe—Wyatt's rancher father hasn't always been the best of fathers. But how far will he be willing to go to save his daughter?

Morgan McCabe—Wyatt's older brother has spent years away on commando missions, but now that he's home again to help out his family, will he be sticking around? Or is the draw of danger and adventure too much to resist?

Virgil "Bull" McCabe—It took the kidnapping of the half sister he didn't know he had to bring the cop back home to Texas. Does he have it in his heart to forgive his difficult father?

For Julie and Dana.
Thanks for being so much fun to work with.

Chapter One

Serpentine, Texas, shivered under a gray December sky, a cold north wind blowing across the scrubby grassland and swaying the bare trees dotting the landscape around the fairgrounds on the southern edge of town. The *Feria de la Navidad* had been an annual festival since long before Elena Vargas was born, and she had a feeling it would be there long after she was gone. Some things seemed to hang on forever.

And some things, she thought blackly as she spotted her prey across the crowded market square, *just won't go away.*

Her target on this blustery day wore a black Justin wool hat low over his dark eyes and a black Western shirt with an embroidered rose pattern across the shoulders. His boots were silver snakeskin and black leather, embellished at points with silver and turquoise.

El Pavón. The Peacock. He lived up to the name.

His real name was Tomás Sanchez, and he was one of Javier Calderón's top lieutenants. Calderón's cartel, *Los Jaguares,* had been tormenting towns across the Mexican border for the last seven years. For the last two years, they'd been bringing their ruthless brutality into Texas.

It had to stop.

Sanchez strutted across the square toward a couple of women swaying to the street band's lively rendition of *"La Rama."* He coaxed one into a dance in the middle of the square, drawing claps and smiles.

"Do you think they laugh because they like him? Or fear him?"

The low voice in her ear made Elena jump. She whipped

around to face the gray-eyed cowboy who had slipped up behind her without a sound. "Go away, Sheriff."

Wyatt McCabe's dark eyebrows notched upward. "*Feliz Navidad* to you, too, Agent Vargas."

She turned away, trying to pretend she didn't know him. There was no way McCabe could blend in with the crowd in this part of town the way she could. "You're blowing my cover, cowboy."

"Aren't you supposed to be on vacation?"

Damn. He'd heard. "I'm spending my vacation pretending to be a human being," she covered lightly, although she knew Wyatt McCabe wouldn't buy that excuse for a second.

"A human being keeping an eye on *El Pavón?*" He ignored her obvious attempt to distance herself from him, closing the gap between them. He held out a bag of freshly roasted pecans, the warm, nutty aroma reminding her she'd skipped breakfast that morning. "Nuts?"

"I'm trying to pretend you're not here." She clenched her fist to keep from grabbing a handful of pecans.

"You know how to make a man feel wanted." His tone as dry as the north wind, he cocked his head to one side. "Your hair looks different."

Her clenched fists tightened, this time to keep from self-consciously finger-combing her curls. Instead of her usual struggle to tame her unruly hair into the sleek, professional bob she wore on the job, she'd let her hair air dry after the shower this morning. She'd also skipped applying makeup, she realized with a grimace. She probably looked terrible.

Not that she cared how she looked to Wyatt McCabe. She squared her jaw. "If I let you tell me why you're here, will you go away?"

"Morgan's found out where Calderón is keeping Brittany."

Elena tried not to react, but she couldn't keep her gaze from straying to Wyatt's face. "Where?"

His gaze swept the square. "Dance with me and I'll tell you."

"What?" He'd lost his mind.

"We're the only folks here not dancing. Do you want to blend in or stick out like a sore thumb?" He folded the bag of pecans and stuffed it in the pocket of his jeans. Holding out his hand, he gave her a pointed look.

She took his hand and let him whirl her out into the square with the others. "Where is Calderón holding your sister?"

"Somewhere around Los Soldados, down near Malachi."

She knew the place. "There's nothing in Los Soldados but scrub grass and alpaca dung."

"Well, that alpaca dung belongs to our friend Javier. Calderón owns majority interest in *Rancho de Las Crías.*"

She stopped pretending he wasn't there. "What?"

"Yeah, came as a shock to me, too. The task force has been busting our tails trying to sniff out any business holdings Calderón has in the southwest and apparently the slimy *cabrón* has been shoveling alpaca droppings ten miles away for two years."

"I doubt he does any of his own shoveling," she muttered as he tugged her closer to avoid a collision with another dancing couple. As she leaned in to speak quietly in his ear, her cheek brushing against his, she felt the light bristle of his beard stubble and suppressed a shiver of attraction. "What makes you think he's keeping Brittany there?"

"Morgan got the information out of one of our ranch hands who was working for Calderón."

She leaned her head back to look up at him, struck by his bitter tone. "Got it out of him how?"

"Morgan has his ways," Wyatt said flatly. Elena had a feeling some of Morgan's ways of getting things done wouldn't please her superiors at Immigration and Customs Enforcement.

Then again, ICE had made her take a three-week enforced vacation when she was hot on Calderón's trail. They weren't her favorite people at the moment.

"What are you going to do?" she asked Wyatt.

"Morgan, Bull and I went to Mexico earlier this week, but we got nowhere. Everybody's terrified of Calderón. Nobody's talking." He pulled her back to him, resting his cheek against hers so he could lower his voice. Again, she felt a tremor of sexual awareness dart through her, as unstoppable as a south

Texas flash flood. "But you know more about Calderón than anyone. It was criminal of ICE to tie your hands, which makes me wonder if Calderón has people in the San Antonio field office."

She sucked in a sharp breath. "Do you know something?"

"Just speculating."

She was almost certain there was a mole at ICE, as Calderón constantly slipped through their fingers just as they got close to bringing him down. "What do you want?"

"I want to see your personal files. Maybe there's information there we can use to open up some doors."

She shook her head quickly. "Nobody sees my files. Not even ICE."

His voice hardened. "Calderón has my sister, Vargas."

"I don't let people look at my files," she said more quietly. "I have my reasons. But I'll dig through them myself for every bit of information I've collected about Calderón's movements along the border and see if there's something we can exploit."

She saw he wasn't pleased with the compromise, but he gave a brief nod. His hand moved lightly against her back, tracking fire along her nerve endings. "I can be at your place by one. Will you be there?"

She looked across the square, where Sanchez had moved on to another pretty dance partner. Her stakeout here at the fair had been a desperation move anyway, she thought. If McCabe was right about the alpaca farm in Los Soldados, it could turn out to be a far more productive lead.

"I'll be there," she said.

He let her go and reached into his pocket, retrieving the bag of pecans. He put the rumpled paper sack in her hands. "Here. You look hungry."

Before she could come up with a retort, he'd disappeared into the crowd, blending in far more easily than she'd expected.

She checked her watch. Only eleven-fifteen. The drive back to her house would take less than fifteen minutes, and thanks to McCabe, she now had a bag of pecans for lunch.

It might have been a desperation move, but she could stick
ith her surveillance of *El Pavón* a little while longer.

Better than waiting at home like a desperate spinster for the
xy cowboy to show up.

HAT'S ALL SHE'D AGREE TO?" Morgan sounded disgusted.

"It's more than I expected," Wyatt answered quietly.

"I've met a few difficult women in my time," his older brother
irgil muttered, "but your ICE queen tops them all."

"ICE queen," Wyatt repeated. "Cute. What are you, thirteen?"

"She's in our way," Morgan growled.

"She'd say we're in hers."

Both of his brothers turned to glare at him. "You're taking
er side on this?" Virgil asked, his demeanor reminding Wyatt
`his nickname—Bull.

*Turn him out in a rodeo arena with a wrangler on his back and
'd give you one hell of an eight-second ride,* Wyatt thought,
ding a grin because he had a feeling Bull was in the mood
punch it right off his face. "I don't think we *are* on opposite
des," he answered his brother's question, keeping his voice
lm. He'd gotten good playing peacemaker over the years, first
tween his brothers and their father and later as a lawman.

"You trying to handle me?" Bull asked.

"No more than usual," he shot back, grinning this time.

Bull's belligerent look faded into a grin as well. "Clearly
ou're not related to me. You're entirely too diplomatic."

"And you're conveniently forgetting my adolescence," Wyatt
id with a laugh. "I know you and Morgan have a lot at stake
ere besides our sister. But try to see it from Agent Vargas's
oint of view—"

"Look, Wyatt, I know you like the woman—"

"I value her insight. I think she's a damned fine investigator.
he's courageous, determined—"

"Not to mention hot as a Texas summer," Bull murmured.
Suppose that might have something to do with your admira-
on for her fine attributes?"

Wyatt shot Bull a withering look. "I'll let y'all know wha
find out."

Morgan followed him to the door. "There's a lot riding
what you can get out of her."

"I know." Wyatt kept his voice low, aware his father was t
doors down in the study, within earshot. Justice McCabe's u
characteristic lethargy over the past few days had begun to wor
Wyatt. Was the old man thinking about caving to Calderó
demands?

Javier Calderón's ransom for Brittany had been simple t
devastating: if he wanted his daughter back alive, by midnig
Christmas Eve, Justice was to sign a lease allowing Calder
to use the western valley, which included thousands of acres
prime pastureland, as a through-point for his trucks.

The valley provided the shortest, most accessible route t
tween the border and I-10, the east-west interstate highw
stretching across the country from California to Florida. A
Wyatt and his father both knew very well that it wouldn't be
paca wool the trucks would be hauling.

Wyatt couldn't let his father capitulate and turn the ran
into a drug highway. Not as his son—and not as the sheriff
Serpentine.

"Be careful," Morgan said.

"I will be. You do the same. Keep Bull out of trouble."

Morgan smiled at that, the expression a striking change fr
his usual grim seriousness. "I reckon Tracy may have more lu
at that than I will," he admitted quietly, referring to Serpenti
school teacher Tracy Cobb, the pretty, tomboyish high sch
teacher who'd stolen their elder brother's heart.

"Does Dakota keep *you* out of trouble?"

Morgan made a face. "She tries."

"You think you could hang around Texas this time?" Wy
asked. "It's not right to expect Dakota to wait around while y
disappear for months or years at a time."

"I've been thinking about retiring, before I ever came he
Dakota and Cody are making the idea a lot more tempting."

"Good. It's time the McCabe brothers got to know each other again." Wyatt held out his hand.

Morgan shook it. "Call if you need me."

Wyatt found himself still thinking about his brothers as he neared Elena Vargas's rented stucco bungalow in Eastside, a neighborhood situated on the eastern boundary of the Serpentine town limits. She'd been living in Serpentine for over a year now, preferring to rent in the area rather than make the six-hour round trip from San Antonio when most of her work these days was here on the border.

Wyatt couldn't tell that she'd made many friends since she'd lived here, even though it was hard to remain a stranger in a town the size of Serpentine. She could be prickly, he supposed, trying to picture her the way other people did. The way his brothers obviously did.

She was a good investigator. A very smart woman. Resourceful and insightful. But she tended to hide all those good qualities behind a defensive streak as wide as the Rio Grande.

He parked his truck across the street, next to an empty land parcel full of scrub grass and weedy shrubs. A skinny-looking stray cat watched him with wary gold eyes from across the empty lot, streaking away the second Wyatt made a move toward his Stetson lying on the truck's passenger seat.

He didn't want to call this area blighted—a lot of hardworking, good-hearted people lived in Eastside—but the recent economic doldrums had hit the area particularly hard. Many of the people in Eastside were first-generation immigrants who'd come here, legally or illegally, to take advantage of the higher rates of pay in the U.S. But higher pay only mattered if there were jobs to be had, and with the shutdown of the chicken processing plant outside Serpentine, many of the laborer jobs had dried up.

Lack of money had given Javier Calderón and *Los Jaguares* a foothold in the area, Wyatt knew. But proof was difficult to come by. The people who might have information to share usually ended up dead or cowed into terrified submission by *Los Jaguares* and their ruthless threats and actions.

He suspected Elena had chosen this particular rental house, in

this specific neighborhood, because of its volatility. She liked to
be right in the thick of things, and Eastside qualified.

Her car, a compact blue Ford, sat under a narrow stucco car
port on the left side of the bungalow, so she was home already,
beating their one o'clock meeting time by a quarter hour. He won
dered if she'd eaten the pecans or if she was still hungry enough
for him to coax her out of the house to lunch.

It's not a date, McCabe. No matter how pretty she'd looked
today at the *feria,* with her dusky hair falling in unexpected soft
curls and her expressive face free of cosmetics, making her look
younger and more vulnerable than normal.

She'd hate that description, he thought with a half smile. Elena
Vargas prided herself on her competence and strength.

He had just reached for the door handle of his truck when he
noticed movement on the porch of the house next door to Ele
na's. A woman and three young children were hurrying down
the steps, the children holding hands and looking puzzled, while
their mother appeared terrified.

She spotted Wyatt watching her and turned her face away
quickly, looking ashamed.

He got out of the truck and approached her, but before he made
it across the road, she had already shoved her children in the back
of the rust-flecked station wagon parked at the curb, cranked the
rattling engine and pulled away in a cloud of Texas dust.

Wyatt watched her go for a moment, then looked down the
street for other signs of oddness. Three doors down, the sagging
front door of a turquoise-colored clapboard house stood open, as
if the occupants had left in a rush, forgetting to close the door
behind them. As he watched, a man in a dark fleece hoodie came
out of the next house down, talking with a raised voice and ani
mated gestures to a gangly Hispanic teenager. Wyatt could only
make out a word here or there, enough to glean that the man in
the hoodie was trying to get the boy to leave the house.

"*¡Vete, tonto!*" the man in the hoodie shouted, turning away
from the boy and running down the steps. He stutter-stepped
at the sidewalk as he spotted Wyatt watching him. The hoodie

covered most of his face, but not the jagged, white knife scars that traversed his copper-brown face like streets on a roadmap.

Memo Fuentes, Wyatt thought, shocked. *Son of a—*

Fuentes whirled around and started running up the road.

"Stop! Sheriff's Department!" Wyatt shouted, starting to take chase.

But a deafening concussion split the air around him, a shock-wave hurling him off his feet. He landed on his side ten feet away on the hard-packed dirt of the empty lot, his breath exploding from his lungs.

Gasping for air, he pushed himself to a sitting position and stared at the spot across the road where Elena Vargas's stucco bungalow had stood.

There was almost nothing left but jagged timbers and rubble.

Chapter Two

Her ears were ringing.

Elena tried to lift her hand to her throbbing head but something was holding it immobile. She blinked her eyes open and stared up into a gunmetal-gray sky.

Why was she outside?

"Elena!" That was Wyatt McCabe's voice, she thought, trying to clear her head. He sounded distant through the ringing in her ears. "Elena, can you hear me?"

She lifted her head, wincing as pain darted through her skull, leaving a path of agony in its wake. It took a second for the reality of her surroundings to form a coherent picture for her sluggish brain.

She wasn't outside. She was lying on her bedroom floor, surrounded by chunks of wood, metal and stucco, all that was left of her house.

"Elena!" Panic rose in Wyatt's voice. He sounded closer now. She heard the faint sound of falling debris coming from somewhere near what had been the front of her house.

"I'm here!" Her voice came out in a croak, the effort setting off a painful coughing spell. She covered her mouth with the one hand she could move until it subsided, then checked her hand for any sign of blood. Nothing but dust and grime. No lung injury, then.

She looked at her other arm, the one that had refused to move, dreading what she might find. But the limb seemed to be intact and, if her wiggling fingers were any indication, mostly uninjured. It was just pinned beneath the weight of her fallen armoire, a heavy oak monstrosity her father had built for her when she had graduated from college. Grimacing, she rolled onto her side and tried to pull the armoire off her arm. It didn't budge. Too heavy.

"Wyatt!"

"I'm right here." And he was, suddenly, a cowboy-shaped silhouette against the winter sky. Relief swamped her, bringing tears to her eyes. If Wyatt was here, she was going to be okay.

"Are you hurt anywhere?" Though she couldn't make out much about his features, backlit as he was against the daylight, she couldn't mistake the real concern in his deep voice. The tears trembling on her eyelids started to spill, and she blinked hard to hold them back.

She started to say, "I'm fine," but stopped before she formed the words. She wasn't fine. Her head was killing her, which might mean a closed head injury. And her arm was pinned under a three-hundred-pound armoire. It was starting to go numb. It would be stupid not to say so. "My head hurts and my arm is pinned."

"Okay, I don't want you to move anymore, in case that head-ache is more than just a bump. I'll do all the heavy lifting." He threaded his way through the debris field and hunkered down next to her, smiling at her briefly before he examined the armoire pinning her arm. "Can you move your arm at all?"

"I think so."

"Okay, then when I say go, I want you to try to pull your arm across your chest to get it out of the way. Ready?"

She nodded, grimacing at the resulting pain in her skull.

He bent over the armoire, sliding his hands on either side of her trapped arm. "Here we go." He took a deep breath and pushed upward with his legs. She felt the pressure on her tingling arm ease. "Go!" he said.

She rolled a little to the side, pulling her arm out and over her chest. With a thud, Wyatt let the armoire drop to the ground and turned immediately to her. "Thank you," she said as he carefully examined her arm. "What happened?"

"Bomb, I think."

"Bomb?"

"Well, some sort of explosion." He pressed the bones of her arm from shoulder to wrist. "Anything hurt?"

"It's still a little numb from the pressure," she answered, flexing her fingers. Her wrist twinged, but not badly. "I think it may be sprained but not broken."

"Good. What about your legs?"

She hadn't even thought about her legs, she realized, panic starting to rise in her throat. Were they there at all? Raising her head again, she looked down at her legs. Both were still intact and attached. She released a gusty sigh and tried to move her legs. To her relief, both limbs shifted in response to her mental command.

"Very good." Wyatt smiled at her. He was a little scuffed up himself, she realized as her eyes adjusted to the daylight. He had a scrape on his jaw, and a spot on his elbow was still oozing blood.

"You're hurt." She lifted her hand to his face, gently probing the area around the scrape without touching the wound itself.

"Just scrapes," he assured her lightly. "If you think you can move, we should get clear of here. In case there's a secondary device."

"You should have stayed out there and waited for first responders," she said with a shake of her head. "This place can't be stable, with all the structural damage."

"I *am* a first responder. Remember?" He wrapped his arms around her shoulders and pulled her carefully to a sitting position. "How's that?"

"I can get up," she assured him.

He stopped her from trying by herself, slipping his arms around her waist and pulling her up to a standing position as effortlessly as if she'd been made of balsa wood. He didn't let her go, giving her time to steady herself as her vision swam from the change in positions. But even after the dizzy spell faded, she still felt shaky and vulnerable, and it took every ounce of her inner strength to push his arms away so she could stand on her own.

"I made a path out. We need to hurry."

Already she heard sirens wailing in the distance. "Where did the bomb blow?" she asked as he guided her through a maze of ebris, taking care not to touch anything that looked ready to rash down on top of them.

"At a guess, it was somewhere in the carport. The blast blew our car into the house next door." Even as he spoke the words, ney emerged from the wreckage and into the front yard, where its and pieces of her shattered home lay sprinkled across the round like confetti. To her right, the neighbor's house was a alf ruin, the wall nearest her house collapsed under the weight f the blast and the airborne Ford Focus that lay upside down in vhat had once been the neighbors' living room.

"Was anyone home?" she asked in alarm.

"No." There was an odd quality to Wyatt's brief answer, but he didn't have time to ask more questions, for the Serpentine ire Department truck had arrived, and the next few minutes of onsultation and examination resulted in a trip by ambulance to ne regional medical center about an hour away in Del Rio. To er surprise, Wyatt rode with her in the ambulance, leaving the omb scene investigation to a couple of his deputy investigators.

"I'm okay," she said as he settled down next to her, holding er hand while the medical technicians got her hooked up to an V cannula and periodically checked her vitals.

"I know," he said. "Just try to relax. We'll be in Del Rio be-ore you know it."

VAITING FOR THE DOCTOR to bring him news of Elena's condi-on, Wyatt spent the next few hours on the phone with his of-ce and his family. On the work front, his deputies had cordoned ff the bomb site and were guarding it while they waited for an xplosives investigation team from the Texas Ranger division. t home, Bull and Morgan had offered to help with the bomb nvestigation any way they could, although Wyatt assured them nat protecting Tracy, Dakota and the rest of the J-Bar-J Ranch nhabitants was the most vital job they could have at the moment.

"Why don't you talk to Julio Rivas, see what he knows about uillermo Fuentes?" he'd suggested to Bull, knowing his brother ad formed a tentative truce with the scared young troublemaker ho'd gotten their sister Brittany into trouble in the first place.

It had been Julio, whose dalliance with *Los Jaguares* had nearly cost him his life, who'd provided their first clues toward locating Brittany. Wyatt still wanted to give the kid a good whomping for being foolish enough to get mixed up with such dangerous thugs in the first place, much less drag Brittany into the mess, but Julio was still just a kid. A stupid, stupid kid who might be able to help them save their sister.

"Will do," Bull had assured him. "Is Vargas going to be okay?"

"Hard to say. Depends on the verdict on her head injury." As both a sheriff and a cowboy, Wyatt had seen his share of simple-seeming knocks on the head turn into crises. "I'll call when I know more."

By the time the doctor came into the Emergency Department waiting room, Wyatt's nerves were beginning to fray, the relief of finding Vargas still alive inside that bombed-out ruin of a rental house beginning to give way to a gnawing fear that bringing her out alive and conscious had been only a reprieve. What if that knock on her head was worse than they'd thought? Blood could be clotting from a hidden bleed, putting pressure on her brain.

People could die from little knocks on the head—

The thought of Vargas lying lifeless in a hospital bed made him physically ill. Elena Vargas, for all her annoying flaws, was the most vibrant person he'd ever known. Life radiated from her in almost tangible waves, as if she generated her own electricity from some inner dynamo.

She couldn't be dead. What would the world do without her?

What would he do without her?

"Sheriff McCabe?"

The doctor's quiet voice drew him to his feet, his heart knocking wildly in his chest. *Please tell me she's going to be okay,* he thought. *Please.*

"Ms. Vargas can see you now."

"Is she okay?"

"As okay as one can be with a slight concussion and a sprained wrist," the doctor said with a wry smile. "She also has contusions and scrapes, as you'd expect. I just saw the images from her house on the news. She's a very lucky woman to have survived the blast."

Wyatt nodded. There had been several hellish minutes when he'd been certain she hadn't.

The doctor handed him off to an E.R. nurse, who took him to Elena. She was sitting up in the E.R. bed, looking rumpled but very much alive. "They're talking about keeping me overnight," she said, clearly annoyed.

"If they think you need to stay—"

"I don't. I'm okay. My head's not even really hurting anymore." She held up her bandaged wrist. "And this is a sprain. It'll go away in a few days. McCabe, you've got to get me out of here."

"And go where? Your house is gone."

She closed her eyes a moment, her jittery irritation giving way as if the full weight of all she'd lost had just landed on her in one heavy thud. "Oh, God. All my stuff is gone."

Including her notes, he thought. Funny, they had seemed so important before but were an afterthought now. All that mattered was that Elena was going to be okay. "If there's anything left, we'll get it for you." He sat on the edge of her bed and took her uninjured hand in his. "Do you remember anything more about the blast?"

In the ambulance, she'd confessed the last thing she remembered before opening her eyes to see her house blown up around her was walking into the bathroom for an elastic band to put up her hair.

"No." Her eyes narrowed suddenly. "What about you? Did you see anything before the bomb blew?"

He hesitated, knowing that anything he said about spotting Memo Fuentes would set her off. But she deserved the truth, didn't she? She was the one who'd lost everything she possessed, right down to the roof over her head. She'd damned near lost her life.

"I saw Guillermo Fuentes down the street from your house."

Her gaze snapped to meet his. "Memo Fuentes? Are you sure?"

"Yeah."

"I thought he was dead."

"So did I." Guillermo Fuentes was one of Javier Calderón's lower-level henchmen. Earlier that year, he had been driving a truck packed with undocumented workers crossing the border illegally when a flash flood from a spring thunderstorm had turned the Rio Grande River into a death trap. The van had hit a slick patch and run off the road into the river.

Of the thirty-five people aboard, including Fuentes, only eight had survived. Nine, Wyatt corrected, counting Fuentes. Had the heartless bastard run away from the van and left all those people to drown?

"Did he see you?" Elena asked.

"Yes. He ran. I started to take chase when the bomb blew."

"What was he doing when you spotted him?"

The doctor came in at that moment, stopping him from responding. He nodded to Wyatt and turned to look at Elena. "You won't rethink sticking around overnight?"

"I'm not sick. I don't need to be here. Leave the bed free for someone who really needs it. I just want to go home."

"Your home is gone," Wyatt repeated, keeping his tone gentle.

The look she gave him was pained. "So I'll get a motel room for a few days. The one in Davenport is supposed to be nice—"

"No." Wyatt and the doctor spoke in unison.

She looked at them both through narrowed eyes, as if she suspected they'd been colluding behind her back. "It's my decision."

"You have a concussion," the doctor said in a firm voice. "Just because I don't think it's a bad one doesn't mean it's something to ignore. You should have someone with you for tonight, at least, in case something goes wrong."

"Is there someone I can call for you?" Wyatt asked, realizing he didn't know whether Elena even had any close friends who'd be willing to come to her aid when she needed them. He had worked closely with her for over a year on the Border Security Task Force, but how she spent her time outside of work hours was a blank spot in his store of knowledge about her.

"No," she admitted, looking embarrassed.

"Then you'll stay with me," he said.

"YOU CAN STILL TAKE ME TO the Davenport Inn if you want. I won't tell the doctor if you won't." Elena watched Wyatt's clever hands unlocking the dead bolt on his front door and wondered, not for the first time, what else those long-fingered hands could do in a more intimate setting.

Really not a good time to be thinking like that, Vargas, she scolded herself as he let her inside.

"I know I'm not the neatest housekeeper in the world, but staying here for one night isn't going to kill you. I promise."

She looked around the small living room, saw that he was neater than she was by several degrees and tamped down a hint of dismay. "Yeah, you're a total slob."

"You feel like eating anything? I'm pretty sure the last thing you ate was that bag of pecans."

He was right. And now that the worst of the trauma had passed, she was starting to feel pretty hungry. But she didn't want him to think he had to wait on her. "Don't go to any trouble."

"I'm starving, so I'm going to make something for myself, anyway." He was already halfway into the small kitchen just off the living room. "Soup? Sandwiches?"

"Whatever you're having." She dropped into the nearest chair, resting her sore skull against the soft back cushion. As if she'd been running on fumes for the past few hours, she felt all her energy starting to sputter to a standstill. She let her eyes drift shut, lulled by the sounds of Wyatt moving around in the kitchen.

"Elena?"

Her eyes snapped open. Wyatt crouched beside her chair, his gray eyes warm with concern. "I'm sorry. I wanted to let you sleep, but the doctor told me to be sure to wake you every couple of hours."

Her gaze drifted to her wrist, where she'd returned her watch after the E.R. had given her back her personal effects. The watch crystal was cracked but the inner workings still ran, or they had, at least, when she left the hospital. But if the time on her watch was correct, she had been at Wyatt's apartment for nearly two hours already.

"I fell asleep."

He smiled. "You did. I put your sandwich in a plastic bag so it wouldn't dry out. You want to try eating something before you go to bed?"

She looked back at him, unarmed by his gentleness. The Wyatt McCabe she knew was all spurs and leather, a hardworking, no-nonsense cowboy cop. She wasn't sure she liked this softer side to the man. It made her feel entirely too vulnerable.

"Or," he added, a hint of rawhide returning to his voice, "you could tell me how long Javier Calderón has had a bounty on your head."

Chapter Three

Elena's dusky eyelashes dropped to cover her dark eyes. "How'd you figure it out?"

"Well, the bomb was a big clue," Wyatt answered, his tone drier than he'd intended. He softened his voice. "And seeing Memo there, running your neighbors out of their houses to protect them from the bomb—"

"Altruistic of him." She sounded skeptical.

"I've been thinking about that, too." He sat on the end of the coffee table so he could look her in the eye. "Guillermo Fuentes may be a killer, but he's always been workmanlike about it. He doesn't kill for fun, and he's never been known as cruel or ruthless."

Her brow creased. "True. Except if he's still alive, that means he left a whole bunch of poor, desperate people to die in that truck while he ran to protect his own hide."

"I don't doubt that's exactly what he did," Wyatt conceded. "I just don't think he felt good about it."

"So he risked his neck sticking around there long enough to warn my neighbors to get out?"

"Yes."

"Well, if we ever catch him, I'll be sure to send him a thank-you note." Her voice flattened with anger. "Oh, wait. He didn't warn me."

"Because you were a legitimate target from his perspective."

"Pardon me if I think his perspective is a crock of—"

"Yeah. Same here, believe me." He pushed back a wavy lock of hair that had fallen into her face. Her eyes fluttered up to meet his, and the heat he saw in their smoky brown depths scorched him to the bone.

He dropped his hand away, feeling shaky in his gut. He repeated his earlier question. "How long?"

Elena's gaze dropped to her lap, where her fingers twined together so tightly her knuckles had gone white. "At least two years."

"Two years?" And he'd never heard a word about it?

"Since I killed Antonio Calderón."

Wyatt sat back, caught off guard. "You killed Calderón's brother? I thought he died in a boating accident."

"That's the story the *federales* told the Mexican press, and ICE didn't try to contradict them. They thought it would keep me safe."

"How did you kill him?"

"Shot him. To protect myself and another ICE agent."

Wyatt heard a thread of pain beneath her otherwise uninflected answer. Clearly, there was more she wasn't telling him about what happened between her and Calderón's younger brother. "Calderón knows you killed Tonio?"

She nodded. "He'd sent Tonio there to kill me. He knows."

"So he wanted you dead even before you killed his brother?"

"Not exactly. I mean, it wasn't personal then." She looked down at her hands again, a frown creasing her brow. "It doesn't matter, anyway. What matters is that he wants me dead now, and it's very personal."

"Does Agent Howard know Calderón has a hit out on you?" he asked, referring to her supervisor at ICE, Clive Howard.

She shook her head. "I don't think so. Clive wouldn't let me anywhere near the Calderón investigation if he did. He probably wouldn't even let me out in the field at all."

He put his hand over hers where they twisted anxiously in her lap. "Do you have a death wish, Vargas?"

Her dark eyes met his. "If you tell anyone at ICE what you know—"

"I'm not going to promise to keep your secret at the risk of your life."

"Fine." She pulled her hands away from his. "I'll go now."

He stopped her, closing his hands around her arms and holding her in place. "We'll table all of this until you've had a good night's sleep. Okay?"

Wariness blazed in her tired eyes. "You won't make any calls tonight while I'm asleep?"

"Not to anyone who could put you out of a job."

She released a slow breath. "I'm too tired to eat. Put the sandwich in the fridge and I'll eat it for breakfast." She started out of the room, then paused, turning to look at him. "Where am I sleeping?"

"My bed," he answered, not thinking how the statement would sound.

Elena's lips curled with a sudden flash of humor. "Sorry, cowboy. I don't think I'm capable of staying in the saddle long enough to do either one of us much good tonight. We'll have to play rodeo another night."

Good grief, the woman could make his jeans tight with a few saucy words faster than any woman he'd ever met. "One of these days, Vargas, I'm going to call you on all that trash-talking you do."

"Preferably when I'm fully conscious," she said around a yawn.

"The bedroom is the door on the right. There's a bathroom with a shower inside if you need it."

"Where will you sleep?"

His other bedroom was a study, but it had an old bunk he'd confiscated when his father was refurbishing the bunkhouse at the ranch. "Got it covered," he assured her.

She started toward the door on the right but stopped, turning back to face him. "We never did talk about Los Soldados."

"Your notes are somewhere in the rubble, remember?"

"Right," she said. "Good night." She continued on to the bedroom, closing the door behind her.

Wyatt stared at the closed door, unsettled. Because Elena Vargas had just lied to him. He didn't know where her mysterious notes might be, but clearly they weren't in the rubble of her house.

Just what else was the beautiful ICE agent hiding from him?

ELENA DIDN'T DREAM about the explosion.

She dreamed about Tonio. And not those last moments of his life, when he aimed the shiny Colt .45 at Sam Benson, forcing her to pull the trigger of her own service weapon and kill the man she thought she loved.

No, she dreamed about the weekend they'd spent together on South Padre Island, a brief moment in time when she'd believed Tonio was nothing like his brother Javier and meant it when he said he loved her.

He'd been tall and handsome, with a movie-star smile and a mind as sharp as the razor blades his brother liked to use for torture. U.S.-educated—a graduate of Harvard Law and destined for greatness.

Or so she'd thought.

She'd met him through her undercover work in Ciudad Acuña, the Mexican city across the border from Del Rio. She'd been playing the role of an American grad student, studying in Mexico, whose ethics were on the shaky side. She'd hoped to work her way into a position with Calderón's cartel as a mule, smuggling drugs from one point to another.

Instead, she'd drawn the attention of Calderón's handsome younger brother and fallen hopelessly in love.

The last night on South Padre Island, she'd almost told Tonio the truth. Only the knowledge that her fellow ICE agent, Sam Benson, was already halfway inside the organization had kept her from risking it.

In her dream, she went with the impulse. She blurted her deceit in a single breath, eager to get it out of the way so that nothing else would stand between her and Tonio.

The words were still ringing in the soft Gulf breeze when Tonio pulled out his Colt .45 and shot her between the eyes.

Elena woke with a jerk, her pulse pounding in her head, beating a swift cadence of pain. All around her was darkness, and for the briefest of moments, she thought she was dead, awaking in the afterlife in some dark, unfamiliar limbo.

Then a door opened, streaming light into the darkness, and she saw she was in a small, spare bedroom. The silhouette in the open doorway was tall and rangy, broad-shouldered and cowboy-lean.

Wyatt, she remembered, swamped with relief.

But her relief was short-lived. "We have to go. Now."

The anxiety in his voice terrified her. "What's going on?"

"Someone roughed up your ER doctor in the parking deck to find out who you left with. They know you're with me." He grabbed a gym bag sitting by the door, hurried to the chest of drawers across from the bed and started pulling clothes out and stuffing them into the bag.

She squelched a streak of modesty and rolled out of the bed, pulling on the jeans she'd talked the E.R. doctors out of cutting off her. The T-shirt she wore was one she'd borrowed from Wyatt's drawer, a long-sleeved cotton T-shirt that wouldn't be much protection from the December cold outside. "What are we doing? Where do you plan to take me?"

He tossed a sweater to her. "Put that on. We won't have time to warm up the truck and the temperature's dropped a lot since sundown."

"That's not an answer."

He zipped the bag. "I'm taking you to the J-Bar-J."

His father's ranch? "Won't that be the first place they look for me if they don't find me here?"

"Maybe. We have a lot better chance of holding them off at the ranch, though." He pulled open the bottom drawer, withdrew a gun case and pulled out a small pistol—a Kel Tec P32, Elena saw as he slid a loaded ammunition magazine into the grip. Good ankle-carry weapon.

Sure enough, he took out an ankle holster and started strapping it to his right leg. "How're you feeling?" he asked as he buckled the holster in place.

"I'm okay," she answered, and was relieved to find she was telling the truth. Her head had stopped pounding and her heart rate had returned to normal after the heightened stress of her nightmare. "Don't suppose you have an extra weapon lying around?"

"I have your Smith & Wesson. I spotted it in the rubble and grabbed it." He dropped the hem of his jeans over the ankle holster. He'd eschewed his usual cowboy boots, she saw with a hint of surprise, in favor of simple hiking boots that would better accommodate the holster. "I checked for damage. It's fine."

He led her into the living room and unlocked one of the drawers of the writing desk by the window. Her M&P40 and hip holster were inside.

She took the weapon and checked the magazine. Ten rounds, plus one in the chamber. "My spare ammo's back at the house. Assuming it survived the bomb."

"I think my brother Bull has an M&P40. You can borrow some rounds from him when we get to the ranch."

"What if I need the ammo before we get there?"

Wyatt strapped on his regular service pistol, a large gray GLOCK 31, and shrugged a denim jacket over it. "If we need more firepower than we're carrying, running out of ammo will be the least of our worries." He opened the front door and looked at her. "Ready?"

With a nod, she followed him out to the truck.

The night was cold for south Texas, with a dry wind that seeped through the layers of clothes she wore to chill her right down to her bones. Wyatt started the truck and turned the heat up to high. "Buckle in."

She fastened her seat belt, careful not to let the belt block her access to the shoulder holster she wore strapped outside her sweater. "Are those lights coming toward us?" she asked in a hushed tone as they started down the street in front of Wyatt's house.

Wyatt didn't answer, turning into a nearby driveway and parking. He cut the engine and the lights. "Hunker down."

He slumped in his seat as well, keeping his head below the seat. In the rearview mirror, the reflection of headlights moved past so slowly that she was ready to scream before the vehicle finally passed the driveway where they sat parked.

Wyatt lifted his head a few inches, looking past her out the passenger window. "They're stopping at my house."

Elena risked a quick look. The vehicle, she saw, was one of the large panel vans *Los Jaguares* favored. Eight men got out of the van and moved in silent concert toward the front of Wyatt's house.

"We can't stay here," she whispered.

"I know. But we can't risk being seen leaving."

She looked around them. The house where they had parked had a fence around the small backyard but the one next door had a flat, bare yard behind the house that led to an alley about twenty yards away. Moonlight shining down from the clearing sky shed enough light to show an obstacle-free path to the alley through the yard. "Leave your lights off and go through that backyard," she suggested.

He followed her gaze and nodded. "Good idea."

He started the truck's engine and eased the gear into Drive. With a light bump they left the concrete driveway and started across the grassless yard behind the house next door.

As they neared the alley, lights came on in the backyard, a spotlight that illuminated the truck so brightly that it made Elena's eyes hurt. Wyatt growled a sharp profanity and hit the gas, his wheels crunching and popping against the gravel surface of the alley.

Elena twisted in her seat, looking for any sign of pursuit. So far, nothing, but the homeowner had run out into the alley, no doubt trying to get their license plate number. A flood of panic rose in her chest, making her voice come out tight and strained. "If he makes too much of a ruckus, one of those thugs is going to come find out what's going on."

"So let's make sure we have a big head start," Wyatt shot back, whipping the truck onto the crossroad and driving as fast as he dared.

They reached the highway leading to the J-Bar-J Ranch within minutes, weaving into the light flow of vehicles, mostly eighteen-wheelers and delivery trucks, that made up the usual late-night traffic. The pickup's dashboard clock read eleven-forty-three. Almost midnight.

"Did you call ahead to let them know we're coming?" she asked a few minutes later, after her heart rate had settled down.

"No." He shot her a grin. "One of the benefits of being family. Nobody turns you away, no matter how late you show up."

Chapter Four

"Why'd you bring her here?" Bull's jaw jutted about a mile from his face, his gray eyes dark with anger. "What if she tells someone at ICE or the FBI that Julio's hiding here?"

"Nobody at ICE or the FBI gives a damn where Rivas is. They don't think he's anything more than a peripheral witness at best." Wyatt was already tiring of his brother's third degree. So he'd formed a soft spot for their sister's troublesome boyfriend. And maybe Tracy Cobb was right about the kid having potential. But Wyatt had his own fugitive to guard. *Los Jaguares* might want to eliminate Julio Rivas from their list of potential prosecution witnesses, but that was business.

Elena Vargas had shot and killed Javier Calderón's younger brother. His vendetta against her was very, very personal. But he couldn't tell his brothers that part of the story. Not without Elena's permission. So they were understandably skeptical of Wyatt's certainty that she was a target.

"What makes you think Calderón's put a price on her head, anyway?" Morgan asked.

"Besides having her house blown up with her in it?"

"That could have been a random attack on any law-enforcement agent."

"Trust me. It wasn't. She was the target, and she will be again if we don't stop Calderón." Wyatt shot a pointed look at Bull, who was blocking the path to the study door. "I need to make sure she's comfortable in the guest room and not having any symptoms of a closed-head injury, if that's okay with y'all."

Bull moved aside. "How long's she staying here?"

"As long as necessary. So grit your teeth and bear it."

Dakota Dayton, his father's finance manager, was still in the guest bedroom with Elena when Wyatt knocked on the door. She smiled at him, reminding him why his brother Morgan found her so irresistible. Dakota was good people. A tough, hardworking, softhearted Texas woman. A man couldn't go wrong with one of those.

"I'll be around if you need anything," Dakota told Elena as she started out the door. "Like a break from all the testosterone floating around this place." She winked at Wyatt as she left the room, closing the door behind her.

"I work in law enforcement. I'm probably leaking a little testosterone myself," Elena said with a dry laugh.

She looked about as far from masculine as a woman could get, Wyatt thought, especially freshly showered and dressed in some soft blue froth of a nightgown Dakota had lent her. She was sitting up against the pillows at the head of the bed, the comforter up to her chest, allowing Wyatt only a tantalizing peek at the shadows of her breasts beneath the gown's silk bodice.

She must have caught him looking, for she sank a little farther under the covers, pulling the comforter up toward her chin. "I never figured Dakota Dayton for the frilly type."

"It's a good look for you," he said, waiting for her caustic comeback.

But she just smiled at the compliment. "Thank you."

"Not that other looks are bad looks for you," he added.

Her smile grew wry. "You just prefer the soft, girly look?"

He eased closer to the bed. "I didn't say that."

She lifted her chin to keep her gaze locked with his. "Most men do."

There it was again. That minor chord in her voice that made him think she'd been hurt, and badly. He hadn't heard any stories about her love life in the years he'd known her, and law-enforcement circles were just as bad as any about spreading gossip.

Maybe that was something he and Elena Vargas had in common. He didn't go around sharing his secrets, either.

"How long do you expect me to stay here?" Elena asked. "I'm

not an invalid and I'm damned sure not going to hide out here like a coward while you menfolk look for Calderón. So if that's your plan—"

Unfortunately, that was exactly his plan. "If you're already in their crosshairs, the last thing you need to do is go out there with a big bull's-eye painted on your back."

"Even if I can help you get your sister back?"

"You don't have to martyr yourself to do it."

"I don't intend to." Her voice darkened with determination.

He felt his blood pressure rising at her stubborn bravado. "How are you going to avoid it?"

"The same way I've avoided it for the past two years."

"Because that worked so well this afternoon."

Her dark eyes flashed with annoyance. "I started to get complacent. I won't let that happen again. But I'm the best person to help you find Brittany. I know more about Calderón than anyone around here—I've been studying him for years now."

Damn, but she was gorgeous when she was stubborn. It was well after midnight, and she'd had her house blown up around her and a knock to the head that had sent her to the hospital for treatment. She'd just had a harrowing near miss with the ruthless cartel that had put a price on her head and spent the last hour in a car driving lickety-split across ranch country to escape an ambush. But Wyatt had never seen her look more appealing.

Anger pinked her cheeks, and gritty determination sparked in her eyes. Her hair was a wavy, tumbled mess and somehow, in the middle of their argument, she'd forgotten she was in bed and let the comforter slip, revealing just how damned good her breasts looked in that silky nightgown.

He'd been lusting after her for almost as long as he'd known her, though he'd kept his urges to himself since Elena had made it clear in her behavior, not just to him but to every man on the task force, that she was off-limits sexually. As far as he knew, he was the only one who'd had any trouble following her unspoken rules about sex in the workplace.

Most of them thought her too prickly and reserved. But Wyatt found the emotional barriers she erected around herself to be intriguing, a mystery to be solved. And this might be his best chance to breach her defenses, he realized. While she was here, on his turf.

He crossed slowly to the side of the bed, careful not to move too quickly, knowing how easily she spooked. "Mind if I sit? It's been a long day for me, too."

Her eyes narrowed but she nodded.

He sat beside her, close enough that he felt her hip warm against his, only the comforter and their clothes between them. "What is it that you think you can give me that nobody else can?" Although he hadn't intended for his voice to come out in a low, sensuous growl, he couldn't really regret it, not when he saw a deep flush spread across Elena's throat and chest. Her eyes darkened, and an answering heat flooded into his lower belly and slid south.

Her long black eyelashes dropped to hide her eyes. A curl of black hair slid into her face, falling over her brow and across her eyes. He reached out and pushed it behind her ear without thinking. But at his touch, her gaze snapped up to meet his, and the heat in his gut ignited, spreading fire through him, out of control.

He saw an answering blaze reflected in her eyes. "Elena—"

She touched his jaw, her finger tracing across a tiny scar on his chin he'd earned years ago at his first youth rodeo. "You have the worst timing, cowboy." She dropped her hand to her lap.

He tipped her chin up, making her look at him again. "It doesn't have to be bad timing. Maybe this is the chance we never gave ourselves. I can't be the only one who feels the sparks we strike off each other."

"You're not." Her voice softened. "But all that means is we know how to push each other's buttons."

"You don't find me at all attractive?" His question came out sounding cocky, which he hadn't planned. But at least it made her laugh.

"Nobody with eyes and a libido would find you unattractive, McCabe."

"Wyatt," he murmured, leaning closer, pressing his advantage.

She flattened her hand against his chest. "You're trying to

find your sister. I'm trying to take out Calderón. We don't have time for this."

"We never have time for this." He stood up, starting for the door.

"Wait," she blurted.

He turned to face her again. "What?"

"I have an idea about getting your sister back."

He came back to the edge of the bed. "What's that?"

"We make contact with *Los Jaguares* in Los Soldados. And we offer them a trade."

Wyatt narrowed his eyes. "What kind of trade?"

Elena's spine straightened, and despite the filmy nightgown and her tousled hair, there was no mistaking the return of tough, composed Agent Vargas of Immigration and Customs Enforcement.

"Your sister for me," she answered.

WYATT MCCABE COULD BE the most hardheaded creature this side of a mule pen, Elena reflected the next morning when she dragged her bleary-eyed self out of the too-soft bed, driven to speed by the late hour. She'd told Wyatt to make sure someone woke her at six, but apparently he'd taken it upon himself to control her sleep time as well as the rest of her life.

It was seven-twenty and the sun was already up outside her bedroom window, pouring in through the brown muslin curtains to cast a bar graph of shadows on the hardwood floor. On the floor by the bed, someone had put a blue gym bag that hadn't been there when she went to bed. She checked inside cautiously and discovered a couple pairs of jeans, a cotton sweater, a denim jacket and two pairs of shoes—tennis shoes and hiking boots. They were a half size too large, but the thick socks she found in the bottom of the bag made them fit better. The jeans, on the other hand, fit fine. She put on the blue sweater and checked her reflection in the mirror.

Not quite the composed and competent ICE agent she was used to seeing, she thought. But she'd looked worse.

Hearing voices coming from somewhere in the house, she

followed the noise until she reached the great room to find Justice talking in quiet tones to Dakota Dayton, while Dakota's three-year-old darted around the Christmas tree nearby, gazing with toddler wonder at the wrapped presents nestled under the branches of the massive fir.

Justice turned at the sound of her steps. He looked at her a moment without smiling, as if trying to assess her motives for being here.

"Thank you for your hospitality, Mr. McCabe."

He nodded formally. "You're welcome, Agent Vargas. How are you feeling this morning?"

Sore, she thought. But clearheaded. "Fine," she said. "Is Wyatt around?"

She expected the answer to be no, to discover that he'd left for Los Soldados without her. But the door from the veranda opened and Wyatt entered, followed by a Mexican teenager who went stone-still at the sight of her standing in the middle of the great room.

With a sharp profanity that sent Dakota diving to cover her son's ears, Julio Rivas backpedaled toward the door. Wyatt grabbed him by the back of his jacket and hauled him around to face Elena.

She stared at Julio's terrified expression for a second before shifting her glare to Wyatt. "So. I see he didn't run off to Mexico after all. Let me guess, you just ran into him outside?"

Wyatt's lips pressed to a thin line. "He's been here for about a week."

"You know that could be seen as harboring a fugitive?"

"We like to think of it as protecting an endangered witness." Wyatt's older brother, Virgil, entered from the veranda, his broad shoulders nearly brushing the door frame. Instantly the room seemed about two sizes smaller than before.

Elena wanted to chew out the whole family for keeping Julio's location from the rest of the task-force agencies who were looking for the kid as a material witness, but she had to admit, if she'd found him first, she'd have done the same thing and kept his whereabouts to herself. "Any other witnesses against Calderón stashed around here I should know about?"

"Just you," Wyatt answered. "Have you had breakfast?"

She shook her head.

"Come on." He handed Julio off to his brother and walked to where Elena stood, her arms crossed with annoyance. If he noticed the speculative look his father was giving him, he showed no sign of it.

"Miguel made biscuits this morning." Wyatt led her out of the great room and into the kitchen—a large, warm room down the hall. "They should still be warm. We have honey or strawberry jam, or Miguel could probably whip up a batch of milk gravy—"

She caught his arm and pulled him around to face her. "Did you think about what I said last night?"

His expression hardened. "I couldn't think of much else."

"You understand this has to be how we handle it. It's the best way to get a foot in the door with the cartel."

"What makes you think he'd be willing to trade the leverage Brittany gives him for a chance to get his revenge on you?"

"He can find other leverage against your father," she answered. "You or your brothers. Dakota and her kid, even. But he's never going to get a better chance to get his hands on me."

Wyatt's gray eyes locked with hers, his conflicted thoughts almost readable in their gunmetal depths. Suddenly, he curled his hand around the back of her neck and pulled her to him until she was pressed flat against the solid wall of his lean, muscular body.

He was going to kiss her, she realized, her heart stuttering into a frantic sprint. He was going to kiss her, and God help her, she was going to let him.

She tasted coffee on his tongue as he skipped the preliminaries and went straight for seduction. She didn't resist when he walked her back against the kitchen counter and lifted her onto the granite top. When he stepped between her knees, she opened her thighs and wrapped her legs around his waist, tugging him closer.

Anyone could come in here any minute, argued the sliver of sanity left in her spinning head. But she didn't care. Wyatt's hands were like pure magic against her body, burning past the thin layer of cotton sweater to scorch the skin beneath with fiery pleasure.

A couple of quick footsteps were all the warning they got.

It wasn't enough.

"Oh, my God, I'm so sorry."

Wyatt pressed his head against the side of Elena's neck. She forced her eyes open to see Dakota Dayton's flushed face staring back at them.

"I'll just go."

Wyatt stepped back and lifted Elena down to the floor. "It's okay," he said to Dakota, managing a smile, which was more than Elena could come up with. She just wanted to run the woman out of the kitchen and finish what Wyatt had started.

"Cody wanted another biscuit," Dakota murmured.

"Go ahead. We're done here." Wyatt slanted a look at Elena, a silent invitation to follow him. He headed out the back door without another word.

Elena averted her gaze from Dakota's curious look and followed Wyatt outside. The north wind that had chilled the previous day was back with a vengeance. Elena wished she'd grabbed a jacket from the duffel bag.

"I'll do it," Wyatt said.

Elena arched an eyebrow. "You mean—?"

"I'll set up the trade. On one condition."

"What condition?"

"You give me access to those notes you're hiding. Because I know they didn't get lost in the fire."

Chapter Five

"They're not keeping her on the alpaca ranch." Elena set a cup of coffee in front of Wyatt and pulled out a notepad. "Are you ready to order?"

If he hadn't helped her transform herself into the cantina waitress himself, he might not have recognized her. Long, black hair extensions gave her a thick, wavy mane, and dramatic makeup and a low-cut peasant blouse erased almost all resemblance to the ICE agent who spent most of her time in conservative business suits. Inside the purse she wore bandolier style over her neck and shoulders, her Smith & Wesson M&P40 lay nestled in a built-in holster. He'd bought the purse the day before from a gun shop in Serpentine.

He hadn't liked her suggestion that she get a job in Los Soldados, fearing she'd put herself too obviously in the line of fire. She had chosen this particular undercover setup, and after reading through her copious notes, kept in a password-protected web archive Elena had set up to protect her notes from exactly the kind of destruction that had happened to her house earlier that week, Wyatt couldn't really argue.

Los Jaguares were known for their womanizing. Who better than a sexy woman to get the goods on them? So far, members of *Los Jaguares* who'd come through the cantina hadn't looked any higher than her cleavage. He supposed there was something to the idea of hiding in plain sight.

He was doing a bit of that himself, playing tourist from somewhere up North. The Western shirt he'd bought at one of the shops in Serpentine that catered to tourists was too ornate and obvious to ever pass as authentic Texas gear. His jeans were too new and too tight, and he wore his most expensive pair of running shoes instead of boots.

He'd even gelled up his hair, at his brother Morgan's suggestion, and borrowed his father's horn-rimmed reading glasses, though he spent most of his time looking over the tops of the rims because the view through the lenses was a blur.

"I'll have a Buffalo Burger and Texas fries," he ordered, mimicking his brother Morgan's neutral accent and hoping his Texas twang wasn't bleeding through. Lowering his voice, he added, "Then where are they keeping her?"

"My shift ends at one. Stick around and I'll pretend I'm taking a tourist home for a little Texas hospitality." She winked at him and went to turn his order in.

He waited patiently, enduring the badly spiced abomination Avalina's Cantina called a Buffalo Burger and, more annoying, at least three attempts by customers to grope Elena as she took their orders.

She came back near the end of her shift, bending close enough that he could see right down her shirt. Wicked woman wasn't wearing a bra, he realized, heat flushing through his body. He looked up and saw laughter in her eyes. "Tip me big, fella, and you might get lucky." She flashed him a flirtatious smile.

He added a twenty to the bill and caught her hand as she started toward the back of the bar. "You get off any time soon, gorgeous?"

She pretended to consider her answer. "Five minutes. You have something in mind?"

He rose and whispered in her ear. "I'm seeing a whole new side of you, Vargas."

She laughed softly. "My side isn't what you were looking at a minute ago." She patted his cheek. "Stick around till my shift is over and I'll show you around town, *gringo*."

He waited around outside the cantina until she emerged, stuffing something into the pocket of her skirt. She feigned surprise at finding him waiting. "You waited, *hermoso!*" she exclaimed, loud enough to be heard by passersby. "You have a car? Maybe something big and powerful like you?"

She was laying it on thick, he thought, his concern for her tempering his amusement a bit. He showed her to his father's Mercedes coupe, which he'd talked the old man into letting him borrow, and opened the passenger door for her.

Once he was safely behind the closed car door, he asked, "Where is Calderón keeping Brittany?"

"There's apparently some sort of enclave on the Mexican side of the border, about three miles from the packing plant. The people at the cantina say he must have found himself a young *concubina,* because lately he's been sending lackeys into town to buy tampons, soft drinks and chocolate bars."

"So how do we get in there and get my sister?"

"From what I heard just today, the place is always under guard." As she spoke, Wyatt saw her gaze drift toward the side mirror of her door. He'd been checking the rearview mirror himself, in case they were being followed. So far, he hadn't spotted anything suspicious.

"Wonder why they shared all this information with you on your first day at work," he said.

"I was suspicious about that at first, too, but it didn't take long to figure out most of these people are genuinely afraid of Calderón and his thugs. They were trying to watch out for me, best I can tell. Pointed out the men I'd want to stay away from. I didn't tell them that I have pictures of most of those bastards hanging on my office wall."

"You're either brave or crazy going in there right under their noses."

"Yeah, their noses never got out of my cleavage long enough to be a threat," she drawled. "I think we have to go ahead with the plan for the exchange. Tell them you can hand me over and see if you can talk them into letting you see your sister."

"And then I just hand you over?"

"ICE has been trying to get people on the inside for ages. We might never get a better chance than this."

"You think he's just going to hold you there? Let you learn all his secrets?" Wyatt shook his head. "Elena, he tried to kill you two days ago. If he gets you in his sights, he'll pull the trigger."

"Not if I offer to be his eyes and ears at ICE."

"You think he'll believe you?"

"I made a stink about being put on mandatory vacation. there's a mole inside ICE, and I'm pretty sure there is, Calderó already knows I'm crossways with ICE. I might be able to convince him I want payback for how they're treating me."

"But the second you go back to ICE and tell them what you' doing, the mole's going to know you're a double agent."

She shook her head. "Who says I'm going back to ICE?"

She'd lost her mind. Maybe that concussion had been wors than she thought. "You can't go rogue."

"Nobody in this part of Texas will ever be safe as long a Calderón's running drugs through here and sending his murde squads to keep people terrified." Elena's expression darkene "It's got to stop."

He wanted to argue with her, to beg her to reconsider. But h knew it would do no good. Elena was right. Calderón's reign terror had been going on far too long as it was.

But he didn't intend to let her make the sacrifice to bring to an end.

Elena had booked a low-rate room at a local motel for the du ration of their plan, giving them a base of operations and some where to rest. The room was small but it had two beds, givin Wyatt a place to stay as well.

"I don't normally pick up guys at cantinas," Elena said, a smil in her voice, as she unlocked the motel room door to let them in side. "But you were awfully cute, *gringo,* and you tip well....'

He closed the door behind them. "You enjoy playing wit fire, Vargas?"

"Sometimes," she answered seriously.

"You know I want you. Don't you?"

She nodded. "I want you, too."

He shook his head. "You've hid it pretty well."

"I know." She stepped closer, her finger plucking at the to button of his shirt. "I've made mistakes where men are con cerned. Very big mistakes. I don't want to make another one."

"And you think I'm a mistake?"

She flattened her hands against his chest and looked up at him, her dark eyes shining with a curious combination of excitement and fear. "I don't know. I don't trust my instincts about men anymore." She pushed away from him and sat on the edge of the nearest bed, sliding her shoes off and rubbing her feet. "Been a long time since I waited tables. I forgot what hell it could be on your feet."

He sat next to her and patted his lap. "Put your feet up here and I'll see if I can rub out the kinks."

She shot him a look of pure suspicion but did as he said. "Is this part of your sneaky plan to seduce me?"

He massaged her instep, electricity zinging through him as she threw her head back in pleasure. "Is it working?"

"Yes it is, you bastard."

He laughed softly. "I hate to bring work into this very promising situation, but we can't wait much longer. The deadline is approaching quickly. Christmas is the day after tomorrow."

"Raul Santiago is Calderón's main enforcer in Los Soldados," Elena told him. "If you want to talk to Calderón, you have to go through him."

"You learned a lot in one day of waitressing."

"Mmm-hmm," she murmured, her eyes fluttering shut as he started caressing the ball of her foot. "You should really reconsider careers, cowboy. You could make a fortune massaging feet for a living."

"I don't know. I'm pretty picky about my clientele. And my terms of payment," he added, moving his hand up her ankle to her calf.

She opened her eyes and shot him with a scorching look. "Are we going to have sex?"

He couldn't hold back a soft laugh. "You're such a romantic, Vargas."

"I just need to know what you're expecting from me."

Her question caught him flat-footed. "I don't know."

"You don't strike me as a guy who does one-night stands, Wyatt. And I'm not sure I can promise anything more than that."

She was right. He wasn't a player. And one night with Elena

wouldn't be nearly enough. But could he walk away from th
possibility just to hold out for something more, something sh
might never be able to give him?

"If you have to think about it this hard, it's probably a ba
idea." Elena swung her legs over the side of the bed and stoo
pacing to the front window of the motel room. "Santiago's sleep
ing with one of the waitresses at the cantina. I might be able t
use that to get you a meeting with him."

"You think she'd be willing to set it up?"

"I could tell her you're a middle man to the drug gangs in th
North and Midwest. You're willing to be Calderón's distributo
to markets he'd have trouble breaking into otherwise."

The story might be enough to tempt Calderón, or at least hi
henchman, into meeting Wyatt in public. He could then make th
offer to trade Elena for Brittany. But he still had no intention o
letting Elena go so far as to leave Los Soldados with Calderón

"She's working through the afternoon," Elena said, puttin
a jacket on over her low-cut blouse. "I can see if she'll set it up
I'll just tell her the guy I picked up did a little business talkin
in between the pillow talking." She winked at him.

Damn, but he wanted her. Right here in this flea hole of
motel room, on the table, on the sink, on the bed, up against th
wall. He could already imagine how she'd feel under him, ski
to skin. Soft and hard, sweet and tart, difficult and easy. All th
things she was outside of bed, all those delicious contradiction
that had fascinated him from the moment he'd crossed sword
with her on a joint task force border-breach case almost tw
years ago, she would bring with her into bed. A challenge lik
none he'd ever come across, with a promise of reward beyon
anything he'd ever known he wanted.

But one taste, one brief taste, would never be enough. And i
that's all she had to offer—

"What are you thinking about, cowboy?" She turned to loo
at him, her coal eyes smoldering.

"What it would feel like to be inside you," he answered hon
estly. "And if I could be satisfied with just one night."

She stared at him for a long moment before she turned back to the window. "I thought I'd found forever once."

He knew an important concession when he heard one. He prodded carefully, afraid to spook her into silence. "You did?"

She nodded, her throat bobbing as she seemed to search for words. "It was almost three years ago. I was still working undercover for ICE and I managed to get really close to the edge of Calderón's operation."

"How?" he asked, surprised.

"Through his brother Tonio."

"Honey trap?"

She turned to look at him, her expression raw. "I fell in love with him. Or, at least, who I thought he was."

The pain in her eyes made his gut clench in sympathy. "Oh."

"I knew trusting anyone connected to Calderón was dangerous, but Tonio was very convincing. He was educated, urbane, charming—all the things Calderón isn't. He had me convinced he hated his brother's crimes and wanted to restore honor to his family name."

"And you believed it."

She turned away. "Stupid, I know."

"I don't think it's stupid to want to trust someone you care about," Wyatt disagreed, thinking about his mother, Jeanne. She'd loved his father, even when he'd been fooling around on her. She'd put up with a lot of pain and humiliation to keep the family together. She'd wanted to believe Justice's promises that he'd stick to the straight and narrow this time.

Who knows, maybe one day he would have. He was certainly a changed man now. Now, when Wyatt's mother was dead and no longer able to enjoy who he'd become. But if anyone in that scenario was foolish, it was Justice, not Wyatt's mother.

"It was such a risk to take," Elena growled. "I never should have been arrogant enough to think I could take it and win."

"What if you'd been right about him? You might have found the love of your life."

"But I wasn't right. And I didn't. I ended up shooting a man I loved because he was going to kill me and another agent." She leaned her head against the window. "I can't trust my instincts where men are concerned. I clearly have no judgment."

"Because of one mistake?"

"A mistake that ended with one man dead, another wounded badly enough to be forced out of his job, and a dangerous drug lord gunning for me." She laughed bleakly. "I don't do things halfway."

"No, you don't," he agreed, pushing off the bed and crossing to stand beside her. He curved his palms over her cheeks and drew her gaze up to meet his. "But maybe that also means when you make the right choice, it's going to be one hell of a good decision."

Cocking her head, she grinned at him. "You are entirely too nice a guy to be hanging around with a curmudgeon like me, Wyatt McCabe."

He grimaced. "Shh, don't say that. You'll ruin my bad-boy mystique."

She wrapped her arms around his waist and laid her head against his chest. "Are you sure you want to take on Calderón head-to-head? He might enjoy taking out a Texas sheriff just for the reputation it'll give him."

"He wants access to my father's land. If he kills me, he'll never get it."

"Are you sure he'll be thinking that logically? It's not exactly wise business to blow up an ICE agent." She rubbed her cheek against his chest, making his heart rate climb. "The world needs more Wyatt McCabes, not fewer. If you're going to do this, I need to be nearby."

"Not a good idea. If anyone takes a good look at you, they're going to see through that makeup and those hair extensions."

"So I won't let anyone take a good look at me." The firm tone in her voice was like a roadblock, Wyatt knew. Nothing would get through her steely determination once she'd made a decision. She'd be there, having his back, whether he liked it or not.

"Okay," he said, though he wasn't happy about it. "But you stay under the radar."

She pulled back and looked at him. "Pretty bossy for sheriff of a tiny little Texas town, cowboy."

"I just want to keep you alive," he said seriously, making her smile fade. "When I saw that bomb go off with you inside the house—"

She put her fingers over his lips. "Don't get all mushy on me. I don't think I can take it."

Cradling her face between his palms again, he kissed her lightly, more a promise than a challenge. "Let's see if we can get this meeting set up today. The sooner the better."

She squeezed his hands and let go. "Take me back to the cantina."

Chapter Six

Elena hadn't counted on Raul Santiago being at Avalina's Cantina when she and Wyatt arrived. While Wyatt settled in a corner booth, Elena found Mariana, Santiago's woman, cleaning up in the back to finish her shift. "Back so soon, *chica?*" Mariana asked in rapid-fire Spanish.

"Remember the *gringo* who tipped me so big?" Elena replied, feigning naive excitement. "He wants to meet your boyfriend, Raul."

Mariana looked immediately wary. "Is he the police?"

"God, no," Elena said quickly. "Unless cops go around offering you blow. And lots of it."

Mariana's eyebrows arched. "Did you take it?"

"No. I don't do the stuff myself. Certainly didn't need it to have fun this afternoon," she added with a laugh. "He may look like a professor, but he's all stallion in bed."

Mariana looked across the room at Wyatt with a salacious smile. "It's always the quiet ones."

"He's a—what do you call it? Distributor. He's a distributor for the drug gangs up North." Elena lowered her voice. "When I told him I'd met one of the infamous *Jaguares,* he wanted to meet him. Maybe he wants to make some sort of deal with *El Jefe.*"

Mariana's voice lowered to a whisper. "Good luck with that. Señor Calderón meets with few. I have never seen him on this side of the border, myself." For all her bravado, she clearly feared Calderón. Elena couldn't blame her. *"El Jefe,"* as she'd called him, was the chief indeed, but he was no benevolent dictator. If he thought Mariana was in his way, he'd cut her down with no remorse. Probably even enjoy it.

If Elena had been able to think of a way to arrange an introduction between Wyatt and Calderón's henchman without using Mariana, she'd have done it. But Wyatt would need a personal voucher to get anywhere close to Raul Santiago, much less Calderón. "So there's nothing you could do to help him?" she asked Mariana.

"You like him that much?"

"I do," Elena answered, surprising even herself by the fervor in her tone. She looked across the room at Wyatt, who was nursing a Corona and people-watching from his corner booth. His gaze shifting to lock with hers, he lifted his bottle in salute. Elena almost forgot to smile, overwhelmed by a powerful tug of attraction. It wouldn't be hard to convince anyone she'd fallen hard for the sexy *gringo,* she realized, because she had.

Mariana's eyebrows twitched again, but she just patted Elena's arm. "Are you sure you know what you'll be getting into?"

No, Elena thought. *I don't. And that scares the hell out of me.* "I may never have a chance like this again, Mariana. He's handsome and rich and he wants me."

"Are you sure he wants you? Or just what you do in bed?"

"Does it matter?" she asked, a hint of pragmatism in her tone. "If I help him get this deal, he'll be very grateful, yes?"

"Perhaps," Mariana said. "I'll do this. I'll tell Raul about your *gringo* and what he does for the Americans. If Raul thinks Señor Calderón might wish to know more, he will approach your lover himself. What is his name?"

"Roger," Elena answered. "Roger Hines. He's from Illinois."

Mariana patted her hair into place. "I will do what I can."

"Wait." Elena grabbed Mariana's arm. "Be sure Raul tells Roger that this was my idea. So he will be grateful to me."

"I will." Mariana's smile held a hint of sadness. Perhaps her love affair with one of *Los Jaguares* hadn't lived up to her expectations, either.

As the other woman crossed to speak to Raul, Elena made eye contact with Wyatt again. His eyebrow quirked and she gave a quick nod. He smiled at her so warmly, she thought she might melt into a puddle right there in the middle of the cantina. She'd been attracted to him since the day they met, but she had been fresh off the Tonio Calderón disaster, wary of men in general.

When had she dropped her guard and let Wyatt become so important to her?

"Señor Hines?"

Wyatt had seen Raul Santiago coming, but he feigned surprise and just a hint of wariness. "I'm Roger Hines."

Raul's accented English was quite good, suggesting an American education at some point in his life. "You are a brave man, coming here to seek out Señor Calderón."

"Who told you that?"

"Your whore."

Wyatt felt a surge of rage run through him at Santiago's cold words, but he kept it hidden. "Then she was worth every penny I paid," he said with an equally cold smile. "I can be of great service to your boss."

"I will pass along the message."

"No, I believe it would better if I spoke to Mr. Calderón face-to-face." He deliberately used the English title rather than the Spanish, a show of power rather than deference.

Santiago didn't miss the shift. "Señor Calderón meets with only a chosen few. I don't expect you will be among them."

"Isn't that a decision Mr. Calderón should make for himself?"

Santiago was silent for a long moment. Wyatt could tell he didn't want to lose this particular battle of wills. But finally, he nodded and stepped back. "I will pass your message to Señor Calderón and give you his answer."

Wyatt breathed a little easier as he watched Santiago walk toward the back of the cantina and pull out a cell phone. Calling Calderón, he hoped.

He let his gaze wander around the bar, looking for Elena. But she was nowhere in sight. Had she gone to the bathroom? Outside for some fresh air?

Or had she run into trouble while he was distracted by Santiago?

He spotted the other waitress—Mariana, Elena had told him.

He crossed to the table where she sat drinking a glass of wine. "You're Carlita's friend, aren't you?"

Mariana looked surprised to be approached. "I know her," she said cautiously.

"Do you know where she went?"

Mariana looked around the bar. "She was still in the back the last time I saw her. Maybe she's in the bathroom?"

"Perhaps," he agreed. It was the most likely answer.

But his gut crawled with alarm.

THE VOICES DRIFTING TOWARD her through the night air were hard and mean. The voices of men used to doing what they wanted when they wanted, and to hell with who got hurt. Elena had known too many men like that in her thirty years of life, mostly professionally but sometimes personally.

Had she not heard the words, *"la gringita,"* she might have gone back inside the cantina, back to the noise and liquor and the unmistakable odor of desperate people living desperate lives. Places like Avalina's weren't often frequented by happy tourists. No, these small, seedy cantinas catered to downtrodden locals and the occasional weary traveler looking for something raw and authentic to break up the monotony of his life on the road.

They were also magnets for the predators, as potent a draw as carrion to a hungry coyote. From the next words she heard from the voices drifting down the narrow alley, she knew these men were predators of the worst kind.

"*El Jefe* is coming here to meet someone. It's our chance. He'll be away, and the others'll keep our secret if we let them in on it." She recognized the voice, she realized. *El Pavón* himself, Tomás Sanchez.

Elena pressed her back flat against the exterior wall of the cantina. Despite the cold wind, the adobe was surprisingly warm, having retained some of the sun's heat from earlier in the day.

"If Javi finds out—"

"Who will tell? The girl? She's already lied to try to get away. We'll be careful. Leave no marks. She's no virgin at her age, anyway. The *gringas* never are. She might even like it."

Elena covered her mouth, feeling sick. They were talking about Brittany Means. She knew it, gut deep.

"He is already on his way here. If we go now, we can get what we want and be gone again before he returns."

"And if José doesn't go along?" The second man's protests were halfhearted. Elena could tell he would do what Sanchez suggested. He was just looking for assurances that he wouldn't get caught.

"He will disappear," Sanchez said flatly. "Let's go now, while we can."

Elena slipped silently down the alley and searched the street on the other side of the building for the two men she'd overheard.

There. They were heading for a large truck with a canvas covering over the truck bed. Old Mexican army surplus, she guessed from the desert-camouflage pattern of the paint job. She edged closer to the truck, keeping out of the line of sight. Once Sanchez and the other man climbed into the cab of the truck, she made a snap decision.

Grabbing the tailgate, she stepped onto the bumper and climbed into the truck bed, staying low to keep herself hidden from view. The canvas covering blocked the view from the truck's back window, which meant that while the men inside couldn't see her, she couldn't see them, either.

For however long it took the truck to reach Calderón's compound, she had to stay quiet and stay put. She reached into her pocket and put her cell phone on vibrate, for she knew without a doubt Wyatt would be calling her the second he realized she had disappeared.

And boy, was he going to be pissed.

"Señor Calderón has agreed to meet with you." Raul Santiago merely stopped by Wyatt's table, speaking with cool formality, as if he couldn't be deigned to treat Wyatt as an equal.

Putting me in my place, Wyatt thought. "When?"

"He's on his way now."

Wyatt looked up at the man, surprised. "Now?"

Santiago slanted a disdainful look at him. "Is that a problem?"

"No. Of course not."

"I will introduce you when Señor Calderón arrives. You may wish to be less…American when you meet him. He has little affection for *gringo* arrogance."

What a coincidence, Wyatt thought. *I have no affection for psychopaths who terrorize and murder innocent people. Whatever their race or nationality.*

Santiago left the table, giving Wyatt a chance to compose his scattered thoughts. Calderón was coming here? Everyone had seemed so sure he'd never agree to the meeting, which meant one of two things. Either the head honcho of *Los Jaguares* was in desperate need of distribution for his goods in America, or he already suspected Wyatt was a plant and he was coming to Los Soldados to handle things personally.

Wyatt hoped it was the former, not the latter. But the light weight of the Kel Tec P32 strapped to his ankle offered a little comfort.

He was more worried about Elena. She clearly hadn't gone to the bathroom, or she'd have been back by now.

Keeping an eye on Santiago, who was at a table with Mariana, Wyatt pulled his cell phone from his pocket and checked for any missed messages. Nothing. He dialed the number for Elena's cell phone and got no answer.

Damn it. Where the hell was she?

THE BUZZ OF HER CELL PHONE was muted by the flap of her purse but it still sounded unnaturally loud in the empty bed of the cargo truck. Elena curled herself around the phone to muffle the noise. It was the second time her phone had vibrated in the last five minutes. It had to be Wyatt, looking for her. When the phone hummed a third time, it was two short buzzes, signaling she had a text message.

She risked a look at the screen. It was from Wyatt. Where are you?

Typing slower than she'd like, since she could barely see the keypad of her phone, she typed in a terse explanation and hit Send. Before he could respond, she added a second message.

Calderón's on his way there. Keep him occupied and I'll get
Brittany out.

She could only imagine his reaction to that message but hoped
he'd see the wisdom of letting her do her part to save his sister.
She wasn't some civilian who didn't know how to handle herself in a sticky situation, after all. She was a field agent for ICE.
This wasn't her first rodeo.

The sound of the tires on the road changed, and she dared a
quick peek under the canopy. They were on a bridge crossing
the Rio Grande. No checkpoint that she could see. This bridge
must have been built by one of the cartels as a border crossing.

She had a GPS tracker on her phone that could give her the
exact coordinates of her position. Huddling with her back to the
truck cab, blocking any light the phone display might cast, she
checked the program and got her coordinates. Now she knew
where she had to head once she got Brittany out of that compound.

As she was about to close the phone again, she stopped and
texted the coordinates to Wyatt. It wasn't backup, exactly, but it
was better than going in completely alone.

The truck began to slow, and Elena closed her phone, sliding
backward into the corner of the truck bed, where some smelly
old horse blankets lay in a wad. She made herself as small as possible, covering up with the blankets. The smell of horses made
her need to sneeze, but she fought to keep it inside.

She heard Sanchez and the other man talking as they got out
of the truck and started walking away. The tickle in her nose in-
creased until she could barely keep her eyes open.

A little farther, she thought. Let them get just a little farther
from the truck....

She couldn't stop the sneeze. Or the next two. But she pressed
her hands over her nose, doing her best to muffle the sound.

The sneezes subsided and she froze in place, listening for any
sign that the men walking away from the truck had heard her. She
heard only the sound of cattle lowing in the distance and,
somewhere nearer, the plaintive howl of a coyote.

She let a minute pass in silence before she ventured toward

the back of the truck. A peek outside reassuring her that she was alone, she climbed out of the truck bed and dropped to the hard-packed ground below.

Some sort of outbuilding sprawled about a hundred yards away. Perhaps housing stables at one time, it had weathered in the desert sun and harsh north wind until the wood siding was a pale, bleached gray. But it was not entirely abandoned. She saw lamplight shining through the window.

Two dark figures, silhouetted against an open doorway, caught her eye. Sanchez and the other man, perhaps? They seemed to be talking to another man who was blocking the doorway.

Suddenly, one of the two men outside made a quick movement and the scene lit up with a soft flare of light. Almost simultaneously, a crack of gunfire carried through the cold night air. Elena ducked behind the truck, peeking around the corner to see what had happened.

The man in the doorway crumpled to the ground.

They hadn't been able to talk the guard into joining them, Elena thought. Once the other two men entered the building, she started running as quietly as possible toward the outbuilding.

There was enough light inside the building, and so little outside, that she dared to peek through the high-set windows to get a better look at what was going on inside. She had guessed right about the building's former use. Definitely stables of some sort, with concrete and wood stalls to house a large number of animals at once. Might be part of the alpaca ranch. Or maybe the alpaca ranch had formerly been a horse ranch.

She edged her way down the outside wall, keeping an eye out for anyone approaching from nearby buildings or the hard-packed dirt road leading from the bridge. As she neared the end of the stable, she found what she was looking for.

Brittany Means, locked in one of the stalls. And the two men from the truck approaching her with clear intent.

It was now or never.

She reached the edge of the building and looked around the corner. There. A large set of double doors leading into the building. No padlock to impede her entry. But opening the large pair of doors would draw the attention of the men long before she could make her move.

She had to lure them outside instead.

Slipping back around the corner of the building, she reached into her purse and brought out the Smith &Wesson tucked in the built-in holster inside. Aiming for the rusty metal barrel standing about ten yards away, she squeezed off a round. The gunshot made her ears ring, but the round hit its mark, drilling a hole into the barrel.

Exclamations and curses in excited Spanish immediately followed the gunshot. Elena hurried back around the corner and set up for their reaction.

What she didn't expect was to see them both burst from the stable, guns blazing. The one she didn't recognize ran around the corner and skidded to a stop at the sight of her, his expression almost comical. But when he brought his gun up and took a shot at her, she had no choice but to shoot back.

His bullet fired well wide, slamming into the wall above her head. Hers hit him center mass. He fired another shot as he went down, the bullet pinging against the rusty metal overhang of the stable roof. It ricocheted into the ground fifteen yards away.

Elena set herself for Sanchez to come running. But all she heard was a loud cry of pain and then footsteps pounding away at a sprint.

She grabbed the gun from the fallen man's hand and peered around the corner. Tomás Sanchez lay facedown on the ground, a pitchfork sticking out of his back.

About thirty yards away, she saw a slim figure racing into the desert, silhouetted by moonlight.

Brittany, she thought.

She took off after her.

Chapter Seven

When this was all over, Wyatt thought, and Brittany and Elena were both safe, he was going to have a long talk with Elena about going off on her own without backup.

Not that she'd listen. And, if he was being honest with himself, he probably would have done the same thing. He couldn't have let the opportunity to hitch a ride to Calderón's secret compound go by, either.

At least she'd texted him her GPS coordinates. Wyatt had mapped the location and found that she'd been somewhere just south of the Rio Grande, where the Texas scrub grass gave way to the matorrales of northern Coahuila.

"How sure are you this isn't a trap?" Morgan, always the suspicious type, sounded skeptical as Wyatt outlined the situation over the phone. "You've been wondering if there are *Los Jaguares* spies inside ICE. What if Elena's the spy?"

"She's not," Wyatt said without hesitation. Elena Vargas might be frustrating, prickly as hell and hard to get close to, but no way was she a spy for Calderón. "She's in danger. She's trying to find our sister and bring her home safely."

"She should have waited for us."

"Someone has to stay there at the ranch and protect the others."

"Bull can do it." Over the phone, Morgan was already on the move. Wyatt could hear his feet crunching on the river-stone walkway to the ranch-house garage. "Give me the coordinates again."

Wyatt repeated them. "I'm not waiting for you. Just get here and wait to hear from me."

"Don't go there alo—"

Wyatt hung up, made sure his phone was set to vibrate and stuck it in the back pocket of his jeans.

He'd never met with Calderón, despite Elena's request. As much as he might want the drug runner dead or captured, he wanted his sister and Elena alive and safe even more. The battle with Calderón had been going on for years and it could go on a little longer, as long as he knew Brittany and Elena were okay.

He had no trouble following the path of the truck in which Elena had stowed away. It was apparently a heavy vehicle, with newer tires that left easy-to-track prints in the sandy dirt road. Wyatt came to a bridge, fashioned with concrete blocks and a few steel girders. It looked steady enough to allow for the weight of a large military-style truck like the one Elena had described in her text.

But it would never hold up to the strain of an 18-wheeler, he thought. Which explained why Calderón wanted to use J-Bar-J land for his shipping routes. He could easily bribe some border guards to look past any irregularities in his shipping manifest, but the more time he spent on U.S. roads with his contraband, the more danger he was in of discovery. Taking the private road that wound through the J-Bar-J, he could take his trucks almost all the way to I-10 without scrutiny.

Wyatt parked his father's Mercedes on the Texas side of the bridge, put on the emergency blinkers and got out to go the rest of the way on foot. He could make a more stealthy approach that way.

Wyatt hadn't gotten far past the bridge when he saw a small compound of buildings in the distance, seemingly slumbering in the pale moonlight. But after a couple of seconds, he spotted lights inside one of the buildings, dots of gold in the ghostly bluish-white color of the structures.

A truck sat parked about a hundred yards from the building. Wyatt headed for the vehicle as silently as possible and laid his hand on the hood.

Still warm.

He moved toward the building with lights on and peeked inside. It looked like some sort of commercial stable no longer in use, though the stalls seemed to be in decent shape.

Then he saw the dark shape lying in the open doorway.

Kel Tec in hand, he edged toward the figure. It was a man, lying in a pool of his own blood. A large hole in his chest told the tale. He was dead.

Wyatt turned away, flattening his back against the outside wall of the stable. He listened carefully for any sound that might give away the presence of another person. But all he heard were animals moving in the underbrush and, somewhere not too far away, coyotes baying at the moon.

Nearing the end of the building, he stopped just short, spotting another crumpled form lying in the shadow of the stable eaves. A second man's body, this one gut shot. A couple of feet in front of Wyatt, something had gouged a hole in the concrete siding of the stable building.

A bullet gone awry?

As he started around the corner, a faint crunching sound was his only warning. Something swung through the air and hit him square in the chest, knocking him to the ground. His weapon hand hit the hard dirt first with a jarring crack, shooting numbness through his fingers and wrist. His Kel Tec fell away from his nerveless grip.

"¿El policía?" The voice was male. Close. Tight with pain. Wyatt looked up and found himself staring into the prongs of a pitchfork. And clutching the pitchfork handle in one hand, his face contorted with pain, was Tomás Sanchez. *El Pavón.* Blood ran down his forearm and dripped on the ground next to Wyatt.

"No," Wyatt answered. *"Ranchero."* He knew *Los Jaguares* loved taking police scalps. Sometimes literally. And while he knew who Sanchez was, he didn't think Sanchez knew who he was.

"Why are you here?" Sanchez asked in English.

"Looking for a lost calf," Wyatt answered. "Have you seen her?"

Sanchez just laughed. "You're funny, *vaquero.*"

The sound of a vehicle approaching drew Sanchez's attention away from Wyatt for just a moment, but when Wyatt tried to make a move to roll away, Sanchez drove the pitchfork downward, barely missing Wyatt's wrist, and pinned his sleeve against the dirt. "You stay put," he said.

Wyatt considered making another attempt to escape, but he'd never get his arm unpinned before Sanchez used the weapon hanging from his belt holster and finished him off.

He still had a chance to help Brittany and Elena. But not if he was dead. So he stayed put, as *El Pavón* demanded, and waited with dread for the vehicle still moving toward them to come to a stop.

The tires popped and hissed on the stony driveway before the vehicle pulled to a halt. Footsteps crunched on the ground toward him and his captor, and Wyatt turned his head to see who had arrived.

The vulpine features of Javier Calderón were unmistakable, even in the pale moonlight. He walked forward, ahead of the two men accompanying him, and looked down at Wyatt.

"Sheriff McCabe," he said in his lightly accented English. "What a mess you've made of my property tonight." He crouched by Wyatt, his dark eyes shining with malice. "You'll pay dearly for the trouble you've caused."

THE GIRL WAS FASTER THAN Elena expected, though her path over the scrubby ground cover was erratic and panicked. Elena could hear her crying, terrified sobs that were beginning to take on a tone of despair. She was lost, and she knew it.

"Brittany!" Elena called, praying this time the cold wind blowing across the matorrales wouldn't carry her voice away before the girl heard her.

Brittany stutter-stepped, her head turning toward Elena's voice, but she didn't stop running.

"Brittany Means, stop running! My name is Elena Vargas. I'm a friend of your brother Wyatt."

Brittany's head whipped around that time, and she stumbled, falling hard to the ground.

Elena raced to her side, reaching her as the girl was struggling to her feet. "It's okay, Brittany. I'm here to help you."

"I didn't mean to kill him. I just wanted to get away. I climbed out of the stall and I—I didn't want him dead. I just wanted him out."

"I know." Carefully, Elena reached out and touched the girl's dark hair, brushing it out of her eyes. "I was there. I know what happened."

"The police here are on their side," she wailed. "They'll put me in jail and throw away the key."

"We're not staying here," Elena told her. "We're going back to Texas."

Brittany sniffed back tears, but they kept coming. "I don't know how to get back to Texas."

"But I do," Elena assured her. She helped the crying teen to her feet. "Do you think you can walk a little farther?"

Brittany nodded. "Do you know—do you know Julio Rivas? Is he—?"

"He's fine. He's safe. Now let's get you to safety, too." Putting her arm around the girl, Elena checked the coordinates on her cell phone to get her bearings. They were less than a mile from the border. Once she and Brittany were back in Texas, she'd feel safer.

As they neared the border bridge, she pulled out her cell phone again and tried Wyatt's number. No answer.

Brittany grabbed her arm, stopping. "There's someone there," she said, pointing toward the bridge ahead.

Elena followed the girl's gaze and spotted a Mercedes coupe parked at the side of the bridge, emergency lights flashing. Relief washed over her. Wyatt. "It's your brother's car. Come on." She started running, pulling Brittany along by the hand.

But as they got close to the car, Elena's earlier relief began to seep away. Why wasn't Wyatt getting out to greet them? Why were the flashers on? She peered at the interior of the coupe, trying to see beyond the moonlight glare on the windshield.

There was nobody inside.

"Where's Wyatt?" Brittany asked, sounding bleak.

"I don't know," Elena admitted, although her chest was beginning to hurt as the obvious answer occurred to her.

He was looking for her. And since he hadn't stayed to meet

Calderón, the leader of *Los Jaguares* might be on his way back here right now.

Without a key, she couldn't move Wyatt's car out of the way. So there was no way to keep Calderón from knowing someone had invaded his territory.

Wyatt was in serious trouble.

"Brittany, listen to me. You have to find somewhere to hide while I go find Wyatt. And you need to stay quiet and still, no matter what happens. Promise me."

The girl sniffled. "Okay. I promise."

Elena looked around, wondering where the girl could hide. Her gaze ended up on the river below the bridge. This part of the Rio Grande wasn't particularly wide, though it had cut a furrow through the land deep enough to create a sloping bank on either side. Beneath the bridge, there was a narrow ledge of land that would accommodate a girl Brittany's size.

"Under the bridge," she said. "Do you think you can get down there?"

Brittany nodded, already heading down the bank on the Texas side of the river. Elena waited until she heard the girl settle into place before she started walking across the bridge into Mexico.

She checked the magazine of her Smith & Wesson M&P40. She'd fired the round she'd had chambered, but there were still fifteen rounds in the magazine. She chambered another round and started hiking south.

"ELENA VARGAS WAS HERE?"

From the stall where he was tied up, Wyatt could make out only snippets of what Calderón and Sanchez were talking about in rapid Spanish. But Calderón's mention of Elena came through loud and clear, along with the seething hatred that infused his voice when he spoke her name.

Elena had been right. Calderón's reasons for wanting her dead seemed to be deeply personal.

"And you're sure she and the sheriff are involved?" Calderón asked, this time in English.

"Positive," came a new voice, also speaking English with a

mild Texas accent. "At least, she spent the last few nights with him, either at his place or at his family ranch. And they spent the afternoon together at a motel at Los Soldados."

Wyatt shook his head, recognizing the voice. Unbelievable.

Elena had suspected a mole in the San Antonio ICE office. And she'd been right.

The voice belonged to the ICE agent who'd been her supervisor for the last two years, Clive Howard. The man who'd put her on enforced vacation leave. No wonder Memo Fuentes had known to set the bomb in the middle of the day. Howard had known she'd be home.

"They're probably heading for the border bridge," Howard added. "We should go look for them. We don't need them to get back to Texas and start talking. When it was just the girl, that was one thing—nobody's going to believe the little liar. But Elena—"

"She is a knife in my heart," Calderón growled in Spanish. "Every day she lives is a twist of the knife."

Wyatt kept working on the thick cord they'd used to lash him to the stall support, but Calderón and his men had stripped him of anything he could have used to free himself.

He should have fought back. What good did it do for him to be alive if he couldn't even get his damned hands down from over his head?

Calderón and his men left the stable, their voices fading as they moved farther away. A few minutes later, there was only silence in the cavernous abandoned stable.

Damn it. Damn it, damn it, damn it—

"Cowboy!"

The word was a whisper, so soft he thought he'd imagined it. "Wyatt, where are you?"

It was Elena's voice, still barely a whisper. She sounded close. "Stall ten," he answered with equal quiet.

He couldn't hear footsteps, but he sensed her coming closer. Felt her, like lifeblood coursing through him, warming him from the inside out.

"Why didn't you stay in Los Soldados?" Suddenly, she was there, in the door of the stall, gazing at him with soft brown eyes. Her hair was a mess, her wrinkled clothes were dusty, and a streak of dirt ran down her face from forehead to chin. But he'd never seen a more beautiful woman in his life.

"Why aren't you halfway to San Antonio?"

With a knife from her purse, she cut through his bindings in a few seconds. "Leave you behind? I could never do that."

He caught her hand. "Is this a bad time to tell you I think I love you?"

She stared at him for a moment, surprise and pleasure shining in her dark eyes. "It's a terrible time. We have to go. I left Brittany out there alone." She pulled a pistol out from behind her back. "I got this off the guy who shot at me outside." Her voice darkened. "He's dead. He won't need it."

She led him quietly out of the stall, heading for the side door of the stable. "They left Tomás Sanchez standing guard out front," she whispered. "Brittany pitchforked him, but I guess he lived, huh?"

"He's wounded, but it's not a mortal injury, apparently," Wyatt answered, checking the pistol's magazine. It was a GLOCK G17. At least one round missing. Two, if he'd had a full magazine and one in the chamber. It looked clean enough, at least. Maybe it wouldn't jam on him at a bad time. "How do we get past Sanchez without his seeing us?"

"He was already nodding off when I sneaked in here," she answered. "He's playing it tough for Calderón's benefit, but I think he's hurt more than he realizes. I think we can get out of here without being spotted."

Wyatt wasn't as confident that Sanchez would be oblivious to their escape, but she turned out to be correct. They reached the cargo truck without raising an alarm and headed north toward the border.

This had to be the third time Elena had walked the mile and a half between the stables and the border, Wyatt realized as they neared the river, but she showed no signs of flagging. He wondered if she was that strong and fit, or if she was running on pure adrenaline.

His father's car was still where he'd left it, he saw with some surprise. He'd figured Calderón and his crew might have taken it. Of course, they also might have tampered with it, he realized, remembering the powerful bomb that had blown Elena's car into the house next door.

"I'd better check it out, make sure it hasn't been booby-trapped," he said as he crouched by the left front tire and peered under the chassis.

"Wyatt?" Elena's voice sounded strange.

He pushed to his feet, looking at her across the hood of the Mercedes.

But she was not alone.

"Did you really think I would leave an injured man to guard you, sheriff?" Calderón's smug voice froze Wyatt's blood. He had a gun to Elena's head. "I have been tracking you since you left the ranch."

"How?" Elena asked. Her dark eyes darted around, looking for a way to escape. Determination squared her jaw, and Wyatt knew that she'd rather die trying to get away than to play passive to Calderón's whims.

He admired her for it, even as he feared the outcome of her intentions.

"Check your pocket, sheriff."

Elena's eyebrows twitched, and he knew without her saying a word what she wanted him to do. It was a big risk, but if he was going to make any kind of life with a strong, independent-minded woman like Elena Vargas, he was going to have to trust her instincts.

He reached down to his pocket, as Calderón suggested. At that moment, Elena began to struggle, earning a clout to the face with the butt of Calderón's weapon. But it was distraction enough. When Calderón got her back under control, he was staring down the barrel of the borrowed GLOCK.

Elena smiled at Wyatt.

"You should have brought your thugs to watch your back, Calderón," Wyatt said. "Why didn't you?"

"Put the gun down or I'll kill her."

Wyatt knew Calderón wasn't bluffing, but he had to give Elena a chance to make another move. "I think you don't trust your men at all. They're in it for money, not out of loyalty. And surely some of them must realize that if you were to die, they might be able to take over your empire."

"My men are loyal to the death."

A new thought occurred to Wyatt. "Is that why you sent your brother Tonio after Agent Vargas and her partner? You had to know one or the other of them would kill Tonio. Two against one."

"I did not think she would shoot. She was my brother's whore." Elena's expression darkened, her nostrils flaring with rage.

"She was an ICE agent, and you knew it. You sent your brother to get what he could out of her. And then you sent him to die. Because he was a threat to your control, wasn't he? Your men liked Tonio better. They trusted him more. Admired him more. After all, he was charming and handsome, and you…" Wyatt let the words hang in the cold night air.

Calderón's gun hand twitched toward Wyatt, all the opening Elena needed. She rammed her elbow into his gut and tore free of his grasp, rolling out of the way.

Calderón's gun moved with her, tracking her. *"¡Puta!"*

"Put the pistol down," Wyatt ordered.

Calderón fired a shot toward the side of the Mercedes. At the same time, Wyatt fired at Calderón. The round struck Calderón in the side of the neck, tearing through his throat. Calderón's gun went off one more time as he started to fall. The pistol slid from his grasp as he put his hands to his ruined throat and crumpled to the ground.

Wyatt circled the Mercedes carefully, looking first for Calderón to make sure he was no longer moving. "Elena?"

"I'm okay." Her voice came from behind the Mercedes. "But you have a hole in your back tire."

With his foot, Wyatt nudged Calderón's pistol out of reach. Calderón was dead. The blood pouring from his neck had already slowed to a trickle, no longer pumped by his heart.

He reached in his pocket again and pulled out something Calderón or one of his men must have put there while he wasn't looking. It was about the size of a quarter, with a small antenna built in. He dropped it to the ground and crushed it to pieces beneath his heel.

"Brittany?" Elena called. "It's Elena and Wyatt. You can come out."

There was a scrabbling noise from under the bridge. A few seconds later, Wyatt's half sister crawled up to level ground and ran to Elena's outstretched arms, burying her face in her shoulder.

Wyatt crossed to them, blocking Brittany's view of Calderón's body. "Hey, kiddo. I'm your brother Wyatt."

Brittany looked up at him with tear-stained eyes, her lips trembling. "He said you wouldn't come. He said none of you cared if I lived or died 'cause I was just a bastard from one of Dad's whores." Her jaw squared. "He made me so mad I wanted to shoot him!"

"We've all been looking for you, short stuff." Wyatt pulled her into his arms, an unexpected rush of love spreading through him. "All of us, even Virgil and Morgan. They're here and they really want to meet you."

"Just in time for Christmas," she said with a weary smile.

"Just in time for Christmas." He looked away, his gaze drawn by lights moving through the darkness about a mile away.

Elena had already drawn her pistol, taking cover behind the truck. Wyatt joined her there, coaxing Brittany down to the ground. But before long, he made out the shape of his brother Morgan's rented SUV. The vehicle stopped several feet away and Morgan called out from an open window. "Wyatt?"

"It's Morgan," he said. "Weapons down."

Elena put her Smith & Wesson back in her purse. "I never thought I'd be so glad to see one of your brothers."

He looked at her across the hood of the car, his heart rattling like a snare drum. "We have to talk. Alone. Promise you'll stick around until we sort everything out."

She smiled at him, her expression as warm as a spring day in Serpentine. "I'm not goin' anywhere, cowboy."

Epilogue

Christmas Eve dawned unseasonably warm, even for south Texas. The north wind that had chilled the area for over a week had shifted, leaving the weather calm and sunny. The night before, with its drama and death, seemed to be some point in distant history. Brittany was home safe with her family and Javier Calderón was dead.

Wyatt had been up half the night dealing with the fallout from the events of the evening. Even ICE had gotten into the act, although Wyatt had refused to let them take Elena out of his sight. When he'd told the agents who'd shown up about overhearing Agent Clive Howard colluding with Calderón, they agreed that she'd be safer with Wyatt while they put out an APB for Howard. He, Morgan, Brittany and Elena had arrived at the ranch well after midnight.

But he dragged himself out of bed at six-thirty, mostly from habit, and showered himself to consciousness. Morgan had disappeared at some point in the night without waking him. Wyatt made a mental note not to open the hall closet under any circumstance as he dressed and made his way downstairs.

His brother Bull was awake, along with Justice and Julio Rivas, who seemed to be in a cautious mood. Apparently, Bull told him as he poured a cup of coffee, Justice had found the boy in a clinch with Brittany the previous night and had given the boy one of his famous "talks."

"I told Justice he should put the kibosh on their dating," Bull said flatly. "But the old man's getting soft in his old age."

Wyatt sipped the cup of black coffee, letting the bitter burn wake him up a little more.

"Where's Morgan?" Bull asked.

Wyatt just shot his brother a look.

"Oh."

"Have you seen Elena?"

"Yeah, she went out on the veranda a few minutes ago." Bull grinned over the top of his coffee cup as Wyatt headed for the veranda door at a clip.

Elena sat on one of the stone benches that lined the veranda, sipping a cup of coffee. Her back was against the wall of the house, her feet up on the next bench over. She was wearing faded jeans and a long-sleeved, red T-shirt that hugged her figure like a lover.

At the sound of his footsteps, she turned her head and smiled. "Another early riser."

"Scoot forward." He straddled the bench behind her, putting himself between her and the house wall. She leaned back against his chest, warm and sweet-smelling. "Good morning."

She rubbed her temple against his jaw. "Good morning. Did you get any sleep?"

"Not much. You?"

She shook her head. "It's strange to think that Calderón is dead. I've been chasing him so long."

"Someone else will take his place."

"Someone always does."

They fell into comfortable silence for a while. Wyatt broke it a few minutes later. "We still haven't had that talk."

Elena set her coffee cup on the bench in front of her and stood up, looking down at him. "No, we haven't." She straddled the bench as he had, facing him, sliding her long legs across the top of his until she nearly straddled him as well. "By the way, did you know there was someone having sex in the hall closet this morning?"

Wyatt grinned. "Yeah. We have horny ghosts."

She laughed, sliding her arms around his neck. "I think I love you, too, Wyatt McCabe."

Well, he thought. That was easier than he'd expected. "So, what now?"

"There are other closets in this house, right?"

He tugged her wavy curls. "Yes, but I can lock the door to my room, too, and my bed doesn't smell like mothballs." He bent and kissed her, slowly and thoroughly, tasting the sweet hint of hazelnut coffee on her tongue. She slid closer to him, her jeans creating delicious friction against his own jeans in all the right places.

"Hey, y'all!" That was Brittany's voice, sounding excited. With a soft groan, Wyatt set Elena away from him a few inches, turning to look at his sister. She stood in the veranda doorway, her eyes wide and her mouth forming an "O."

"So sorry!" She blushed madly. "But Bull is going to be going with Ms. Cobb to meet her family for Christmas tomorrow, so Mr. McCabe—Dad—thinks we should open our gifts together today." Brittany dashed back inside.

For the moment, she seemed to have recovered from her ordeal, though Wyatt suspected she'd eventually break down and have to deal with the emotional fallout. At least she'd have family around to help her through it.

"Gifts," Elena said with a groan. "I haven't done a bit of shopping."

"Yeah, well, you know what gift you can give me later." He slid his hand over the curve of her pretty little jean-clad backside.

Inside the house, both Bull and Morgan were watching their father with narrowed eyes as he sat on a small stool next to the beautifully decorated fir tree, a red and white Santa hat on his head, and started handing out gifts. The children got their presents first—Cody, Brittany and even Julio had multiple gifts under the tree.

Tugging Elena's hand to keep her with him, Wyatt crossed to where his brothers stood. "He's mellowed, hasn't he?"

Bull looked at him. "So you keep insisting."

"I didn't buy the old man anything," Morgan said.

"You came home," Wyatt said. "That's what he wanted the most."

Bull looked at Wyatt for a minute, then crossed the room and stood next to his father. Justice looked up, a wary smile on his face. He struggled to get up from the low stool, and Bull reached out a hand to help him up. They stood there, hands still clasped, for a long moment. Then Bull pulled his father into a quick hug. "Merry Christmas, Dad."

"Ah, hell," Morgan said. He crossed to his father's side, reaching out to catch Dakota's hand on the way for a quick squeeze. He gave his father a quick hug and wished him Merry Christmas as well.

"You have to go home for Christmas?" Wyatt asked Elena, blinking back the unexpected moisture in his eyes.

"Mom's in Florida with my sister for the holiday. I'll call them tomorrow." She slid her arm around his waist. "Are you sure about this, McCabe? You and me, I mean."

He looked down at her, drinking in the desire in her dark eyes. "Yeah. I am. But there's something I should warn you about."

"What's that?"

"I don't do things halfway. If we're going to do this, we're going to do it right. Understand?"

She arched an eyebrow. "As in rings and mortgages and little rug rats running around?"

"Eventually. Would that be a problem?"

She thought about it a moment. "No. Not a problem. I may be looking for new employment, though."

"Lucky for you, I know the local sheriff." He pulled her close, lifting her chin for a kiss.

"I don't see any mistletoe," she murmured, smiling up at him.

He made a face. "Mistletoe? Who needs mistletoe?"

Bending his head, he kissed her again.

* * * * *